BirthStone

LA PATRON SERIES – BOOK FOUR
The Alphas Alpha

Sydney Addae

BirthStone: Book Four of the La Patron Series
Sydney Addae
Copyright 2013 by Addae, Sydney
First Edition Electronic November 2013

This is a work of fiction. Names, places, characters, and incidents are either the product of the author's imagination or are used fictitiously, and any resemblance to any actual persons, living or dead, businesses, organizations, events, or locales is entirely coincidental. All trademarks, service marks, registered trademarks, and registered service marks are the property of their respective owners and are used herein for identification purposes only. The publisher does not have any control over or assume any responsibility for the author or third-party websites or their contents.

All rights reserved under the International and Pan-American Copyright Conventions. No part of this book may be reproduced or transmitted in any form or by any means, electronic or mechanical, including photocopying, recording, or by any information storage and retrieval system, without permission in writing from Sydney Addae.

BirthStone

Book 4 of
The Patron, the Alphas Alpha

When you're the top wolf on the continent with the backing of the Goddess, how does an enemy topple your kingdom? By challenging you to a fight?
No.
By changing the rules.
In BirthStone, Silas and Jasmine finally christened their pups and become frantic when the babies become sick and are at risk of dying. Silas is ready to clean house and accuses the five people who are new to his home. Unfortunately, that includes Jasmine's mom and her fiancé, her sister, and her former pastor. Jasmine is unwilling to believe her family would do anything to hurt her babies. Silas disagrees and battle lines are drawn.
Since his enemies have not abandoned their plans to destroy him, Silas is under attack within his home and from outside. Determined not to lose hope or the war he comes to some startling conclusions just as Jasmine realizes she is much stronger than she realized before. Can the two of them work together to push back the threat out to destroy their home before it's too late? Or will they lose it all?

This is the fourth book in the La Patron series.

Book one is BirthRight,
Book two is BirthControl
Book three is BirthMark and should be read first for a better understanding of this book.

Thanks
Sydney

Chapter 1

ANOTHER SLEEPLESS NIGHT RESULTED in hours of counting small black wolves running through the darkness. A smidgen of light appeared in the distance. Her heart pounded as she rushed toward the glimmering orb, desperate to escape the gloom of the clingy shadows. Heat, amazing in its intensity, splashed over her, battling the perpetual cold just beneath her skin. All night she had longed for the beauty of the sun, the life it produced, the bright glimmer of hope that often trailed in its wake.

Caught up in the majestic beauty and peacefulness of the sun-dappled woods, Jasmine Bennett heard her bedroom door creak open, but refused to turn over or acknowledge her mate and top wolf in the nation, Silas Knight. Instead, she tried to return to the dreamy place she had been enjoying a moment ago.

"What's wrong?" he asked, his deep voice filled with compassion.

Ignoring his pesky question, she again sought the sunny park with its green grass and long wooden benches that had been a premier location in her musings. The heat from the blazing sun-warmed some of the coldness lodged in her chest, allowing her to breathe better than she had in months.

"Jasmine?" The depression of the bed behind her halted her mind wandering and catapulted her into the here and now.

"What?" She gritted her teeth at the ill-timed interruption. After another night of restless wolf counting and sleep chasing, she invoked her right of irritability.

"You're in bed, have been in bed all morning…is everything alright?" Silas asked as his hand rested on her arm.

Inching forward to dislodge his limb, she closed her eyes and released a breath. "I need a minute or two alone." She emphasized the last word, hoping he'd leave. Where his hand sat on the comforter covering her thigh, he pressed down a bit. Heat flashed through her, zipping to her head through her chest and lower, but fizzled before it banished the remaining cold blocks of ice inside her. She tugged on the comforter.

"You've been alone for a few days, and each time I ask, you say the same thing, you are resting. You have not been to the nursery or allowed the twins to visit. For the past week, you haven't left our suite, and you barely allow me to touch you. I held you last night while you cried for no specific reason, yet you refuse to allow the doctor to examine you."

She forced herself to roll over and meet his concerned cobalt blue eyes. Today he wore his long black hair pulled back in a ponytail, giving him a rakish appeal like a pirate. Her lips curled at the mental image of her tall wolf with his deliciously sinful body on a pirate ship leading a raid. His intense gaze normally created a firestorm in her core. He was that potent and never failed to please her. She wanted to tease him but lacked the energy to follow up on the thought.

"I'm fine, just tired."

His eyes roamed over her body. In her mind, she ran her hand over her wild hair, bringing it into some semblance of order, and then exchanged her short gown for a clean one. But reality was a stickler for the truth, reminding her she had done neither of those things.

He shook his head. "Normal tired would not keep you from the pups or the twins. Everyone is worried." His voice had taken on an authoritative tone he rarely used with her, which meant he would not be swayed. She tried to get angry but lacked the energy at the moment. A wave of lethargy rolled over her as he continued to stare at her.

"With the recent bombings and drugs floating around, I have called the doctor to check you out. I need to do something because this is not you," he said sternly when she turned away from him.

"Not me?" She leaned up on her elbow and then fell back to the bed. Wrapped in a cloak of heightened anger, and pleased that she felt something, she snapped. "I have been locked up in this prison for months, and now I'll never be able to go outside to have a picnic in the sun. On a pretty day," she added, peeking at the slack-jawed expression on his face. "I'm telling the truth and you know it. With all the recent stuff and them taking Rese, I can't go shopping or out to dinner for a nice meal. I have to buy my clothes online. Half the fun of buying clothes is walking into the store, Silas," she said, her voice raised as every injustice against her, real or imagined, rose to the surface.

He continued to stare at her as if trying to figure out the pieces to a puzzle. Inexplicably, that fired her anger.

"You get to talk to people and see people all the time, but I don't. It's like

I'm nothing, no job, no responsibilities in your world. I'm not a wolf. The babies will turn into wolves one day, but not me. No sir. I'm not a good example of a wolf mother. The babies are fine with the nurses. I don't want my boys to see me like this, not when I can't give them good advice or cook a meal to feed them. I'm not ready. Not ready to do it." She sniffed without realizing her face was wet with tears. "I need to take my time, damn it," she yelled when he didn't respond.

"Jasmine…"

"You see it, you know I'm right. Just go…go, and let the nurses take care of our wolf-babies, and don't you dare call them pups. They are babies, half-human, so that makes them babies," she screamed. She covered her face as her chest expanded before releasing a huge sob.

Everything inside her ached. Worse, she was cold. The kind of cold that stops you from placing one foot in front of the other without Herculean effort. And she was plumb out of effort.

"I'm not losing my mind," she whimpered.

Each word she uttered contained a price tag and payment was in the currency of energy dollars. Her eyelids lowered as her breathing slowed. The darkness wooed her like her favorite treat. Eventually, she would get up, apologize to her lover, talk to her sons, and kiss her babies. But not right now, now all she wanted was rest. Her bones ached along with her head.

She wanted to play in the park she had been daydreaming about earlier, the sun had felt nice…warm. Warmth was good. She snuggled deeper beneath the comforter, covering her head. Darkness welcomed her. It hid her. No one could see her shortcomings, not even Silas, who thought he saw everything.

Silas's stomach clenched in agony as his mate wiggled beneath the covers. Initially, he gave her the benefit of the doubt. She had said she was tired, so he left her alone. In hindsight, that may have been a mistake. Earlier, when he entered the room, his heart had stopped and then slammed in his chest at the sight of her lying so still on the bed. He'd stumbled before he heard her light breathing. It had been the most precious sound imaginable.

She had shuttered their link to the point he couldn't gauge her true condition. The idea that he was losing her played on a constant loop in the back of his mind. The possibility of her not being in his life paralyzed him. He hadn't been able to oversee his Alphas or competently perform his everyday duties as La Patron. Each day she remained in bed filled him with impotent dread. He couldn't shake the dark loneliness that dogged him without her. Every thought, every action led him back to their suite where he waited for his mate to complete her requested respite and then rise. Not wanting anyone to know of his debilitating fear of her death, her request for privacy became his.

He welcomed her outburst, although it made little sense. It proved his Sweet Bitch was still with him. But, something kept her fire banked. For a moment he'd thought she smiled, there had been a flash of sparkle in her otherwise dull eyes, then it was gone. He may have been projecting his desire to see his interest reflected in her eyes and that was what he'd seen. This whole listless, disinterested thing puzzled him.

What happened to his mate? She had been fine after the pups had been born and even after living through the most recent spate of attacks, but then she had simply stopped getting out of bed in the mornings. Now she spouted ridiculous comments regarding everything from motherhood to being a good mate to being a good person.

It was as if a switch flipped and his loving, confident woman disappeared and someone else now resided in her body. Not knowing anything about this weird behavior ended today, the doctor would tell him what was wrong with his mate…or else.

Silas had talked to the twins, Tyrese and Tyrone, about taking her shopping or out to a restaurant since it had been a common theme of her infrequent rants. Tyrese completely shut down when Tyrone mentioned the previous bombings and refused to entertain the idea of his mom in a public place. Despite her requests, all of them agreed that exposing her to the type of danger a shopping expedition would produce was sheer insanity. They all agreed an angry Jasmine could be dealt with; the alternative did not bear thought.

Stretching out behind her on top of the covers, he lay on his back, aching to hold her. He hadn't missed her drawing away from his touch earlier. Instead of thinking about the pain of her rejection, he covered his eyes with his arm and focused on her getting better. It took a day longer than he'd anticipated locating Dr. Ross. Jasmine's new doctor had been out of town and just returned today. He glanced at the clock, it was ten minutes before the doctor was to arrive. *Good.*

Bottom line, he wanted his mate back. And he wanted her now. A light tapping on the door signaled the doctor's arrival. Silas slid off the bed and headed to the living area. Tyrese, Tyrone, and Rose, his mate, stood next to a strange female.

"I'm Dr. Ross. I've been Jasmine's gynecologist since the birth of her babies."

Pleasantly surprised, Silas shook the human's hand. "When Jasmine said Dr. Ross…nice to meet you." He shut up before his tiredness caused him to say something stupid. As La Patron, he knew better than most that women were more than capable of doing most things. In this instance, he and his wolf were happy Dr. Ross was female. "She's in there." He pointed to the bedroom door.

Dr. Ross held up her hand, halting him. "First, can you tell me what's wrong? Are there symptoms?"

Silas glanced at the concerned faces of his new family members as he told the doctor everything he knew. For a moment he thought about sugar-coating his mate's failings to ease the bad diagnosis. But he preferred to know the truth. He stiffened his commitment to get Jasmine the best care possible to help her through this illness.

When he finished, the doctor smiled.

Silas frowned at her response, rethinking the whole female doctors are just as qualified as male doctors thing. No male would smile at a personality disorder in the woman he loved.

"I will check Jasmine just to be sure, but I will say it sounds as if she's experiencing a bad case of postpartum depression." The doctor typed on a large tablet as she continued. "Half the women who give birth experience this in some form. It's not uncommon. If it's what I think it is, and that's based solely on what you've told me, I will prescribe an anti-depressant for her. It might help if she talked to a therapist as well. I can give you a list of qualified doctors."

Ignoring the therapy, his thoughts lodged firmly on the depression. "So she is depressed because she had my babies?" Being depressed because you gave birth? He had never heard of anything like that, not in his world. Bitches recovered fast after birth and went on to take care of their pups.

"No, no, this is not personal," she said quickly, her face a mask of concern. "It's a collection of things. Fast drops in her hormone levels after the birth, any kind of extraordinary challenges she's gone through recently, plus just taking care of four babies. That does a lot to your body and in some women, their minds. It's not you, her body is going through all types of changes and this is a by-product."

The doctor's answers rolled around Silas's mind for a moment. He had no idea about the hormone stuff. Extraordinary challenges? Jasmine had been dropped down a cavern and gone into labor, plus she had been thrust into a world she'd had no idea existed and was now mated to him, Alpha of the Wolf Nation for the North American continent. He had thought she was handling the challenges well, perhaps he had been wrong.

"How long until she's back to normal?" Tyrone asked the question that had been on the tip of Silas's tongue.

"A week, a month, or a day, although that's rare. The answer is I don't know and can't give a specific time. The medicine will work, and a lot depends on her. From what I remember, I don't see her allowing her condition to keep her down long. The good news is, she will get better, postpartum depression is curable." She smiled. "Now, I'd like to see Jasmine."

Chapter 2

"OBVIOUSLY ASKING AND ALLOWING you an option was the wrong thing to do. As your Alpha, I order you to return to West Virginia, to the compound. I need you. Be here within the next forty-eight hours. Is that understood?" Silas growled into the receiver. Frustrated that it had come to this point, he waited for the only acceptable answer.

"Yes, Sir."

Silas leaned back in his chair, the creak of the leather familiar and comforting as he exhaled. His tense gaze relaxed as it welcomed the sunrise, signaling a new day of confrontations.

It had taken a week of medication and some heartfelt conversations, but Jasmine fought her demons and won. Once again she ruled his den with an air of fairness and confidence few could resist. Her tigress returned to his bed and he couldn't be happier with the marks she scored on his back. Despite his fast healing capabilities, a slight sting remained from their play last night.

Her return to normalcy signaled his return to a desk full of work that accumulated while he tended his mate. He needed assistance to catch up and had no qualms ordering his former assistant to change personal plans and hasten across the world to his side. He tapped his finger on his desk, the wood solid beneath it. Three separate stacks of paper filled with reports and supporting documents waited for his attention. He had been working on them the past three hours, but it seemed longer.

"Good, do I need to make arrangements or will you handle them yourself?" The answer to this question would determine how much damage control would be required later.

"I believe I am capable of making arrangements. Will I stay in the compound or should I reserve a room in town?" Jacques said.

Silas gritted his teeth. The man refused to give an inch. That was the danger in allowing someone to get too close, they knew just how to push your buttons without taking it too far. Normally, this back and forth wouldn't bother him, but these were not normal times. "At the compound."

"Yes, Sir." Despite the correctness of the words, the delivery had a mocking quality. "Is there anything in particular, other than myself, you require I bring with me?"

Silas wiped his face with his palm and closed his eyes. "Your crystal ball. I would have you tell me where the next attack will come from and how to prevent the loss of lives. When I close my eyes I hear explosions and see walls covered in blood. I would have you look into your magic mirror and tell me my pups are safe and will live to our age or longer, and that I will not bury my mate. If you can bring the answers to the questions and problems that plague me, I would most appreciate it, my friend."

There was a pause of silence.

"I wish I could, Sir. Perhaps that would atone for my previous lapse." This time Silas heard remorse mixed with sympathy. "It seems my ability to sense upcoming events is broken. Lost on the same battlefield that stole my mind. Truly I am sorry for that, Sir." Jacques released a long sigh. "But I will see you in less than forty-eight hours and offer my assistance in whatever manner you require."

The sun seemed brighter as it rose across the mountains at that declaration. "Your help and presence at this time are appreciated." He disconnected the call and continued to gaze out the window. Jacques had a way of connecting dots and seeing patterns that amazed him. Over the past few weeks, Silas was inundated with truckloads of information, so much that most of it made little sense. He needed Jacques to process everything so he could go on the offensive and stop the bastards before more of his people died.

Each day he prayed to the Goddess to spare them from another attack. A few weeks ago he experienced what had to be a trek through hell. For five days straight, his enemies had bombarded him with new technology that threatened to wipe out his compound and cripple the Wolf Nation. Deadly situations arose daily. It had come down to a last stand effort to survive.

That his enemies had breached his facilities still sent a chill of fear through him. All his Alphas were on alert and putting out fires in their back yards. He shared information with them as it came in, but they were at a disadvantage in catch-up mode. The enemy had new technology he and his people just learned about. He needed a break to change the narrative in this battle.

A glance at the clock and he stood. *"I'm on my way down, meet me in the tunnels."* He sent Tyrone and Tyrese the message through their links as he left his office.

Silas strode through lower tunnels made of polished gray concrete walls and reinforced with tons of steel. Quarry stone gleamed beneath bright lights. The steady sound of their footfalls echoed in the hall. Tyrone and Tyrese were already on his heels as he turned the corner to the labs.

Three weeks had passed since Tyrese had been captured by a faceless enemy who'd injected some type of serum into his body, which changed his physiology forever. Jasmine had been worried and wanted a full-scale examination done immediately after he'd returned from capture.

According to Dr. Matt Chism, the mate of the twins' father, some of the blood and muscle tissue work had to be studied over a period of time. The results had come in last night, and it was Silas' promise to get the information first thing this morning that kept his mate in their room.

Silas had spent hours successfully training Tyrese to control his hybrid beast, except for the run. No one had been able to run in the forest for weeks, that would need to change so Tyrese's hybrid beast could practice operating in the wild.

Once Jacques arrived to take over the office, Silas would make arrangements for them to continue their training in the forest.

Remembering a conversation he and Jasmine had last night, he stopped in front of the lab door and spoke over his shoulder. "I will discuss the markings if I'm inclined, do not mention them. The human breeders believe the marks have a certain significance and I do not want them or anyone else knowing anything. Is that clear?"

"Yes, Sir."

It wasn't that he didn't trust the young wolves, he trusted them implicitly. But they might encounter their father and things had a way of slipping. He simply wanted to cover his bases. Jasmine urged him to keep the knowledge of the marks a secret. The breeders had sent a suicide bomber into his compound to kill him because of their beliefs. Neither he nor his mate wanted to stoke the fires of their fanaticism. The nurses assisting in the care of his pups were randomly scanned to ensure they kept their vow of secrecy about the sudden appearance of marks on all four of his pups. He and Jasmine sought the wisdom of the Goddess for answers regarding the strange phenomena. To date, they were still waiting for answers regarding the marks and other things.

He opened the door. Cooler airbrushed across his cheeks as he quickly moved into the large ventilated room. Various personnel in the midst of research were bent over equipment and speaking into shoulder-mounted recorders. Pleased with the level of activity, Silas stopped at a long metal table and waited until Dr. Passen and two other men finished their discussion. As soon as they saw him, they stopped, bowed from the waist, and left the doctor.

"Good morning, Sir." The doctor bowed to Silas and nodded to the twins.

"Morning. I need to know about the test results of the shot administered to Tyrese. Have you discovered the type of metal used in Asia?"

"Metals."

Silas's brow rose. "They used more than one?" He gauged the doctor's excited expression and assumed he had more news regarding what he termed, "Asia, the walking miracle."

"Yes, yes, they did." He pushed his glasses up his nose. "It is amazing how they took something so simple and forged it into her body, making it a part of her." He widened his gaze and stared at Silas. "It is cutting edge and Asia has been so helpful. Studying her has placed us leap years ahead in research. We should be able to help thousands of our people with this new technology." He paused, sucked in a breath. "The possibilities are endless. Please, Sir… come, let me show you what we've learned."

Silas exhaled. While pleased the doctor was excited about the future, his interest was more in the present. His enemies had not let up. There had been random killings and maimings in nearby communities. Attacks were not limited to West Virginia where his compound was located; many of his alphas reported an increase of unprovoked attacks in their states as well.

His adversaries were determined to destroy him and his family.

Family. He tried to remember if he had ever equated his younger years in the Pack as having a family. He barely remembered the bitch who birthed him. She'd died while he was but a pup. His father had been Alpha of their pack, but he too had been taken and killed before Silas reached adulthood. Most of his experience had been with Pack; the bitches who'd cared for him when he was small did not birth him, but that didn't matter. There were no accidental pregnancies or births. All wolves had inherent value and were protected.

His mate definitely impacted his life. A year and a half ago, the only meaning that word had for him was in regards to the Wolf Nation as a whole, it was not personal. Now, with a mate, four pups, two stepsons, a godson, and their mates, he had a family to live for and with.

"This way." Dr. Passen stood back and allowed Silas, Tyrone, and Tyrese to enter the observation room ahead of him.

Silas took a seat in front of a large window. A dark sparsely furnished room lay on the other side of the glass. He thought of Asia and wondered who she was and why the Goddess wanted her spared. "She still refuses additional furniture?"

Dr. Passen sighed as though pained. "Yes, Sir. She cooperates fully with our research but does not want any additional comforts."

That bothered Silas. These past two weeks since her capture, he had grown to admire and respect the young, feisty bitch. "She is eating well?"

Dr. Passen nodded. "Yes, her appetite and her body are healthy."

When Asia first arrived at the compound, she'd gone through withdrawal from whatever drugs she had been on. Her high-pitched, agonized, screams and contorted body had been difficult to hear and see. Since the doctors had no idea what drugs were used, they couldn't offer any assistance, and she went through withdrawal cold turkey. It lasted three long days. Afterward, she had been catatonic for the next twenty-four hours. Slowly, she regained control of her bodily functions and was moved into the room next door in the lab for research. It had been a rocky road, but now she seemed better of mind for it.

"Does she know we are here?" Tyrese asked while staring at the glass.

"She may," the doctor answered. "With Asia, you never know exactly how her senses are firing." The hum from the curtain lowering slowly over the glass blocked their view of Asia's room and muted the doctor's clicking keyboard noise.

"Let's start with the shot of serum both Asia and Tyrese received from those assholes. What are the lasting effects and will it cause any problems for his health?" Silas asked as he waved toward Tyrese.

Dr. Passen nodded and dimmed the lights. A screen appeared on the far wall. He typed a command into the computer and pages of data filled the screen. "Dr. Chism said he explained the nature of the serum to you already, so we won't spend a lot of time on that. The black case Tyrese submitted for testing confirmed Dr. Chism's original assessment that the drugs amplify an individual's core. There were a couple of vials of the drug they used to knock Tyrese out in that case as well. We have the chemical compounds of both of these now and will begin work on possible antidotes."

Pleased with the progress so far, Silas nodded for him to continue.

"I'm going to start here, at the cellular level." He pointed to a picture with a group of cells. "We pulled some of his older records." He glanced at them. "This is Tyrese's blood from before the shot." The red clusters looked normal to Silas. Another picture filled the screen for a moment, and then the doctor finessed the screen so that they were side by side.

"There's not much difference," Tyrone said, voicing Silas' thoughts.

"No. On a cellular level, there was very little change. But there was some change and that's all that is necessary for what happened to cause the hybrid shift. I'll explain more in a few moments. Take a look at this." The next screen showed a group of cells that were smaller and double the number of the other cells. "This is Asia's cells. Notice she has twice the number."

"They look different, smaller," Tyrese said.

"Yes, her cells have been manipulated to work with the metal in her body. As she uses her titanium arm or legs, her human cells require faster delivery of oxygenated blood. Whoever worked on her devised a method to change her cells so they work in perfect harmony with her mechanical parts. It's brilliant and eons ahead of its time. I have a team working on her blood and the titanium so we can understand and possibly duplicate the technology."

Silas nodded. "The effects of the shot?" While he appreciated the doctor's enthusiasm for new discoveries, he had a full agenda today and needed to get this discussion back on track.

Dr. Passen's face reddened. He wiped his mouth with his handkerchief before stuffing it back into his lab coat. "Of course, of course." He tapped the keyboard again and another page filled the screen.

"Dr. Chism was lead on Tyrese's examinations and here is a copy of the report. These findings were uploaded last night after he received the final lab reports." Squinting, he gazed at the screen a moment.

"The formula set the stage for the hybrid shift, but would not necessarily work that way in another hybrid?" Tyrese turned from the screen to gaze at the doctor. "I don't understand. Is the hybrid shift permanent or not?"

"Yes, it's permanent." The doctor's gaze flicked at Tyrese before returning to the document. "But if I gave your brother the same shot, chances are it would not react the same way on him."

"Why not?" Silas asked, glancing at the frowning twins. He suspected Tyrone would take the shot if it would give him the same ability as his brother. Although neither ever said, he believed they needed to be equal in every way and Tyrese having this ability that Tyrone did not threw things off-kilter for them.

"Tyrone is mated," Dr. Passen said with a touch of amazement in his voice that they asked something all wolves knew. "Anything that happens to him should be filtered through that bond." His frown deepened. "At least that's the way it is with full-bloods. If his mate did not receive the shot at the same time with the same intent, the shot would not affect him other than to amplify whatever is already there. Still, I'm not sure how much that would work because of the mating bond, and with half breeds, I'm not sure how this will play out."

Silas hadn't thought of the mating bond and from the look of the twins' faces, they had not given it much consideration either. "So the hybrid shift is permanent. Will there be any other side effects?" he asked to move the discussion along.

"Yes. The formula enhances whatever is there, so if Rese enjoyed fighting before, he will want to fight more often, perhaps have a quicker temper. If he was peace-loving before, he will be even more so."

Silas nodded in understanding while glancing at Tyrese to see how he took the news. His face was expressionless, as usual.

"You may want to warn your partners of the increase in your sexual appetite," Dr. Passen said, his face serious.

"Will do," Tyrese said in a dry tone.

Pleased with the report on Tyrese, Silas passed the information, minus the sexual advice, along to Jasmine who was in the nursery with their pups.

"I'm so relieved, thanks, baby. Let me know when you finish your meeting."

"Okay."

"I'd like to take the shot," Tyrone said, meeting Silas' gaze with determination blazing in his eyes.

"You cannot take the shot and do the challenge. It might give you an unfair advantage or disadvantage," Silas said, knowing Tyrone had no interest in fighting Cameron, Silas' godson, and Tyrone's brother-in-law. Nevertheless, until Silas voiced his decision on who would fight in the challenge, Tyrone was still a contender.

"I understand." Tyrone gazed at Silas a moment longer and then faced the doctor. "I'd like to take that shot."

Dr. Passen cheeks reddened further as his gaze slid from Tyrone to Silas and back to Tyrone again. "Is that permitted, Sir?" he asked Silas.

Silas glanced at the somber-faced twins; it was obvious they had discussed this. If something went wrong, Jasmine would be furious with him. He shook off that thought. These men fought valiantly by his side every day, he had once accused her of babying them and was about to fall into the same rut himself.

"Yes, as long as you understand the risks and take full responsibility for your actions." He stared at Tyrone to make sure he understood the reference to his mama.

Tyrone's color heightened but he did not release Silas' gaze. Amazing how such a small woman could impact grown men this way. In light of her recent bout of depression, no one wanted to give Jasmine cause for additional stress or discomfort. "I understand."

Silas nodded. "Set it up and give him the shot. Tyrese, I want you with him when he takes it. If I remember correctly, it burns like fire." His gaze slid to Tyrone, who had been merged with his twin when the shot had been administered and had informed Silas of the painful experience. Now he would undergo a similar occurrence, except this time it would be with consent

"Will do, Sir." The doctor sounded skeptical but he scribbled a note on a piece of paper. "As far as the weapons we discovered..." He looked at Silas for permission to continue.

Silas waved him on. He had placed tremendous pressure on the doctor and the researchers to devise a method of detecting suicide bombers who were locked and loaded with the internal bombs. Two people had entered the compound without detection. It had been a surprise when he discovered such devices existed, even more so when he discovered the sophisticated objects were attuned to him. With his mate and pups nearby, he would make sure every entry into his compound utilized this extra security measure in addition to scans.

This was something he wanted to know more about. The speed and commitment in which the researchers and factories worked to get the equipment perfected filled him with pride.

"You are aware we are now able to detect the bombs even when they are disguised in human tissue."

Silas sat back in a chair. "Yes."

"Two weeks ago we sent the diagram of the detection device to the companies you specified to manufacture the equipment parts. The first shipment of the assembled devices arrived last night. I wanted to give you a brief demonstration."

Silas released a sigh of relief at the news. Every wolf-owned company was at his disposal to manufacture parts and additional security features so that all Alphas would have access to these devices for public and private events. It had been a major undertaking to neutralize the threat so quickly, but they had come together as a national pack and completed the project in record time.

"Yes, I would love to see it."

The doctor pressed the intercom. "We're ready for the demonstration." The picture on the screen changed to one of the exterior security checkpoints. "Let's start."

A woman dressed in a lab coat and jeans walked into the security device, a moment later it beeped and the gate opened, allowing her access. The next woman who walked through wore a lab coat as well and a short dress. When she walked in, the side of the device blinked red on the outside. A gate closed behind her and she was trapped between the two gates. The lights flashed on the side of the device for several minutes.

"What's going on?" Tyrese asked, leaning forward in his seat.

Dr. Passen beamed. "We took it a step further and incorporated a series of rays that lock onto the bomb to shrink it so small it can pass safely through the individual's system as waste. I had my best team working on it and we're super excited to see it in action."

Silas smiled. The doctor's eyes had lit up to the point his wolf showed behind his lens. "I'm glad you were able to add that component, it will make a safer situation all around...what's happening?" Silas pointed to the screen where the woman was jumping up and down as though in pain.

"What's going on?" Dr. Passen asked through his microphone. Silas threw out his senses to the woman and discovered the flesh covering the bomb was on fire and she was trapped between the bars.

"*Open the gates,*" Silas demanded of security through their link. The gates opened, the woman dropped the box holding the explosive and ran out, brushing licks of flames from her jacket. Security immediately secured the scorched package and removed it from the area.

No one spoke until the bomb had been replaced in a nearby metal container and locked away. "Seems like you need a bit more work on those devices," Tyrone said dryly

The doctor peeked at him over his shoulder. "I'll get a representative from the manufacturing company here. Each of these was tested three or more times before they were shipped. According to the paperwork I received, they all passed inspection with no problems."

"Is it possible the device was installed wrong?" Tyrese asked, staring at the device on the screen.

Dr. Passen shrugged. "It's possible. The engineer from the factory came along and installed each one." He looked at Silas. "He was the same engineer you scanned and approved a week ago when the other new pieces of security arrived."

Silas had been ready to rip into the man if someone had been allowed on the property he had not personally scanned. "Good job on the identification of the bombs, which was a critical part. Have your men check for errors and make the corrections ASAP. I want these installed yesterday."

"Yes, Sir."

Silas gazed at the twins. "How soon do you want to take that shot?" he asked Tyrone. There was so much work that needed to be done, now was not the best time to lose both men.

"As soon as possible. I've already discussed it with my mate and we both understand there are some risks."

Silas nodded with the understanding he would need to hold some things off until Tyrese and Tyrone were available again. He spoke to the doctor who stood near the computer. "Is there someone available who can administer the shot now?"

"Yes, Sir. I will do it."

"Okay, I'd appreciate it if you take care of it. Rese, I'm going to need you and Leon to work on an assignment later today once Rone stabilizes. We have a lot of information that needs to be checked out. I want to find these assholes and put them down."

"Yes, Sir." Tyrese nodded.

Silas watched the look that passed between the twins. He knew Tyrone wanted to do more fieldwork and now that he was out of running for the West Virginia Alpha slot, Silas would use him more. "Rone, once the effects mellow, meet me in the gym. I need to run you through your paces."

Tyrone perked up. "Yes, Sir."

Silas stood and straightened the crease in his pants. "I'll see the two of you later. Doc?"

Dr. Passen gazed up at him. "Sir?"

"Get that device working, pronto."

The doctor nodded. "Yes, Sir. I've emailed the technicians. They should begin testing within the hour. Do you want to see a demo before they are installed throughout the compound?"

"Yes. Security is too important to me for it to half work. Send me a message after each one is tested. After they pass that bar, I want another demonstration after each one is installed, is that clear?"

"Yes, Sir. I understand." He typed into the keyboard while Silas stepped toward the door. He glanced at the curtain and then back to the twins. "I hope this works, I'm going to be very angry if it comes back to bite me in the ass. Make sure it does not." He stared at Tyrone.

"Yes, Sir. No matter what, I have to try. If I never shift into a hybrid at least I will be amped up enough that we can still spar and train." And that was the root of it. The twins needed to count on the other. Silas hoped it worked for all of their sakes.

Chapter 3

Silas left the room. He didn't travel far, just to Asia's room. He typed in the code and entered, throwing out his signature energy so Asia would know it was him. Once the door closed, he noticed she was on the floor on her knees. Was she praying?

"Asia?"

"Yes, Patron?"

"Rise."

Unassisted, she rose slowly. He took in her appearance. She wore a sleeveless yellow tank top, leaving her arms and neck visible. A twisted vine with thorns tattoo ran up her right shoulder, disappearing beneath her shirt. Gold cotton drawstring pants with small black diamonds printed on the pockets and black sandals completed her attire. He agreed with Dr. Passen's assessment. She appeared healthy if not vibrant. Toned honey-brown skin stretched over a tall, statuesque frame. Long, thin braids fell across her chest and down her back. A leather and metal blindfold with a small locked clasp covered her eyes to block any further transmissions. Silas refused to allow his enemy to see his labs or anything else of his through the camera lens embedded inside her eyes.

"How are you today?" Silas asked as he crossed his arms and leaned against the cool metal door.

She tilted her head to the side before answering. "Today is a good day. The headaches have abated with the blindfold. There is still a deep throbbing in my mind which tells me they know my location but can't reach me. They're attempting to regain control of me." She inhaled deep and then released her breath slowly. "I am forever in your debt, Sir, for the freedom I have experienced these past weeks. For the first time in years, my sleep is uninterrupted from nightmares. Despite the darkness, I'm seeing things clearly for the first time in years."

Her comment piqued his interest. He watched as she navigated the room and sat in the chair without mishap. "Explain."

She folded her hands and placed them in her lap. With a thoughtful expression, she spoke. "I am part human, part wolf, and now…part machine. My wolf hates the machine. She tolerates the human side of me. Internally there was a constant battle between them for supremacy. Since my capture, my wolf and human sides have formed a partnership of sorts to get rid of my mechanical parts."

"That would be your arm, legs, and eyes," Silas said, wondering if she realized just how important those limbs were.

She nodded slowly. "I know. But I am functioning well without the use of my eyes."

"You're locked in a controlled environment."

She chuckled dryly. "That's not new, Sir. I've been controlled for years, either through the camera lens that is my eyes, or the fear they planted in my mind, along with the endless surgeries I had. Every mission I performed, every person I killed, every package I picked up and delivered, was controlled from the moment I left until I returned. I was never alone, not in here." She tapped her head. "Never. There were, and still are to a certain extent, devices to control me. So functioning without the use of my eyes is a good thing."

"You need your arm, and your legs, Asia." He sensed the frustration of her wolf, felt it snapping beneath the surface despite her cool façade.

"Yes, I do."

Neither of them spoke as wafts of determination rolled from her. He suspected she wished to be rid of the foreign objects no matter the cost. There had been cases where a wolf would gnaw his leg to break free from traps, but this was different. He would talk to Dr. Passen to see what could be done to assist the feisty bitch. She had been a tremendous help to them, and he didn't want her to self-terminate over her metal limbs.

"I hate them, Sir. Sometimes it is so strong I can taste it," she said in a ragged whisper. "They turned me into a monster. I will do anything to destroy them for this. I volunteered my body for research to channel my hate into a productive venue. I hope the doc finds something to turn the tides of this war."

"War?" Although he recognized he was under attack, her use of that word surprised him.

"Yes, Sir. They declared war on you years ago, you're just now showing up on the battlefield."

Turn the tides of this war? He stood and braced his legs apart. "You think I'm losing?"

"No disrespect, Sir, but they have you on the defensive. You're just now learning about people like me with merged forms who are difficult to destroy in battle. I'm not the only one created, there are more like me."

That did not surprise him. Her next comment did.

"From what I gleaned, at first they used full-bloods, but they couldn't break through the pack mentality. Too many died in the labs. Then they discovered half-breeds who didn't embrace their wolf as strongly, and that's when their work got started."

"How long ago?"

She shrugged. "I tried to keep track of time, but they have planted so many memories in my mind I don't know what's true. I do remember seeing signs that said 'colored only' while on a mission. I remember sitting in a separate section on the train heading for Washington D.C. I remember wondering why things were so different outside. In the training facility, race was never an issue. Everything, your ranking, your living quarters, even your privileges, was based on how well you did your job." She shook her head. "It wasn't ideal, but it was all I knew at the time. Things were different…back then."

"What do you mean?" he asked.

During the few conversations they'd had before, her thoughts had been chaotic, disjointed. This was the first time she appeared relaxed enough to share her thoughts with logical precision.

"A few years back, there were some changes. The training became more intense. The focus shifted to my wolf. The experiments went from enabling me to merge both sides smoothly to causing tension between the two, to determine how much interference my wolf would tolerate."

"That's probably when the split happened," Silas murmured, remembering the assassin's cryptic words before releasing Jasmine into the ravine.

"Sir?"

"A man attempted to kill my mate months ago. He told me he had been approached by two groups. One wanted to kill me and the other wanted to kill my mate. Is it possible that the group began with the intent of strengthening half-breeds, to prepare them to take over the Wolf Nation one day?"

She frowned. "It's possible. But if so, that group is no longer running the research. Those in charge now want the power that comes with leading wolves. I think they realize they need you to a certain extent, at least for now. The only way to do that is to invade your den, to take and then destroy your mate and pups."

The matter-of-fact words dropped into his gut and detonated. Perhaps if he hadn't believed his mate had been on death's door, or if his pups hadn't received marks the breeders prophesied about, he might not have reacted so swiftly or strongly. Without thought, he reacted to the threat of losing those closest to his heart.

A wild breeze whipped through the room. The glass in the window webbed, pieces of the thick material popped and crackled. Asia's braids flew around her head as she fell from the chair onto the floor. Weeks of watching his mate languish tore at him. Forcibly he fought back the idea of her demise.

Pinging from the exterior door signaled someone's request for entry. Jasmine's frantic calls pierced the blinding rage that engulfed him.

"Damn it, Silas, cut that out and talk to me. Forget it, I'm on my way," Jasmine snapped through their link.

"Sir?"

Through a fog, Silas heard his name and inched back from Asia's quivering form. He had no idea when he had moved to stand above her. The pinging from the steel door increased in frequency and volume.

"Sir?" He recognized Tyrese's voice.

"One minute." He reached forward and touched the top of Asia's head. She shrank back. "I owe you an apology."

"No…no, Sir. I apologize for speaking out of turn." Her shaky voice ended with a sob. She inched back, her body shook as she swallowed hard. "Please forgive me, Sir."

Silas exhaled, regretting his momentary loss of control. Losing his mate was a sore subject and too near the surface. That was no excuse. He needed Jasmine's knack for smoothing awkward situations. "Asia, I need you to listen to me." He waited for her to respond. "Asia," he called her name with a demand that she responded to.

"Yes, Sir?" Her voice sounded weak and uncertain, so unlike the strong Alpha bitch he knew her to be.

He tempered his voice. "I asked you a question. You gave me an honest answer, one I needed to hear. When it comes to my mate and pups…it's a sore spot for me. My anger wasn't directed at you…well it was, but only because…look, I don't want you to stop being honest with me because you're afraid. I needed to know they were after my family and why. I don't like it." That was a mild statement and he knew it. "But I need all the information I can get to win … this war." He waited for her reaction. Her body didn't shake as much and her face hovered above the floor instead of being plastered to the tile.

"Please stand. My mate will be here in just a moment and it will displease her to see you like this." Jasmine was pissed and heading his way. She would have quite a few words to say when she discovered his anger had been directed toward Asia.

Instead of reducing the number of people in her inner emotional circle and taking things easy as her doctor instructed, Jasmine had taken a liking to the young bitch, and worried over Asia's health and well-being. No matter how much he urged her to slow down, she claimed she was better and could handle everything she had been able to handle before her illness. Asia pushed up and stood. Her head remained down, she didn't move.

Silas was unsure if he should help her find the chair or not. He opened the door. Tyrese and Tyrone stood in the entryway. "Right her chair."

Tyrese strode forward, picked up the upholstered seat, and placed it near the wall. He took Asia by the arm and assisted her so that she could sit.

"Thanks," she said softly.

Tyrese glanced at Silas and then spoke. "You're welcome."

Jasmine walked into the room, glanced at Silas, and stood in front of him. "Asia, are you okay?"

"Yes, Ma'am."

"Clear the room," Silas said, gazing at Tyrese and then Tyrone. "You have other places you need to be."

Tyrese glanced at his mother and then Silas. "Yes, Sir." He left the room, closing the door behind him.

"What happened, Asia?"

Silas's brow rose.

Jasmine stroked his arm, the skin-to-skin contact soothed his wolf and excited him.

"I said some things the Patron did not like. I was not thinking clearly and should have answered the question with more finesse. I apologize again for my lack of tact."

"What did you say? And you can say it again, he won't react in the same way, but I need to know. Tell me please."

"You already heard her through our link, I don't want to hear it again," Silas argued.

"I know, but she is our best weapon to get those bastards, at least that's what you told me. She can't do that if she's afraid to offend you at every turn. We need to fix this now before she shrinks back into her shell and rarely speaks. Let me handle this, it requires a softer touch."

He smothered his snort as he backed off. *"Remember, no touching, and do not get close. Otherwise what you felt before will seem like an appetizer."*

"I already agreed to that, so stop with the big bad wolf routine."

Asia's head lifted slightly. She swallowed hard and repeated word for word what she had said to Silas a few moments earlier. Hearing the words burned his gut but lacked the same punch this time. His wolf became agitated. Jasmine leaned back against him, giving him the contact he needed.

"Thanks so much, Asia. That's information we needed to know. We are newly mated and he is extremely protective. You know how mates are, don't you?"

Silas stiffened behind her but remained silent.

Asia frowned. "Yes, he was the same. It cost him…"

"Do you remember your mate? Mother? Or father?" Jasmine continued in a soft voice.

"I think so…I mean I had to be born, but I can't remember." Her hand flew to her head. "Ow…"

"Monitor her," Jasmine told Silas.

Silas probed into Asia's mind. At first, he didn't sense anything untoward. But something caused her pain. He released more energy, seeking the source of the irritant. A few seconds later a small pulse behind the lens of her eyes caught his attention. Gently, his energy surrounded the pulsating vein only to discover something small and hard like a kernel.

Asia moaned as her face dropped into her hands.

Working quickly, he penetrated the vein. There appeared to be a clot in the vein. Silas prepared to dissolve the clot when he realized there was no blood flow. He stopped and followed the vein and discovered a small plate attached to brain matter. No wonder Dr. Passen missed this, it was a cleverly disguised vein that powered their control over her. Eager to pass on this information to the doctor, Silas pulled out of Asia's mind.

Jasmine gazed over her shoulder at him with a worried expression.

"*She needs surgery*," he said through their link.

Jasmine nodded before turning back to Asia. "Sweetheart, do you want to lay down?"

"Not right now. I don't…want to move. My head is spinning…those bastards. I know it's them, they are doing something again," Asia cried.

"I'm going to help you…just like you helped us. We are going to help make this right," Silas said, feeling bad for the young woman. He stepped back, opened the door.

A woman in a lab coat snapped to attention when she saw him. "La Patron, Sir."

"Have Dr. Passen come here immediately." Silas did not contact the doctor via his link to give Tyrone and Tyrese some time to get situated after the shot.

She nodded, spun around, and moved in the direction she had just come.

When he stepped back inside, Jasmine sat in the other chair and spoke softly. "I'm from Colorado originally, a town called Aurora, not far from Denver. I have a sister, she's older and we are close. Growing up, we played a lot of softball at the park near our house. I loved dodgeball. There was something liberating about throwing that ball as hard as you could." She sighed as though she were reliving the games.

"I played volleyball… in school, or at least I think it was a school. My hair was short in a small afro," Asia said softly. "Someone spiked the ball and I dove forward to make the save for our team." Her voice sounded wondrous and then she cringed. "Oh my God, that hurts…it hurts…"

The pinging sound filled the room. Silas opened the door, glad to see Dr. Passen on the other side. "You called for me, Sir?" He glanced around the room before his eyes landed on Asia. The doctor's eyes widened. "Is she okay?"

"No. She has a piece of metal digging into her brain," Silas said in a somber tone.

"What?" Jasmine said, staring at him.

He nodded but continued watching the doctor's expression change. "It's complicated, but I will help you find it again," he explained to Passen. "Right now give her something for pain, and then you can pull a team together to run more tests."

"Yes, Sir." The man left the room.

No one spoke although the atmosphere was pregnant with tension. Moments later the doctor returned and gave Asia a shot. He rubbed her arm a few times before speaking. "Better?"

She nodded slowly. "Yes, it took the edge off. Thanks."

"Sir?" Dr. Passen looked at Silas. "Do you need to talk to me now or…"

Silas glanced at his watch. He needed to talk to Captain Samson regarding Jenkins. The detective had completed his time at the compound and Froggy signed off on the health of the detective's wolf. According to Froggy, Jenkins and his wolf had developed a healthy Pack mentality and the man was eager to assist in any way Silas deemed necessary.

It was time for Detective Jennings to return to work. There were a few things Silas needed to discuss with the captain. The Merriweather's were restless over the stalled investigation of their relative's death. Silas had given the detective instructions to close the case. For that to happen, Jenkins needed to be back behind his desk. The Captain needed to be made aware of the new security devices to be installed in the precinct as well.

Alpha Jayden and Silas officiated the upcoming Alpha Challenge for West Virginia in a few weeks. The Alpha had requested a conference call this morning to discuss the security arrangements. Silas would be tied up in meetings for the next few hours.

"Yes, Dr. Passen we can talk as we walk." Silas held out his hand to Jasmine. "Let's go, she needs her rest. We can visit later to finish that discussion." He softened his tone at the flashing of her eyes. She waited a beat before taking his hand. He loved having his spirited bitch back.

Her eyes softened as he placed a kiss on the back of her hand. "I need you safe. She is still wired to those who would destroy us. I cannot leave you alone with her."

She nodded while glancing over her shoulder. His gaze followed hers. Asia had moved to the bed and lay curled in a fetal position. If anyone deserved a break, the young bitch certainly did. Silas hoped the discovery he'd made would set her free to live a decent life.

Chapter 4

ONCE SILAS EXPLAINED IN detail what he'd seen in Asia's brain, Dr. Passen left at a fast clip to put a team together to re-examine the woman. Jasmine and Silas walked a few feet down the hall. She placed her hand on his arm to stop him. "My mom, her husband, and Renee will be here in a couple of days for the christening." She ignored the tensing of his arm and continued while holding his gaze. "I know you've been busy, I've been busy. Everybody is busy, but we will be having guests soon and you need to spare some time for my family."

He frowned.

"Some quality time, Silas. I mean it." She stopped him from commenting. "My mother remarried and I haven't met this guy. Rose has all the background checks for my former pastor." She glared at him. The man had no shame requiring a man of God to undergo the same scrutiny as one of his Alphas.

"And your mother's husband?"

"Yes, she has Mark's background information as well. I think she even has one on Jacques." She waited for him to defend the need for his trusted friend to receive a clearance, when he didn't, she moved on before he came up with a reason to leave.

"Tonight, I want to go over an outline of how the christening will flow. Since we don't have godparents, I was thinking we could cut out that part."

"God-parents?" He frowned, staring down at her.

Jasmine pointed a finger at him. "Don't."

"What? I've never heard of that term."

She pressed her finger into his chest. "You have a godson."

He stared at her. "But not a god-parent."

"I mentioned it to you, three weeks ago before the depression hit."

"You did not."

She pushed him. He did not move, instead, he wrapped his arm around her waist, pulling her closer. "Silas, I don't like this." Her eyelids fluttered as tingly sparks raced through, awakening her libido.

He inhaled deeply behind her ear and placed a kiss in that spot. "Yes, you do."

"No. I don't like it when I explain things about my culture, things that are a part of my upbringing and a part of me, you don't listen." She shoved at his chest again. But he held fast.

"I do listen. I don't remember the discussion you're referring to. But I listen to you." He tipped up her chin. She searched his eyes. He appeared serious.

"Godparents are individuals chosen by the parents to care for the children in the event of the parent's death or inability to care for the children," she explained, hoping he understood because she would hit him over the head the next time he asked for an explanation.

"No."

"What do you mean no?" Should she remind him of Cameron?

"To set someone up in that position is sending the wrong message to my enemies. I cannot do that. I agree with you, we will exclude that from the ceremony."

"Why is this any different than you calling Cameron your godson?"

"It's not a designation or title, more like an honorarium because of my relationship to the Goddess," he said.

He placed a kiss on her cheek. "I like this dress," he murmured as his palm rubbed over her butt, inching the peach-colored fabric upward.

"I bet you do," she said, glancing around the corridor and removing his hand. Stepping back, she gazed up at him. "I am going to explain the half-breed thing to Mom and Renee. Since Mom is a breeder it won't be too much of a jump. Renee… she's not bringing her girlfriend, Mandy, who would make the leap easier, but I think she'll be okay. Do you need to scan them as well?"

"Yes. When I shake their hands –"

"Mom will probably hug you."

"I'll do a quick mental scan, just to be sure no one slipped anything into their drinks or anything like that."

Although the idea bothered her, memories of recent surprises killed her qualms. "The pastor flies in Saturday morning around eight, does the christening at noon, and then flies back to Washington at four that afternoon. Rose made arrangements through your service."

"That's fine." He gazed up the hall and she knew her few minutes were up, but at least they had covered quite a bit of the event. After her bout with depression, he suggested they postpone the christening, but she'd held firm since almost everything had been done.

"Rone and Rese have to be at the christening, do you have someone else covering security?"

"Yes, Cameron will be in charge."

Her eyes widened. "Cameron's not going to be at the christening?"

Silas met her gaze and responded slowly. "No. Should he be?"

Jasmine's heart plummeted. He still didn't get it. This was a family event. A time when everyone came together to celebrate the newest family members. Cameron was like a son to Silas and in a roundabout way, the catalyst for Jasmine and Silas coming together.

"Yes. He should be there."

He stared into her eyes a moment longer. "Okay," he said softly. "He'll be there. I'll put someone else on security. Tonight, give me the exact date your mother arrives and I'll make sure I'm here to greet her and your sister. Whatever you need to make this a good event, you got it." He squeezed her hand and placed a kiss on her forehead.

He had used his 'I want you' voice', which always turned her to mush. The man still revved her engines when he looked at her with that gleam in his eyes. "I just need you." She leaned into him.

He held her tight. "You have me and everything that goes along with me." He brushed his lips against hers, she grabbed his head and deepened the kiss. He tasted like sunshine and coffee, sweet and decadent.

"Mmmm, I love the way you taste." She breathed deeply as they stepped apart. "You smell so good, too."

He smacked her on her rear cheeks. "Your special scent keeps me grounded and your taste is my morning meal and midnight snack. Now stop distracting me, I've got to get to work. See you later, Sweet Bitch."

Feeling better about the upcoming event, she patted him on the ass and turned in the opposite direction toward the elevator. "Okay, wolfie, it's a date." She watched the smile cross his face and then disappear. No doubt his mind was on the next fire he needed to put out. At least there hadn't been any more bombs or kidnappings recently. While waiting for the elevator, she released her breath. That week had been a living nightmare. Her doctor had no idea the types of challenges she had experienced after the birth of her babies. It was a miracle the depression was the only thing she'd fallen prey to.

The elevator doors opened and she stepped inside. Rose worried over Tyrone's obsession to take the shot to level the field with Tyrese. Much of the twins' identities were locked within each other. Rose tried to talk him out of it, but he claimed his connection with Tyrese was off balance and the shot would fix it. Her daughter-in-law asked her to keep quiet over her concerns. It had been hard. Seeing her sons in the lab earlier, she was certain they were there to get the drug. When the elevator stopped, she headed toward Rose's office.

One thing for sure, if anything went wrong with the injection, Rose would know immediately through her connection with Tyrone. Since Jasmine couldn't sit with him to make sure he was okay, she'd do the next best thing.

She noticed something was off the moment she stepped inside the dimmed office. "Honey, you feeling okay?" she asked Rose as she stepped inside.

Slumped in her large leather chair with her fingertips pressed to her forehead, Rose groaned an unintelligible response. Thick black hair was pulled from her face with a white headband. Her normally dusky complexion appeared two shades lighter, and her pinched lips were pale.

"Not really. I think Rese is blunting it, but some is seeping through." She pushed back, grabbed the trashcan, and pulled it up to her face. Jasmine rushed to the small mini-fridge and pulled out a bottle of water so Rose could rinse out her mouth when she finished vomiting.

"Oh my…" Rose panted. Beads of perspiration dotted her forehead as her small hand opened and closed spasmodically.

Jasmine placed the bottle of water on the desk and rubbed Rose's back. "Come on, you need to lay down, get as comfortable as you can." She thought back to what Silas told her had happened with Tyrese. It hadn't lasted long, but he had been in a life or death situation. Did that have something to do with how the drug impacted a person she wondered?

"No…no. I can't move…it hurts…I can't –" She snatched up the trashcan again. The sound of retching and unpleasant odor rose swiftly, spilling into the air with equal measure. Unable to watch the painful sight, Jasmine strode to the private bathroom in the office, inhaled fresher air deeply, wet a towel, and brought it to Rose, who lay with her head on the desk.

"Let me put this on your forehead." Jasmine eyed the trashcan sitting next to Rose's foot.

Rose whimpered. "I can't move, everything hurts."

"I'm so sorry. So sorry." Jasmine placed the cool towel on the section of exposed forehead she could reach.

"Ah…that feels good, thank you," Rose whispered.

"It's okay. I wish I could do more." Jasmine sat in a nearby chair, prepared to wait until the pain receded, signaling her son was doing better.

The phone rang. "Owww… too loud."

"Who's covering today?" Jasmine asked as the ringing continued.

"I don't remember, but they need to pick up, the noise hurts," Rose moaned.

The ringing stopped. Jasmine released a breath, hoping Rose would feel better soon. It bothered her to see the young vibrant woman in so much pain. Especially when, in her opinion, it wasn't necessary.

Just as Jasmine thought to check on Tyrone, if Rose had it this bad, her son had to be in worse condition, the phone started ringing again. Seeing Rose flinch at the sound, Jasmine picked up the receiver and spoke.

"Silas Knight's office." Out of consideration for Rose, she softened her voice.

"I'd like to speak to Mr. Knight." She knew the person on the other end was human because Silas had another set of protocols in place for wolves to contact him.

"Mr. Knight is unavailable at the moment. Can I take your number and have him return your call." She searched the desk for a piece of paper and grabbed a pen out of a nearby cup full of writing utensils.

There was a long sigh on the other end. Jasmine wasn't sure how much longer she would stay on the phone waiting for him to make up his mind. Rose did not appear to be getting better, which made Jasmine more anxious to check on Tyrone. Normally, the twins didn't give her much reason to stress or worry, but knowing Tyrone was willfully altering his body to be like his brother placed them both in the 'you're stressing me' category.

She frowned.

"Miss…can't he even afford good help…miss," the man on the other end yelled.

Jasmine snapped out of it, catching the tail end of his remarks. If she had not been thinking of other things, and ignoring him she would take offense at his crude remarks. Instead, she sucked it up.

"You'd like to leave a message?" Hell if she called him sir or any other pleasantries.

"Yes. Tell him Alfred Merriweather wants to discuss the situation in the caves. I have some information I think he will be interested in." His voice had taken on a condescending edge that rubbed Jasmine wrong. She took an immediate dislike to the pompous sounding man. Something bogus about him sang through the phone.

"I'll tell him." She scribbled the name knowing Silas would never meet with this creep. First off, he made it seem as though Silas should be happy to talk to him, and second, he had been rude to her. Two things guaranteed to piss her mate off.

"I've left my number before, would you like me to give it to you again?"

"No. He'll contact you if he has time for a meeting."

"The polite thing would be to contact me either way, to say he can or won't meet with me. I'm assuming the great La Patron understands how to conduct himself in business and society."

Anger, hot and potent, flashed through her at the insult. His dig hit its target. Her control over her emotions had been skewed since the postpartum debacle. The only reason she hadn't mentioned the outbursts of rage and tingly hot energy across her skin to Silas is because she wanted to explore this new area on her own. It gave her something to focus on besides her domestic duties.

Jasmine eyed Rose, who lay on the desk whimpering with her eyes closed. Turning, so she could lean against the desk, and knowing that Rose could hear her, Jasmine responded to Merriweather.

"I think you misunderstand, Merriweather." Her tone was low and hard. "La Patron schedules meetings with Presidents of countries, stateside and abroad, he has friends in the Senate, the House, and on the bench. He is the ruler of his nation, and the fact he does not return your call, someone who does not rank on his societal scale, says nothing about him but everything about you."

"Wwwhaaat?"

"I believe we will have a discussion with the good Lieutenant over how you have this very private number. Don't bother calling again, your line will be blocked and I will report you to Captain Samson for stalking."

"I'm not –"

"Of course you are stalking Mr. Knight, Merriweather," she said, grinning, quite enjoying the exasperated sounds he made on the other end as he tried to out-talk her. But the experience of raising two outgoing sons held her steady while she took the conversation in the direction she wanted it to go.

"By your own admission, you've called before, and I know for a fact you've called three times this week." Rose had been complaining about the man's attitude and told her that he was becoming a pest by calling so often. It was a calculated guess on Jasmine's part that it was more than twice.

"I have important business to discuss with him. If he doesn't want to talk to me, then fine, I'll find someone who will listen. We'll see how big he is then, won't we? I promise you this, Silas Knight will pay for killing Robbie. On my honor, I promise you that." His voice had dropped to a low snarl.

The air in her nostrils stilled. Her heartbeat stuttered as each word he spoke registered. Rage, red and potent, curled within her belly. She sensed her mate's attention and shut down their connection. She would handle this.

"Are you threatening Silas?" Jasmine asked in what she hoped was an even tone. Her body tightened at the idea of danger to her mate. She unclenched her fist while waiting for him to answer.

Silence met her question, followed with a delighted chuckle. "Ah…this is better than I hoped. Ms. Bennett, how wonderful to hear your voice. It is truly an honor… I mean I am most fortunate of men to have this gratifying opportunity to speak with you."

Frowning, Jasmine removed the receiver from her ear and then replaced it. "You have been speaking with me for the past ten minutes. I ask again, are you threatening Silas?"

"Not in the sense that you are thinking –"

"You have no idea what I'm thinking," she snapped, aggravated by his about-face. Now she'd have to explain to her mate how talking with a crazy person got her so twisted up she shut down their link. He would think she forgot to take her medication, again. "What the hell is wrong with you?"

"I assure you, nothing is wrong, all is right in my world. To hear the voice of the one… I apologize for being testy before. I would close with these words of caution, be careful and stay close to home."

Brow raised, she glanced at Rose, who remained seated, face down at her desk. She was torn between helping Rose and by extension, her son Tyrone, or listening to information that may or may not shed light on the level of hostility aimed at her or Silas. With her mom and sister arriving soon, she wanted to be sure everyone was safe.

Pushing from the desk, Jasmine pulled up a nearby chair and sat. Crossing her legs, she smoothed down her peach-colored dress and rested her left hand on her leg. "Something tells me that you have more to say. Get it off your chest, big guy. I'm listening," she said, meeting Rose's startled eyes.

"I have been asking for a sign and hearing your voice today, of all days, tells me I am on the right path. You are beauty and grace personified, a worthy choice to lead."

"What?" She sprung forward wondering where he was going with all of this.

"Then once again the glow returns; again the phantom city burns. And down the red-hot valley, lo! The phantom armies marching go."

Since Robert Louis Stevenson was one of her favorite poets, she finished the poem. "The phantom armies marching go! Blinking embers, tell me true. Where are those armies marching to? And what the burning city is that crumbles in your furnaces!" She paused, rehearsing the words over in her mind. That poem dealt with death. What was Merriweather up to? She opened her link to Silas, he needed to hear this.

"Ah, smart and beautiful, a jewel in the crown to be sure. I thank you for taking time to speak with one such as I. Farewell my lady."

"What? Wait," she called out, but he had already disconnected. Jasmine gazed at Rose, who returned her stare. "Merriweather is crazy. Just so you know, he is never to come inside the gate. Never." She slammed the receiver back into the cradle.

Rose jerked as though hit.

"Sorry." Feeling bad that she had caused the younger woman discomfort, but still ticked over Merriweather, Jasmine walked around the desk and placed the back of her hand on Rose's forehead. Sensing Silas's anger, she sent him a message to remain calm before she spoke to her daughter-in-law. "At least you don't have a fever. You need to lie down. Is there someone else who can cover for you?"

"Not right now. I can leave in an hour or so." Rose pushed away from the desk and stood slowly. Color leached from her skin. The milky whiteness of her cheeks surrounded by her wavy jet black hair and smudged red lipstick created a vampire look. Stifling a grin over the thought of vampires and Rose in the same sentence, she offered her arm for assistance.

"No, I can do this. What happened with Merriweather?" she asked, moving toward the sofa.

Jasmine scoffed. "He flipped. One minute he was threatening Silas, the next he started paying me compliments, quoting poetry, and talking like this was the 1800s or something. I'm telling you the man ain't right in the head. Seriously, put him on the 'hell no he can't enter the gate' list."

Rose chuckled and then held her forehead.

Jasmine slowly walked behind her, prepared to assist.

"What the hell happened?" Silas asked through their link.

"I'll tell you later, I'm trying to get Rose settled." After mating with Silas, his gruffness no longer offended her. It had taken some time and lots of conversations, and she knew that while he might get angry, he would never hurt her.

"What's wrong with her?" His tone softened.

"Tyrone took the shot and it's impacting her." She knew he was aware of her son's decision because Silas had to give his approval before the shot was administered.

"Damn. I need to check on him, he should be coming out of it by now. How bad is she?"

"Weak, nauseous, head and body pain. She looks shaky to me, but she won't leave the office until her replacement gets here."

"Tell her to take the rest of the day off. I'll have Hank cover the phones until the replacement comes in. Shut down the office and lock the door behind you. Can she walk, do I need to send someone to help her to their wing?"

Jasmine stooped until she could see Rose's eyes and watch the steady movement of her chest. She informed Rose of Silas's orders. "Can you walk or do I need to get some help?"

"I think I can make it." Rose remained still on the sofa with her eyes closed. "The pain isn't as bad right now."

"She wants to do it on her own," Jasmine told Silas.

"Figures. I've sent Jarcee to wait in the hallway when the two of you leave. If you need him, he's available to assist. Focus on getting Rose back to her wing, Jarcee will shut down the office."

"Okay." She moved back as Rose slowly pushed up from the sofa to a seated position and then stood.

"Jasmine?"

"Yeah?" She walked ahead to open the door for Rose to shuffle through. Her daughter-in-law weaved sluggishly as if she were drunk. It would have been funny if there wasn't a grimace of pain on the younger woman's face.

"I haven't forgotten you shut me down while talking to Merriweather. Do I need to kill him?"

"What?" Shock from his calmly spoken words promoted her to speak aloud.

"What did he say to make you shut me out and then reopen our link moments later?"

Rose walked unsteadily out of the office and turned toward the east wing of the mansion where she lived with her mate and brother. Jasmine walked alongside her.

"Jasmine?" Silas snapped, his irritation flowing through their link.

"Wait a minute, I'm walking Rose to her wing. We'll finish the conversation when I'm done. But I will tell you, Merriweather is unstable and you should do a deep investigation regarding him, somehow he's involved with what happened three weeks ago."

Without seeing him, she knew her mate went absolutely still. *"Why do you say that?"*

"Just a feeling that he's involved. He quoted a poem from Robert Louis Stevenson. It was all about armies and death."

"You were familiar with the poem?"

She exhaled at the skepticism in his voice, refusing to take offense. *"Yes. I knew the poem. I like Stevenson and know his work. Can we talk about this later? I'm about to get Rose settled."*

"Once she is settled I want to know exactly what Merriweather said. I told Jennings to close the case on Merriweather's relative, but we might need to re-evaluate that if your hunch is right, and it probably is."

Blond-haired and green-eyed, Jarcee stood almost seven feet. He bent and knocked at the entry door of Rose and Tyrone's living space. Afterward, he stepped back so he could be seen if anyone was inside. A moment later Tyrese opened the door and looked up at Jarcee, who pointed at Jasmine and Rose. Immediately, Tyrese strode down the hall, picked Rose up, and carried her inside.

"Ow, not so fast, Rese," Rose complained as he set her on her feet inside the living room.

Jasmine nodded her thanks to Jarcee before closing the door. He would wait and escort her to the nursery after she made sure her older children were okay.

"Rone is in bed," Tyrese said, glancing at Jasmine before placing his hand beneath Rose's elbow for support.

"How's he doing?" Jasmine asked, following the two into the back room.

"He'll be fine," Tyrese mumbled without looking at her.

"No doubt. But that's not what I asked, Rese," Jasmine said in a stern voice.

"He's in pain…a lot of pain, but it's waning…a little. Maybe with his mate nearby, it will get better faster," Tyrese said, stopping at the foot of the bed where Tyrone lay on his stomach. The smell of sweaty, unwashed body and vomit stained the air in the dark room. Jasmine was tempted to open the window to let the fresh breeze clear out the odor, but watching Rose slowly climb into bed, fully dressed, and lie next to Tyrone made her ask first.

"Does light bother you?"

"Yes," Tyrone croaked as he touched Rose's fingers and then intertwined them.

Now was not the time to repeat her reservations over what they had done although she yearned to go off on her son. She never agreed this was a good idea no matter how many times both sets of twins tried to explain. Lilly, Rose's twin, and Rose understood immediately 'why' Tyrone needed to take the shot. The fact that Rose was uneasy about *her* mate taking the shot was a different matter in the young woman's mind.

"We grow up in one another's minds, it's like we're one but different," Lilly explained. After going back and forth with the four of them, Jasmine had finally dropped the subject, realizing she would never get it.

Backing up, the ripe odor made her nose itch. She hit the wall and moved to the right of it. "Get some rest, Rone, and I'll check on you both later."

"Thanks, Ma," he whispered.

"Thanks, Mom," Rose said, her voice a little stronger than her mate's.

Chapter 5

DETECTIVE PETE JENNINGS SAT at his desk staring blindly at the blank form on the monitor. La Patron had spoken to the Captain, who had cleared the way for him to return to active duty after his sudden absence. Three and a half weeks ago he had been laid up on an operating table dying because he had no idea his wolf was dying, or how to fix with the problem. All his life he had been taught if he just ignored that side of his personality, it would go away.

When he was a teen, his mom had signed him up for a program where he was given bi-annual shots. At the time he didn't think much of it. There were no side effects that he was aware of and he felt fine. By the time he left for college, he no longer thought of the animal co-existing inside him. He should have known better, it's a miracle he made it as far as he had.

Every once in a while his head would hurt or he'd become nauseous, but those episodes became less over the years. He shook his head at his ignorance. According to the doctor, he would have been dead by the end of the year. His wolf had been that ill. And once his wolf died, he would have simply dropped dead.

Over the past few weeks, Froggy drilled every bit of history of the Wolf Nation into him. He'd been surprised that Silas Knight had been appointed to the position of La Patron by the Goddess, the Supreme Being all wolves believed in. According to Froggy, Silas was the equivalent of the President of any country. An alpha of his training and choosing led every state in the United States. Under Silas's reign, the Wolf Nation had grown stronger and prospered. He wore the title of the Alphas alpha and ran the world's largest pack.

Initially, Jennings had balked. The things he had heard about the Patron over the years didn't add up. But as Froggy trained his wolf, Jennings' mentality transformed. His wolf traits superseded his human side. He embraced the simplicity of Pack rules and craved the comfort and camaraderie of the local Pack. During training, he met other half-breeds like himself from various walks of life, male and female. And for the first time in years, he knew where he belonged.

"Merriweather has been calling and wanting to talk to you," Captain Samson said, placing a file on his desk. "While you were out, I assigned the case to Mirrs, but he never did anything on it. Now that you're back, see about wrapping this up."

Jennings glanced at the file with a sense of foreboding. Neither he nor his wolf cared for Merriweather. Robert had been a hired gun who lost his life on the case. Instead of being glad no one pressed charges against the criminal, the family tried to force Silas' hand in his own yard. Knowing what he now knew, it sickened him how Merriweather used the law with no regard for justice or honesty.

"Yes, Sir."

"He wants to meet with you to show you some information he has discovered. His phone number and address are in the file." The police captain paused. "How are you feeling?"

"I'm good, thank you, Sir." He glanced briefly at the Captain, who frowned at him.

"Good, good, glad to have you back," the Captain mumbled as he strode off.

Jennings wiped his nose. His newly acquired acute sense of smell and the Captain's cologne made his eyes water. Mentally, he dialed back his senses like Froggy had taught him so he wouldn't become distracted by all the body odors in the office.

For a moment, he gazed at the folder. His instructions from La Patron had been clear. "Close the case." It no longer mattered if La Patron was involved in the disappearance of Merriweather or not. If his Alpha meted out judgment, then Jennings would uphold that decree. His job now was to protect his Alpha and his pack. A surge of affirmation from his wolf ran through him. He and his beast were one on this issue. The question now before him was how to follow his instructions without raising a flag.

Opening the file, he re-read his notes from the beginning and smiled. Now that he knew Rose Bennett was bitch to one of La Patron's top security men, he marveled at how well she'd handled him. She could have ripped out his throat and covered it up easily. There might have been a few questions, but his death would have been swept under the rug. He had been rude and disrespectful when he'd interviewed her. Once he discovered who she was, he'd apologized to her mate. The apology had been accepted and he lived to work another day. But the words he had spoken to La Patron's bitch were not so easily glossed over. He had received a well-deserved tongue-lashing from Froggy, and La Patron knocked him down. Lesson learned. It was a good trade-off as far as he was concerned.

The folder was jam-packed with circumstantial data, but nothing concrete connected La Patron to the death of Merriweather. There never had been any substantial clues, other than the ramblings of a rich man yelling for justice for his corrupt relative. And the twisted desire of a dying detective bent on making a name for himself.

Jennings pulled his thoughts together and began filling in the computerized form. Just as he reached the end, the phone on his desk rang. As he re-read the comments he had typed, he answered. "Jennings."

"Detective Jennings, delighted to hear a competent voice on the other end of the phone. I trust your father is better," Alfred Merriweather said. Four weeks ago, Jennings would have wholeheartedly agreed with the man, puffed up his over-inflated ego even more, and pretended they were both on the same team. Now that he knew most of the cops on the force were wolves, he took offense at the dig and didn't respond to the belittling remark.

It took Jennings a moment to remember the cover story Froggy had given him to explain his extended absence. "Thanks, he is doing somewhat better, but he's not quite out of the woods yet. My brother is there with him now." All of that was true except he hadn't been in Montana with his stepfather when the man fell and broke his hip.

"Good, good, glad to have you back. Listen, I know you haven't had an opportunity to do much on the case but I found a folder in Bobby's things. I'd like you to come over and take a look at it. I would bring it to the station but in all honesty, I believe your fellow officers are tired of me and my family. If you don't mind coming out here, I'd appreciate it."

An uneasy feeling skittered down his spine. One thing Froggy had preached the last three weeks, trust your instincts because that's your wolf communicating with you. "I'm sorry but I have to clear my desk. I have a backlog here from being gone so long. If you can, just drop the folder off with the front officer, and I'll grab it from him and take a look at it."

"Yeah, okay, I'll see what I can do. Just trying to get justice for my brother. You understand, right, Detective?"

Jennings heard the curious note in the other man's voice. "Most definitely Mr. Merriweather. We all want justice and will do everything within our power to bring that about."

"Good to hear it, I knew you were a man of value when I first met you. You'll find the people responsible for murdering Robbie. I have faith in your sense of honor." He paused as if Jennings should say something.

He didn't.

"Well, thank you for your time, Detective. I'll get that file to you."

"I appreciate that Mr. Merriweather. Have a good day." He clicked off, gazed at his report for a minute, and then finished his comments. "There is inconclusive evidence that the death of Robert Merriweather was anything other than accidental," Jennings read softly before closing the file and sending it to the captain.

Three hours later, he came back from lunch. The captain had left a message for him to report to his office when he returned. After taking a long sip from his cup, he tossed it and went to see the captain. He tapped on the closed door.

"Captain?"

"Come in, Jennings."

He ran his fingers through his short reddish-brown hair and tucked his shirt into his black pants before opening the door. Unsure what awaited him on the other side, Jennings moved cautiously, listening to his wolf.

Captain Samson sat behind his desk, a large folder sat on the side. He waved Jennings to a chair. "Sit, sit."

Jennings took a seat, trusting his wolf to inform him of any foul play. "Thank you, Sir." He found a comfortable spot and waited for the captain to explain the purpose of this visit.

"Merriweather had one of his people drop this box with folders and other things off while you were at lunch. He called fifteen minutes ago saying a small box with a piece of critical evidence, some clothes or something, was accidentally left out of the package they delivered and wondered if you or one of the other officers could swing by to pick them up. I told him that we could wait until someone on his staff had an opportunity to bring in the additional information, but he insisted this new evidence be looked at today. He went on and on about how patient he's been, and the many times he has come to the station." Captain Samson released a long sigh. Sitting forward, he clasped his hands on his desk and gazed at Jennings. "I'm not going to lie. When you first came here a couple of months back, challenging the status quo, and allowing this man to have a voice, I wondered how long you'd last. When you disappeared, I thought I'd have to write you off. It shocked me when La...Mr. Knight called to tell me you were returning and to make sure you received your back pay."

Jennings hid his surprise at the Captain's candor.

"I read your report, you closed the case that I told you wouldn't go anywhere in the beginning. But in the meantime, you became Merriweather's champion. He didn't stress that you be the one to pick this information up, but it's your case and I want you to handle it. Besides, he thinks you are the only honest cop on the force."

Jenning's cheeks were on fire. "Sir, that was not my intent –"

The captain waved down his explanation. "I am a Black police captain in the mountains of West Virginia, with two more years to serve before my retirement." He eyed Jennings as he tapped a folder on his desk. "How do you think that happened?"

Jennings had wondered but never dared to ask. "I don't know, Sir."

"I applied and interviewed for the position along with a lot of other highly qualified men and women. This…" he waved at his large office, "…is a dream job. This city has one of the lowest crime rates in the nation. My salary is comparable to those of much larger cities and the perks are awesome. My home, car, and insurance…covered…for life."

Jennings stared at the older black man in shock. That was a really good deal. Maybe he should hang around and apply when the old man retired. "Wow." That was all he could come up with and it was inadequate.

"Yeah, but after I interviewed with everyone else, my final interview was with Silas Knight. He approves every government official who works in this State."

Jennings' eyes widened. He didn't know that.

"When he sends a Cop to me for a position, the man is hired, no questions asked. Or if he sends new equipment, like the security monitors his people are installing now, I say thank you and don't ask questions. Silas Knight runs the state of West Virginia, probably a few other states as well," the captain murmured. He hit the desk, garnering Jennings's attention.

"That's why I want this report closed. But you can't close it without at least looking at whatever Merriweather has to show you. He might kick up some dust, have someone start looking into local affairs. I don't want to chance that. Leave early, go to his estate, look at whatever he has so you can make an addendum to the report, and then close this case. Do you understand, Detective Jennings?"

"Yes, Sir." A sense of pride rose within him over the accomplishments of his Alpha. "I will take care of it today." He stood and remained standing next to his chair.

"Make sure that you do. I want to add that the file is closed when I give Mr. Knight my weekly report."

Jennings fought to keep the surprise off his face.

"Dismissed," the captain said. Jennings left the office, his mind shuffling and filing away all the information he had received. One thing stood out above everything else, his Alpha, La Patron was one tough dude.

Chapter 6

CAMERON STRODE DOWN THE corridor searching for Silas. The challenge was in a few weeks and his Alpha had not approved of him entering the competition. He wondered if Silas had doubts over his ability to rule the state or win the fight. If he fought one of the twins, chances were he'd lose. But he had fought Serrano during training and won all of their skirmishes. He believed he could take the man again.

His mate had been urging him to speak with Silas so that he could train better to fight the right opponent in the competition. There were moments when he believed she wanted him to become Alpha more than he did. But at least she talked more freely with him now and allowed him into her bed. It seemed a decent trade-off to him.

He stopped at the door of the lab and saw Dr. Passen speaking to a few men in lab coats. Cameron headed in his direction. The doctor eyed him for a second before finishing his conversation. By the time Cameron reached the man, the other two had walked off.

"Hey Doc, I heard La Patron was down here." He gazed around the large well-lit area seeking his godfather.

Dr. Passen released a breath, his entire demeanor changed as his eyes slid to the floor. "Oh... okay, you're not here for...yes, he was here earlier. But I'm not sure where he is now. I'll be calling him soon to view the testing of some equipment."

"When? How soon?"

"Within the next hour."

Cameron nodded and reached out for Silas via their private link, there was still no response. "I'll come back," he said, backing out of the lab. "Could you tell him I was here looking for him?"

"Yes, sure. I'll let him know." Doctor Passen waved him off and returned to the reports he'd been reading. "Unbelievable," he murmured, looking at the numbers again. Wanting another opinion, he placed a call. It was answered on the first ring.

"Hello."

"Matt, I have some new testing results on Asia. I need another pair of eyes on this, it's too… when can you get here?"

"I'm in the car on my way now. I should be there in ten minutes." He paused. "It's that good?"

"Mind-blowing, high-level security, so make sure you're cleared. I want you to work with me on this. La Patron wants this done yesterday."

"He always does."

Passen snorted. It was true, but in this case, he understood why. Asia was a walking blueprint for at least five key experiments. If they could unravel the codes and duplicate her mechanisms, they could find a way to defend against the technology their enemies threw at them. He still had nightmares over that week when bombs and viruses rendered them almost impotent. They'd had no way to detect the bombs or save the lives of those infected with the unknown virus. He'd left everything behind when La Patron called him for service and was glad he had. The things he had seen and learned in the past weeks were on the cutting edge. Being one of the leaders in this type of research would make his career.

"See you when you get here." He clicked off and stared at the paper. A few moments later he opened the door to Asia's room. She lay on the twin bed, her head bandaged and eyes covered with the locked blindfold. She had been through so much and yet she fought to survive when many would have given up.

"Are you going to remain by the door, Doctor, or do you plan to tell me what's on your mind?" The normalcy of her tone gave no hint of the extreme pain she suffered, which he knew the severity of, given the barrage of testing he'd recently put her through.

He snorted and moved away from the door, pulled the chair from beneath the small desk, and sat. Once he heard the door lock into position, he spoke, "You are an amazing woman."

In the dimness of the room, he noticed she went still. "I am? What have you discovered to make you say that?"

"You know more than you admit, I believe you are prevented from telling us everything by the small lock La Patron discovered earlier. From the x-rays we took this morning, I noticed several small metal teeth digging into your brain to hold it in place. There is a fake vein that travels from a small transmitter behind your eyes to this lock. I would like to remove it to see what's inside."

"And the problem is?"

"We won't remove it if it endangers your life. You are too valuable. I will find another way to access the data if it comes down to that."

"Do I have any say?"

Not really. "Of course, but you realize the final say comes from La Patron, and his mate is against you being permanently harmed in any way. Just so you know, you have a champion in her."

"A champion?" She paused. "I…I'm surprised."

"Me too. But I'm a scientist and a doctor first. You have opened up a whole new world in biomechanical research." Pausing, he shook his head, knowing how easily he went off on tangents regarding his work. "So what do you have to say about all of this?"

"I need to help defeat the people who are trying to destroy my Alpha and his den." Slowly, she sat up and pursed her lips. "It's more than honoring La Patron, although I do honor him and his mate. But as a full-blooded wolf, I've been robbed and violated. My beast demands I never give up or those bastards win, we would prefer death before that." Her head tipped in his direction when she spoke. "If there is anything within me that will help the Pack, take it. I am just one wolf. This war will destroy millions if we do not step up to the plate and neutralize their weapons. What they did a few weeks ago, ramming so much down La Patron's throat to see his response, was just the tip of the iceberg. Multiply that week by hundreds of occurrences all over the U.S."

His throat tightened. "Hundreds of undetected bombs? That would be…catastrophic. We are testing the detectors now, we have had to work fast, and there are still a few bugs to smooth out before we can meet the demand." He wiped his brow. "The virus…will they amp up more breeds?"

"They already have. Unfortunately, they didn't have Dr. Chism on their team, who would've told them straight up the serum only increases performance of what's already in place. Right now, they have a lot of problems with over-aggressive wolves, at least they did the last time I was—ow…" Her hand flew to her head.

He moved so quickly, his chair overturned. "What happened?" He knelt in front of her, holding her other hand.

"When I talk about certain things, my head hurts." She rubbed her forehead.

He rubbed the back of her hand. "Okay, you were saying what you saw the last time you were in a certain place." He squeezed her hand in warning. "Don't say anything, just listen until the pain subsides.

She nodded.

Releasing her hand, he stood and backed up to his chair. He sat and pondered what happened. "Amazing," he murmured.

"What?"

"The device latched into your brain keys into not only your vision but also your speech. The pain comes when you say certain words, which causes you to back off or... modify your words. Have you done that? Instead of saying the lab or whatever the building is where you were located, what if we called it a red site? Can you say that without pain? Red site."

"Red site." She straightened. "The red site was surrounded by a lot of trees with..." she paused. "Give me another word for below..." She pointed downward.

He grabbed his pad from his inner pocket and a pen. "Below ground, like a bunker?" She shook her head.

"Not a basement, an underground facility like this one?"

"Yes."

He wrote red site in his pad, along with the words, underground labs. With his other hand, he pulled out his cell and turned on the mini-recorder. "So the underground lab, red site, is surrounded by a lot of trees. Was it near a main highway?"

"No."

"Okay, to access it, you had to drive down a long dirt road."

"Yes."

He wrote that information down. "The next questions I want you to answer with numbers, hopefully none will be a trigger."

"I'd rather know now and avoid saying it later. Let's get on with it."

He marveled at her eagerness to assist them in this process. "There are three suns in the sky."

"One."

"A hybrid is made up of four beings."

"Two."

"You've had twenty surgeries."

"Forty-seven." Her mouth opened and then snapped close. "That was good. Keep going." She scooted closer to the edge of the bed.

"How many fingers on your right hand?"

"Five."

"How many pups does La Patron have?"

"Three."

His brow rose at that, but he continued. "What state does La Patron reside in?"

"West Virginia."

"And you were born in?"

"Gettysburg, Pennsylvania." She gasped and swallowed hard. "Keep going."

"Your favorite color?"

"Blue."

"The color of your eyes?"

"Dark brown, now reddish-brown."

He wondered if the camera lenses in her eyes were the reason they had changed colors. "Your hair color?"

"Dark brown."

"You are fifty years old?"

"One hundred and forty-four." Her hand flew to her mouth. "Holy shit," she whispered. "Keep going."

"Two brothers, two sisters?"

"Zero."

"Father?"

"Don't know."

"Car color?"

"Silver."

"Mother?"

"Roda-Mae." Her breath hitched and she hung her head.

Dr. Passen wiped his face as he processed the information. After a few generic questions, he asked. "How many doctors worked on you? Five? Ten? Fifteen?" There were only so many men qualified to do the type of research and work that had been done to her over the years. He'd run a check going back a hundred years and ran the names by her.

"Over fifty. They never used names, only codes. The codes were alphabet and numerical combinations. Like ADJK0039." She paused and then relaxed. "He worked the metal in my leg. He's foreign with a German accent. I remember he had thick fingers and smelled like tobacco."

"Okay." He typed that information into his phone and sent the email to his team so they could search. "The metal was placed in your leg ten years ago."

"Twelve. Twelve years."

"You received a metal leg after falling from a moving truck."

"Airplane." She winced.

His eyes widened, she had fallen from the sky? No wonder she had a new leg and arm, her body should've shattered. He glanced at her. She had placed her hands in her lap as she sat perfectly still. Frowning he asked her, "Are you in pain? Does your head hurt?"

"No. It works to empty myself and focus on the questions so I can answer them succinctly."

He nodded with approval. "Ten years ago the first flesh-covered bomb was created."

"Three. It came from another group."

Good, they weren't that far behind. "Five years ago the serum to change wolves was created."

"Eight. First shot."

He glanced at his notes. "A lot of the chemicals in the compound weren't discovered eight years ago. That means this formula has transitioned from the first batch."

"Yes."

He jotted down the information just as his cell beeped. "Excuse me, I have to take this call." He walked out into the hall. "Sir?"

"I am on my way to the labs, I got a message that it was time to approve the bomb detectors. Since the message didn't come from you, I'm calling to make sure you were ready."

"Yes, Sir. I was interviewing Asia. We came up with a way for her to answer questions without causing her pain."

"I want to hear all about it. I'll meet you in the demo area." They clicked off.

Dr. Passen had just typed in the code to open Asia's door when Dr. Matt Chism rounded the corner. He had been so engrossed with Asia, he had forgotten the doctor was on his way. He waved Matt over. "Give me a minute to say good-bye and I'll bring you up to speed."

Matt nodded and stayed next to the door as Dr. Passen walked inside. "I have to meet La Patron, but I'd like to finish this later." He waited for her response, which was slow in coming.

"Yes, but you should know I wasn't in any pain because I didn't think. I just answered. That must mean the lock is somehow connected to the cognitive processes in my brain. Unfortunately, I don't know if the answers are real or planted memories."

He nodded, remembered she couldn't see him. "You're right, but there are ways to verify some things, and that's where we'll begin. I don't want to do your forty-eighth surgery unless it will give you peace without leaving you a vegetable."

She smiled. "I learned some things about myself today. First off, if this thing in my brain could kill me, I'd be dead already."

Silently, he agreed with her.

"Second... dang, I'm old."

He grinned and closed the door.

Chapter 7

LT. JENNINGS CHECKED THE ADDRESS in the folder again and then gazed at his GPS. According to his device, the large colonial-style home in front of him belonged to the Merriweather's. He pulled out his file. Supposedly this family was one of the richest in the state, but judging by the unkempt appearance of the estate, he wondered if that report was true. His car idled at the turn-off into the driveway while he worked out the contradiction in his mind. The building looked abandoned, although he saw lights.

Inhaling, he pulled onto the cracked concrete masquerading as a driveway and inched slowly toward the house. Overgrown grass and debris covered the front yard. He saw loose boards on the wooden porch and wondered if it was safe. He turned off his car, closed his eyes, and inhaled, allowing his wolf to check for danger. There was no response, which concerned him.

He inhaled again, but there was no tingling of danger, no whimpering or barking. No tenseness in his gut like it had been earlier when he talked to Merriweather on the phone. Concerned at the lack of response, he started a mental checklist to determine the status of his beast just as Merriweather stepped out onto the porch with a large smile of welcome.

Trapped, Jennings stepped out of the car and put on his game face. "Mr. Merriweather, how's it going?" He moved closer but remained at the bottom of the steps, not trusting the wood. His host was slightly under six feet, with a head full of silver hair. The older man stared down at him with dark brown eyes that in the waning sunlight appeared to have some sort of glow. Up close, Jennings noted a thin metallic choker around the other man's neck, and the lower half of his face was filled with various sizes of dark brown moles.

"Come on in, we were just having a drink. Let me offer you something." He waved and moved toward the door.

"No, I have a date, I'm sorry. If you could just give me the rest of the information, I'd appreciate it." Even with his wolf silent, the hair had risen on the back of his neck. Going into that house was a bad idea.

Merriweather eyed him over his shoulder for a moment. "You know, son, I'm not sure where you're from. But here in West Virginia, we believe in southern hospitality. A man comes to my door, I invite him in and offer him a drink to wipe the dust from his pipes before he gets back on the road again. Now for some reason, you're being real un-neighborly. I want to know why? Has Silas Knight gotten to you? Has he made you promises? Or did he threaten you to make you close this investigation?" By the time Merriweather asked the last question, he had walked down the steps and was in Jennings' face.

"No and no. I told you I have something else to do. That's all. If you have the information ready, I'll take it with me." He met the other man's stare without backing down.

"Okay." Merriweather nodded, his eyes narrowed into slits. "I'll get it for you." Turning, he strode into the house.

It was all Jennings could do to remain composed. For a moment he thought the older man might hit him, the anger had been wafting off him in waves. Surely his refusal to share a drink with the man wasn't enough to bring on that type of anger.

The front door slammed. Merriweather held a flat box straight out in front of him. When he reached Jennings, he offered it to him.

"Here," he said when Jennings didn't remove it from his hand. Jennings took the box and backed off, intending to leave.

"Aren't you going to look in it?" Merriweather's jovial voice had been replaced with one of exasperation.

"When I get to the station." He opened his car door and prepared to toss the box in the back seat.

"You need to look at it now. If you have any questions, I can answer them for you," Merriweather's tone had changed again, this time it was more conciliatory.

In the back of his mind, he heard the Captain telling him to get this case closed. If looking into the box at the so-called new evidence would hasten the process, he needed to do it. Exhaling, and since there was no outcry from his wolf, Jennings opened the box. Inside there was a lace satchel with some leaves. He picked it up, turned it over, and saw the leaves were dried with some powder. He inhaled "How is this relevant to the case?" he asked glancing at Merriweather and then back at the meager contents of the box.

A spicy scent tickled his nose. He gazed at Merriweather, who stood on the other side of his car, and was surprised when the man multiplied. At first, there were two Merriweathers, then four, then eight, and after that, he stopped counting. Tingles raced up and down his spine. The back of his tongue tasted bitter. His face and neck burned.

"Water," he whispered through a tight throat.

"So you want something to drink now, huh Lieutenant?"

Jennings' head felt heavy. His legs buckled beneath his weight. What the hell did they do to him? The hard earth cushioned his fall. He lay prostrate on the ground looking up at the darkening sky.

"Move his car around back. Pick him up and take him inside. Wouldn't have to do all this if he'd come inside and had a nice drink. Stubborn fool," Merriweather grumbled.

Chapter 8

SILAS SLAPPED A GRINNING Dr. Passen on the back. "Great job, Doc. Everything worked without a hitch. I hope your team sent the corrections to the factory; large numbers of those detectors need to be shipped to every Alpha in the nation. Burn the midnight oil so our people will be safe." The scanners passed each test flawlessly, sending a wave of relief through him. The added ability to shrink the internalized bombs pleased him as well. With Jasmine's family on the way, and the upcoming challenge looming before them, he needed heightened security.

"Yes, Sir." Dr. Passen and Matt walked to the exit with Silas. "As the corrections were being made, they were simultaneously being downloaded to the engineers for modifications. From what I've been told, they've already started on production. Everyone agrees how important this equipment is, Sir."

"I ordered enough for the government agencies nearby. Make sure the detection devices are installed in the courthouse, police station, library, and county offices. I've already explained to those in charge this would be happening as soon as the devices passed inspection, so they are expecting your team."

Dr. Passen nodded. "Will do, Sir." He turned to Matt. "I want you to look at Asia's blood work and see what La Patron discovered." He then proceeded to bring both Matt and Silas current.

"She's over a hundred?" Silas asked to be sure. He hadn't suspected Asia was that old. Arianna, another breeder he had met in Mexico, who'd turned out to be crazy, had been over a hundred but looked to be in her twenties, so he knew it was possible.

"That was her first response, it surprised her," Dr. Passen said, agreeing with Silas' unspoken assessment.

"Well… if she had that many surgeries and they tampered with her mind, who knows what's real and what's fantasy," Matt said, voicing another of Silas' concerns.

"Asia believes if she doesn't think about what to say or not say, the answers come freely without the pain. There may be certain words that act as triggers to prevent her from revealing classified information," Dr. Passen said. "I've heard of a study where this happened. It's been a few years back; I'll have one of my assistants' research it so we can read the results." He pulled out his phone, typed a few instructions, and then returned it to his pocket.

"Plus," Matt said, glancing at Silas, "she has no idea who she is. They stripped her of her identity and gave her so many others that it's hard to take anything we get from her seriously."

"That's part of the plan," Silas said, thinking hard. "Asia is extremely valuable to them, whoever they are, especially if she is as old as she said. Arianna was over a hundred. I don't have to remind you how powerful she was. Must be something about being one of the first," he said, gazing at Matt.

Arianna had come to West Virginia with one goal in mind, to breed with Silas regardless of his mated connection. When she discovered he would never accept her, she'd released a mating call and made slaves of hundreds of wolves hungry to answer her summons. The bloody deaths from her foolish actions were unprecedented outside of war. Killing her had been high on his agenda; pity she could only die once.

"Leon, nor any of the other men we brought in, had the mental safeguards she has. Her eyes, mind, arm, legs, being the recipient of those types of surgeries means they want to keep her around." He gazed at Doctor Passen. "She fell from an airplane?"

The other man nodded. "That's what she said. Shattered her arm and leg, should've killed her." He met Silas's stare. "You're right, Sir. They want her and will probably send someone to take her again. What should we do?"

Silas had been thinking along those lines as well. He welcomed the confrontation. "I'll handle security. But she stays in her room. Right now, she's sleeping and eating well. Her headaches are few because we're not pressuring her for information. I like the code idea. Build on that. When I talk to her, I want the coded names to press for specific data. I have someone coming who will be able to connect the dots, it helps to make sure the information he's processing is accurate." He nodded, thinking fast. Pieces were falling into place. They were on the right path.

"I want Matt to go over everything we have discovered about her." Matt's eyes widened. Silas continued, going with his gut. "Asia is our key to designing a winning defense. I know she is a full-blood on steroids, but there is something special about her. Look for these answers. First off, why her? What makes her genetic make-up such that she has survived all the operations? Why not move to another wolf or breed, even? They kept coming back to her, I want to know why."

A spark of interest lit Matt's green eyes. Silas knew the man wouldn't be able to resist this type of challenge. Energized, he gazed at each man with the intention they catch his sense of urgency. "They placed metal inside a wolf and she can still shift and fight. How the hell is that possible? They made her an altered wolf, yet her wolf responds to me. When she shifts, what happens to the metal? Is it in the wolf? Does it make the wolf faster, stronger? What are the benefits?"

The spark of interest turned into a volcanic blaze. Matt's fingers were rubbing together and Silas knew the only reason the man remained in the hall was that he had not dismissed them. "Here's another thing. If we are going to be faced with altered wolves, how do we stop them? I want answers, I want them now," Silas demanded.

"The metal remains with the shift," Dr. Passen said, frowning. "We took x-rays of her in wolf form when she was first brought in. I'll need permission to take her to the gym to run on the machine to test her speed."

"No, she can never leave this area." Silas shook his head and thought about how to proceed. To get the answers they needed he would need to improvise. "I'll have the equipment set up on this level. Make a list of all the equipment you need and I'll have it delivered. But she will never leave this area until I destroy our and her enemies," Silas vowed.

"Her blood-line," Matt said slowly. Silas turned toward him. "Full-blooded bitches over a hundred aren't that surprising, but the number of surgeries she's had is. She shouldn't be as agile as she is. We age, become slower. Asia looks like a twenty-something, but claims to be almost one hundred and fifty, either that's some serious genetics or those scientists found the fountain of youth."

Silas stilled. "What?" His mind raced over the implications of that statement. Humans were obsessed with looking young, remaining young, and never growing old. Part of the attraction to interact with his nation had always been their longer lifespans. To date, he had not heard of full-bloods being used to fuel this obsession of humans.

Matt straightened and met Silas's gaze. "There is a hell of a lot more going on than we thought, isn't there?" he whispered, his face chalky white.

"Hell…what the fuck?" Dr. Passen said, running his fingers through his hair. "This just got real fucked. If she can regenerate, if they have found a formula that works on her to make her appear young…to remain strong, healthy…they need to reclaim her. Or destroy her to keep others from finding out what they can do." He shook his head.

"They've probably done the same tests on others, but she's the poster girl. The original model. The one who wouldn't die. Probably worked for years," Matt said slowly, his brows puckered into a deep frown.

"Or couldn't die," Silas said into the silence, as another thought, more wicked than the first slid through his mind. "Remember, they shipped her out as a hired gun for years. She's battle-tested. Imagine what someone like her would be worth to any military."

Dr. Passen snorted. "Anyone with enemies would immediately see her worth and pay millions for her skills." He paused and shook his head. "So she was right, they have made others like her. To raise money to continue research or to build an army?" He looked at Silas.

"Probably both," Silas answered as the situation settled on his shoulders. "Are they using full-bloods or breeds?" He glanced at Dr. Passen before his gaze moved to Matt. They moved into a small room and locked the door for privacy.

"Full-bloods are Pack animals," Matt said. "My money says they are taking breeds from the cradle and training them before their wolves develop. By the time they are old enough to shift, the wolf is not the same type of partner as a full-blood, more like a prop used for speed, healing properties, vision, that type of thing. But not the guiding force of a full-blood."

Silas nodded. As much as he hated to admit it, Matt was probably right. No one spoke for a moment. Knowing an enemy had come into his backyard and abused his people was a bitter pill. They'd caught him off his game which rubbed him wrong. During the past twenty years, he had complained to Jacques of boredom. His agenda had consisted of inspecting schools, meeting with heads of state, intervening in small squabbles between his Alphas, nothing more exciting. And during that time, his enemies were violating his people. Shame, thick and vile, rose, choking him. He stood and turned away from the others.

"*Silas?*"

"Not now, Jasmine."

"*What's wrong?*"

He knew she could search him and replay the past few minutes, but she granted him a measure of privacy. "*Just coming to some realizations. Pride is a monster and it does go before the fall.*"

"*Okay. You're arrogant and proud, I knew that when I met you. Why does that bother you now?*"

He should've known she wouldn't sugarcoat anything for him. "*It never occurred to me that humans would be bold enough to attack wolves, to experiment on us. We're stronger, meaner, and in a one-on-one fight, we could rip them apart. Never occurred to me that those I saw as inferior would instigate a war that could destroy my world... and the reason it never crossed my mind is pride.*"

"*What made you open your eyes to all of this?*" There was no judgment, agreement, or disagreement in her voice, and that eased him somewhat.

"*Just going over the information from Asia.*" He shook his head. "*It's deep.*"

"*Okay, the boys are fighting and I have to intervene. But remember this, yesterday's lessons are guideposts for today and tomorrow. Learn from that and change accordingly. No matter what, I love you, arrogance and all."*

He smiled. "*Thanks,* he said dryly. Moments later he turned from the wall, fully aware that he had dropped the ball. But the game was not over yet. "Asia's a full-blood with a Pack mentality, why allow her to get close to me? As the leader of all wolves, I could control her wolf, and through the bitch I control the human. They placed her in a risky position, why? What did they gain? Are they still using her in some way?"

Dr. Passen pushed his glasses up the bridge of his nose. "It was a risk. You've disabled the camera so they see nothing. It's no secret she's here in the compound. Can they hear anything?"

"I don't know, but I doubt they are getting any decent signal from where she is below ground," Silas said, thinking through every test and conversation he'd had with the bitch.

"Don't forget, according to her, their lab is also below ground. Probably lots of steel and concrete, so they may have found a way to receive transmissions through all of that," Matt said.

Silas agreed.

Given the amount of money and knowledge invested in Asia, he knew her creators hadn't given up on her. It was only a matter of time before they attempted to retrieve her, and he would be ready. "I need both of you on top of this. Let's get some answers and find a way to defend against attacks. Asia is willing to help, use her as a resource, but nothing that will cause permanent harm or death. Is that understood?"

Matt and Dr. Passen stood. "Yes, Sir. I'll get started on the reports and then catch up with Passen to sketch out a plan of action." Matt rubbed his hands together. "Is it okay if Davian returns and stays in my old quarters here? Something tells me this project will take most of my time."

Matt was mated to Davian Bennett, father of the twins and Jasmine's ex-husband. She had thought he was dead and was not happy when she discovered her deceased husband was alive and living with his mate. Former husband and wife had met and made peace, but Silas' wolf would never allow her to spend too much time near the man.

Silas nodded. "That's good. Let me know so I can scan him." Silas would explain the limits of his generosity to Davian, which would satisfy his wolf.

Matt nodded as he moved to the exit and glanced back at Dr. Passen. "I still have the same office area?"

"Yes." Dr. Passen nodded and followed behind him. "I downloaded the files and sent them to you earlier after we talked. I look forward to our discussion after you've read the data. This is exciting. I think we are on the brink of something great for our people."

Silas leaned against the wall thinking of the repercussions of what he believed was happening. Asia was in danger. If they could kill her, they would have by now. Obviously, they couldn't destroy her from a distance.

He exhaled. That meant they planned to send someone for her. This was the absolute worse time for Jasmine's family and the minister to visit. Security needed to be on steroids. His phone beeped. Alpha Jayden sent a message regarding the upcoming challenge battle.

"Will Cameron compete?"

Silas stared at the words on the screen. Cameron wanted to fight for the Alpha position, but Silas thought his desire to lead was for all the wrong reasons. He'd had several conversations with his godson over the past few weeks and nothing he said had dissuaded the young wolf. Silas knew Lilly, Cameron's mate and Rose's twin, pushed Cameron behind the scenes. That in of itself was not a bad thing. He would be the first to agree that having a mate in your corner, pushing you to be the best you could be, was part of the mate's creed. But the job of Alpha was about serving wolves beneath your care, not having the number one spot for prestige. And that was the problem he had with Cameron's mate.

Lilly wanted Cameron to have the top dog spot in the state. Silas believed, despite what Jasmine said to the contrary, that the young bitch wanted to live in the Alpha house, to step into the position of the first family for West Virginia. Lilly had no idea the type of work required of Cameron. Silas worried she might bail when she realized being First Bitch was not glamorous; rather it was hard work, long hours, and very public. And then she would convince Cameron to leave the post once reality set in.

He and Jasmine were split over his decision. She believed Cameron would do well and Lilly would make a great First Bitch. The challenge was coming up soon and he had to approve the combatants.

"*Jasmine?*"

"*Yeah?*"

He could tell she was distracted, so he spoke quickly. *I will allow Cameron to compete.*

"*That's good. I've got my hands full right now. Renee and Adam ganged up on David. He is not a happy person.*" Once Jasmine snapped out of her depression, she'd retook the nursery, much to the caregivers' relief. His pups were a handful who required loving discipline; however, no one would do that other than Jasmine or himself.

Silas's brow rose. "*Really? Do you need me?*" David had gone through a recent growth spurt within the past few weeks and was now taller than the others. He dabbled in each of his siblings' interests. He would color with Renee, work through puzzles with Jackie, and chase Adam around the room until his brother collapsed on the floor in a fit of giggles. Seeing David bloom filled Silas with wonder, amazement, and most of all, love.

"*Always.*"

He waited for her to say more. When she didn't, he sent warmth through their link, not wanting to interrupt her longer than he already had. Trusting his mate's opinion, he sent a simple message to Alpha Jayden. *"Yes, Cameron will compete."*

Glancing at his watch, he realized he hadn't heard from Tyrese regarding Tyrone's condition. *"Rese?"*

"Sir?"

"How's Rone?" Silas asked as he stepped out into the corridor. He needed to beef up security both for the christening and Asia. If Tyrone could be left alone, he and Tyrese could get started making plans.

"He and Rose are still resting. I haven't heard much from him in a while."

Silas had forgotten that Rose had taken off because of the symptoms. *"Good. I need you to meet me in my office in twenty minutes. Let Rone know where we are."* Silas paused. *"Davian will be moving into Matt's quarters until his mate finishes a big project for me. Let Rone know that as well."*

"Yes, Sir," Tyrese said slowly. *"I'll tell him and meet you in twenty minutes."*

Silas disconnected and headed for the nursery. He wanted to see his pups and give Jasmine the news in person that Davian would be staying in the compound for a while. His wolf wasn't happy, neither was the other side of him. Jasmine still hadn't worn anything remotely frilly for him like she had for her ex. He planned to remind her of that as well.

Chapter 9

JASMINE HEARD THE SOFT sound of the door closing. Three hours ago a call had come in the middle of their sexual play. Silas surprised her by answering the summons, and then completely blew her away when he lifted her from his lap to the side of the bed. Hurt and disappointment had warred with her need to be wrapped in his arms as she watched him leave their bedroom. He'd thrown a promise over his shoulder to return in an hour.

Stewing with sexual frustration, she had waited. After the first hour, she'd shut down their link so he couldn't hear her horny thoughts and took care of her needs with one of her toys. The vibrator took the edge off, but what she needed was Silas. Seeds of doubt rose within her fertile imagination. It wasn't that she thought he was cheating on her, through their link she would know. Plus, there was the whole 'can't get hard with anyone except your mate thing'. But that didn't mean he couldn't lose interest.

Despite Davian's claim to the contrary, there were many days, before he met Matt when other things had taken precedence over meeting her needs. Many nights he'd slept in the guest room, claiming he didn't want to disturb her. The truth of the matter was she had been so horny, she couldn't get to sleep without battery-operated aid. She never thought she would need a vibrator with Silas. At first, his sexual appetite had been enormous. She would take naps to recover, but lately...he seemed to have lost interest.

For the past two hours he'd attempted to reach her through their bond, but she was so damn frustrated with her needs taking a back seat, she didn't want to be bothered.

His irritation was a living, breathing thing in their bedroom. "Jasmine."

"What?" She didn't bother rolling over. He wasn't the only one in the room unhappy.

"You shut me out. Why?"

"I was busy." She pressed her thighs together as her body vibrated with need.

"With what?" He sounded confused.

"None of your business," she snapped and scooted to the edge of the bed.

The silence in the room stretched taut like a band at the end of its elasticity. "Everything about you is my business."

She squeezed her eyes tight at his soft reply. Damn it, he was supposed to get angry. She could remain pissed at angry, arrogant Silas. Soft, loving Silas…she wouldn't stand a chance. And she needed to keep her wits so that they could make some changes. After spending most of her day in the nursery, she needed some adult time with him.

The bed depressed near her hips. He was too close. "Talk to me, what is wrong? Have you stopped taking your medication?"

She bit her lips as her lids lowered. Now that she thought about it, she hadn't taken her meds since yesterday but she wasn't depressed, she was hurt, angry. A combination of musk and his natural scent wafted across her nostrils, teasing her, tempting her to roll into his arms. Pressing her lips together, she curled into a ball, refusing to speak. She sensed him trying to connect through their link and slammed it down tight.

"Jas…I'm sorry. I was gone longer than I promised. There's the problem with the Lieutenant missing, and some security equipment failure, one thing led to another, delaying my return."

Heat rushed to her face and neck at his explanation. Rolling out of bed, she looked down at him. "I won't do this."

"What?" He gazed at her, his face a mask of confusion. And that hurt even more.

"I played second fiddle for twenty years to one man. I am not doing this again." She shook her head, emphasizing her point. "Nothing you just said could not have waited until tomorrow or least for a few hours. You could have turned any and all of that over to someone else so that we could spend time together. Ever since the bomb scare, and then the depression, we spend less and less time together. I know I went through some health problems, but I'm over that now. You come in too tired to make love. It's been a quick screw, if that, and then you're up and out at dawn. We don't talk, don't cuddle, or do any of the things I need from you. You're so damn busy –"

"Busy making sure you, my pups, and every damn one else is safe," he argued, standing slowly to face her. He wiped his face with his palm before speaking in a low, clipped tone. "A woman sat in my damn house for a month with a bomb inside her body waiting…waiting to blow me up." He slapped his chest. "I fed that bitch, kept her warm, healthy, and for some fucked up reason she probably could not explain, she threatened everybody I love."

She stiffened when he raised his voice. His eyes took on an ethereal glow and changed to a frosty emerald green, a sure sign of his mounting anger. "I am aware of that –"

"Are you? Are you? Because I wonder about that, considering you've invited your family to visit at a time like this. Right after we discovered two bombs and Rese was kidnapped from below. What if something happens while they are here? Huh? How do I keep them safe? How will you look at me if a bomb goes off and they get hurt? Will you still love me? Or leave me?"

Horrified by the scenarios he painted, and that he would think she was that shallow, she blew out a breath. Pointing her finger at him, she spoke through a tight throat. "That's not fair. I have never placed any kind of conditions on loving you. Why are you dragging my family into this? What do they have to do with you not spending quality time with me? What do I have to do to get a few hours with my damn mate?" she screamed, brushing the tears from her face.

He stepped toward her.

She held out her hand as she backed up. "No, Silas. No. I refuse to do this again. It's gotten worse, not better. If dealing with security because of the christening is freaking you out, you should've talked to me. If this is too big of a deal, you should talk to me. Not back off and disappear for hours at a time. I am not doing that with you. Not happening." She had backed up to the door with no clear plan of where she would go. She simply needed time to think.

"You say you never placed any conditions on loving me, but when you're angry, you withdraw. You shut down, cut me off and you know what that does to me. I have told you it's like losing a lung, it's harder to breathe, and yet you do it every time you are angry."

It was the combined hurt and sorrow in his voice that stopped her. She had never heard him sound so mystified before. As if he had shared something with someone and they had turned that knowledge around and used it against him. Surely he wasn't implying she deliberately tried to hurt him when she merely trying to protect herself.

"Stop that. I do not. You are trying to flip this around."

He held up his hands and then stuffed them into his pocket. "No. Honestly, it's not my intention to place the blame on you. You are right, I could have returned sooner. I could have assigned those tasks to someone else. On those issues you are right." He met her gaze. "But you are wrong to say you are second to anything in my life. If I am working long hours, it is to make sure you and my pups are safe. I want all of us to have thousands of tomorrows. How could I pass on the responsibility to someone else to take a look at security equipment when Tyrese was taken from beneath my nose a few weeks ago?" He removed his hands and took a step toward her. "You think I don't hear the bombs going off in my sleep?" he whispered raggedly. "I brought the enemy into my compound and both of them were locked and loaded. Could've killed my pups, my people, my mate. How can I allow anyone else to check security? I can't. That's not the wolf… man I am."

She swallowed hard knowing he was right. Stripped emotionally, she spoke from her heart. "I don't like sleeping alone. I need…I need you. I miss you when you're not here." She paused. "Don't forget, I went through all of that with you. The bombs, Tyrese' kidnapping. Silas, I sat in a room with Siseria while the bomb was inside her. If you think I don't have nightmares about those bombs, you're wrong. I may not have seen the bloody aftermaths like you did. But I sat not five feet from her, talking, trying to get information. So…yeah, I need you to hold me at night. To talk me through my fears, allow me to hold onto you when you're dealing with this shit. We're supposed to be a team, but you've gone Lone Ranger on me. I can't handle this by myself. I miss you so much, I ache with it."

He stepped closer, touched her arms. She trembled at his nearness.

"Jas…I miss you too. I want to ride between your thighs every minute of the day. You know that's my favorite place. But… right now, there is a war going on…"

Frowning, she took a step toward him. "War? Did you just say war?"

He nodded. "Asia gave up some interesting information today. I can't remember if it was before or after you came in, but another group of humans has declared war on us."

"What? Do you mean like a real war? Like they have overseas or the ones they show on TV? Organized crime turf wars, that kinda thing?"

"Wolves being killed in experiments, that's war. Some are being changed into weapons, some are being sent to fight on behalf of the highest bidders. They got the jump on us. I have my teams working around the clock to find answers and develop solutions so that we have a fighting chance. It's going to take some time for them to complete that task. That means I have to play offense to buy them that time."

She searched his eyes, read the sincerity of them, and stepped into the circle of his arms. He wrapped them tightly around her. His warmth filled every nook and cranny of her chilled soul. War? She knew something was off but hadn't expected that. Her sons, her mate, her family were at risk. Prickles of energy raced up and down her spine. She wondered if he noticed. "What do you plan to do?"

"Kick their asses in such a way they never come back at me." His answer was quick, to the point and oh so Silas Knight.

"I'm sorry." Although her complaint was legitimate and something they needed to deal with, the timing sucked. He needed her strength and support right now.

He squeezed her tight and dropped a kiss on her forehead. "I should have told you what was going on. Things changed today, I stepped up security and made other plans. I discovered the location of one of their warehouses and will be sending them a surprise visit." His voice changed to one of gleeful determination. "Like I said, offense."

She nodded against his chest, the feel of his cotton shirt warm against her skin. "Whatever you need from me, let me know."

"Keep my pups safe." He took her arms in his hands and pushed her backward. Their gazes connected and she read his intent. "If anyone breaks through security and comes after you or the children, take whatever you need from me and kill them." He waited a moment. "Do you understand?"

She nodded. "Yeah. I heard you."

He shook her slightly. "I asked if you understood."

"Silas, I'm not simple-minded. I heard and understood what you had to say. Now listen to me." She waited a moment for his attention to shift to her eyes. "If someone breaches security and comes after me or my kids, I will kill them. You evidently don't know me well if you thought for a moment I would do otherwise. But here's where you got it twisted. I will kill them if they come after you as well." She held up her hand to stop him from speaking. "Don't waste your breath telling me to do or think anything differently, because I'm not going to change my mind, you can take that to the bank."

He dropped his hands and took a step back. They continued to look intently at one another. He scowled and she gazed at him until he threw his hands up. "I need you safe."

"Likewise."

His head snapped up, he opened his mouth and then snapped it shut. "Jasmine." His tone held a plea.

"I love you, Silas. Don't ask or expect me to accept something happening to you without doing something to help, I can't do that anymore than you could." She read the resignation in his eyes and released a breath. Her mate could be stubborn but he was realistic.

He snagged her around the waist, their bodies slapped together when he pulled her close. "Be careful, try not to get hurt. You are my barometer for control. If you get hurt, I will lose it and level this place," he whispered next to her ear.

She shivered hearing the ring of truth in his words. Many would die if he lost control, she would need to be extra careful. Damn, this was the worst time to lose control of her emotions. She opened her mouth to tell him about her energy surges and then changed her mind. He had a lot on his plate. She would deal with this.

"I will have my children with me; you know I don't play when it comes to family. You never have to worry about that." She gazed up into his dark green eyes. "With everything that is within me, I will not allow my family to die without a fight. Believe that." As she spoke, a gentle breeze touched the nape of her neck.

"Your eyes changed." He brushed his thumb across her bottom lip.

"Huh?"

"When you made that vow, there was a glow behind your eyes. They became translucent, like liquid gold."

Her brow rose. "Really?" She pretended a nonchalance she didn't feel.

His gaze went from thoughtful to resigned as he placed a kiss on her lips. "Yes. I pity any fool who attempts to come after my mate or pups. I have no doubt you will handle them well. Thank you, love." He took her lips and deepened the kiss.

Her heart jumped and then raced as she sank into his embrace. Familiar heat flared between them as he lifted her in his arms. She laid her palm flat against the hard plane of his chest as he carried her to their bed. Inhaling, her senses were inundated with the scent that was all him, masculinity personified. If she could bottle his unique fragrance, men would pay a mate's ransom for an ounce of the potent cologne. Her tongue flicked into the crook of his neck.

"Mmm…" he moaned, depositing her on the mattress, then falling on top of her. "You are my mate, you can't be second in my mind, we are merged into one. You are the beat of my heart and I am sorry you felt neglected. I will spend all night and tomorrow if necessary to correct my mistake. No one is more important than you, Jasmine. "He gazed into her eyes, holding her captive. "No one."

Tingles of mind-bending pleasure shot through her as she met his unwavering stare. Her eyes filled as his head lowered. "You are my queen." He placed a soft kiss on her lips. "My mate." He kissed her again. "My woman." He brushed the tears from her cheek. "I am sorry you are hurting." Instead of kissing her again, he rolled her over on top of him and held her gently while she pulled her thoughts together. His nearness had a habit of robbing her of her wits at times.

"I know you do. But you have to talk to me, Silas. I don't want to listen to your conversations all day through our link. I have enough just dealing with the kids. I expect you to fill me in on the highlights so I'm in the loop."

He rubbed her back with his fingertips, sending zings of heat rushing to her core. If this wasn't so important, she would demand he take care of her needs right now. But her mate was not fully human and thought in black and white; she needed him to move toward the gray areas and compromise.

"I need a few hours of just the two of us. Doesn't have to be sex, although that would be great," she rushed to say when he stiffened. "We used to do that before the bomb scare, we need to go back to it. As I said, I miss you and need to re-energize. That only happens when we spend time together."

He nodded. "Okay. Whatever we need to do to get back to where you are comfortable, let's do it. I didn't realize how much everything that happened a month ago impacted my actions. I cannot allow that." He squeezed her tight. "Thanks for telling me about it." He pushed her up so she could look into his eyes. "But you can't leave me over stuff like that, or for any reason."

"I wasn't leaving you," she huffed. "I was leaving the bedroom so I could think. It's too hard to gather my thoughts together with you in the same room as the bed."

The arrogant man grinned. "Really?" He pulled her down and kissed her. She forgot the conversation, the war, everything disappeared beneath the fire of his touch. Melting into his embrace, she relished in his possession.

Within seconds he was bare. Their lips broke apart and she sucked down air as she pulled off her tank top.

"Never compare me with your ex again. I am your mate and there are things I can never do, neglect you is one of them. Never mention your time with him in that manner again. I don't like it. My wolf hates it." He paused while searching her eyes. "I promised Matt his mate would be safe here. Don't make me renege on my word and destroy him."

The change in atmosphere caught her off guard. How did he do that? Go from fucking hot to a somber serious moment. Her insides quivered from the promise in his kiss. She nodded, deciding silence was her friend because her only point of reference *had been* her time with Davian. The purpose of the comment was so he understood her feelings, not for Silas to hurt her ex-husband.

His eyes never left hers as his fingertip rubbed and then pinched her pebbled nipple. Fire raced through her stomach as her head fell back. Ridiculous… the effect this man had on her libido was effing ridiculous and she loved it.

"You are so beautiful," he whispered. Her eyes flew open, searching for his. She met his searing gaze and softened. Her mate was arrogance personified, tough as nails, and in some instances, unmercifully brutal. Right now the love and commitment shining brightly from his eyes shoved all of that aside. It spoke to another side of him. The side that was mate, father, and lover. Her lower regions tightened in anticipation.

"Silas," she whispered, her wits evaporating beneath the power of his gaze.

"I love you." He didn't pretty it up with anything extra that was not his way. Her man saw things in black and white, and this time she approved.

"I love you," she said, feeling the coolness of the sheets beneath her as he flipped her over. Her fingertips traced his jaw, loving the stubble on his chin.

"Show me," he whispered.

Smiling she reached low and guided him in. Perfection. That word captured her mind as he slid forward, stretching, claiming, and filling her completely.

"Silas," she said breathily as he placed a kiss on her forehead while holding her tight. Heat from his body set hers aflame. His hardness pulsed inside her like a live wire sending waves of anticipation through her. Need rose with a demand for fulfillment. Lifting slightly, she widened her legs and he slid a bit further in.

"Mmm," he moaned as she rolled her hips beneath him, pushing him closer to the edge.

"You like that?" she whispered, watching him, the tightness of his jaw, the tenseness of his biceps, and the slow dance of his pecs.

"Yesssss," he hissed, and then he moved.

Jasmine thought she was prepared, she truly did. But when he pulled out to the tip and slid back in so slow, she lost her mind. With each hard inch filling her at such an incredibly slow pace, everything inside her tensed in preparation for her climax. Grabbing his butt cheeks, she lifted her hips off the bed and ground into him as hard as she could. If she could climb into his body to ease the itch he created, she would.

He chuckled. "Sweet bitch," he said softly into her ear just before he pulled out and slammed back into her. On edge already, her walls welcomed his thrusts and tightened with each subsequent penetration.

"So good..." she moaned as he continued hitting her spot, taking her higher until she flew over the rainbow. Her body shook beneath the earthquake of her emotions. "Silas," she called, opening their link so he could enjoy her experience.

He groaned as he followed her in orgasmic bliss. She took in large breaths while rubbing his back as he continued to shake and shudder. Moments later he rolled over and pulled her close. She kissed a salty patch of his sweat-laden chest and then ran her tongue across the spot.

Mmm," he moaned. "Such a demanding bitch."

Grinning, she bit his nipple and then laved the abused nub. "Okay, now that you've apologized appropriately, let me show you how much I missed you." She slid down, grabbing his rising wood. He had promised her this night and she intended to take him up on it.

Chapter 10

JENNINGS BLINKED AGAINST THE light as he tried to make sense of where he was. He tried to move and discovered he couldn't. He was strapped to a bed and his head hurt. Inhaling, he refused to panic and tapped into his wolf just as Froggy taught him.

His wolf whined but there wasn't much else. At least his beast was still with him and according to his former instructor that made all the difference.

"How are you feeling, Detective?" A deep feminine voice asked from somewhere in the room.

"I think…water, please." A long straw in a cup was held against his lips. He sucked long draws, savoring the liquid as it coated and saturated the dryness in his mouth and throat. "Thank you." He tried to see more of the person but in the dimness of the room he could not.

"Your mother, Marsha, was a good woman. She would be proud to see you today."

At the mention of his mother, Jennings stiffened. "What are you talking about?" His mother died his freshman year of high school.

"Marsha was a breeder, as was her mother. She fell in love with a wolf, although she didn't know it at the time. They had sex. He left town, not realizing she was one of the few human females who could breed from wolves. She never saw him again, didn't remember his name either. By the time I met her, you were around four, five…tops. She needed help and moved into one of the sanctuaries we have set up around the country for breeders. We offer protection against those who would harm these women, and train them to survive in the world."

Jennings frowned. "I don't remember any of that." He tried to move his arms, but the cuffs were locked tight.

"Of course you don't. But that's another issue. When Marsha left to move out west to be with her new husband, she took an oath to continue your treatment. It pleases me that she was faithful in that task."

"What are you talking about? Oath to who? For what?" His mind cleared at a minuscule rate while he struggled to break free of the bonds.

"Stop struggling, you're only going to hurt yourself, and then how will you drive home?"

He stopped. They were going to allow him to leave? He took a deep breath. "Where am I? How long have I been here?"

"You are in one of our sanctuaries, and you have been here overnight."

"Overnight?" He tried to remember but his mind blanked.

"Who are you?" Quietly he called upon his wolf and was met with silence.

"Corrina Griggs, I'm the founder of the sanctuaries. I knew Marsha personally. She was a sweet woman, so idealistic. I was at her funeral, stood in the back. You probably don't remember, but we sent a large bouquet of pink and yellow flowers. They were her favorite colors."

Jennings swallowed hard. *I'm trapped with a crazy bitch.* "You're a breeder?"

"Yes. I do believe I was one of the first, although I cannot prove that."

He reached out to Froggy through his link and heard static. Fighting down the panic that threatened to choke him, he spoke. "You have pups?"

"No."

He didn't know what to say after that.

"I killed them."

Jennings stilled and then gazed toward the shadowy outline the voice emanated from. "What?" He couldn't wrap his mind around her blatant confession.

She tittered. "Aw, come now Lieutenant, the pups were colored. I lived in the south during that time and they would have been slaves. I could not present either of those little colored girls as mine. I had them drowned by my servant. Since then I have been very particular over my male choices."

He tried to relax so he could remember everything she said. He didn't think La Patron was aware of the sanctuaries or this woman.

"Sounds like you have been around for a while." Since slavery days, that'd place her over a hundred. Knowing La Patron was over three hundred made her declaration easier to believe.

"I have. We have. It has been a long journey but we are near the end. Soon the world will see the beauty and the power of the half-breed nation. Wolf and human, working and living together side by side. Our numbers have finally reached the pinnacle; we are the majority over full-bloods."

He blinked. "Majority of what?" His mind must still be muddled because there were a lot of half-breeds like he had been, totally out of sync with their wolf. To be an effective breed, you had to embrace your wolf or die.

"There are now more half-breeds in the nation than full-bloods," she repeated slowly as if he were incapable of understanding those words the first time she uttered them.

He latched onto a crummy thought. "What about the shots, the ones I've been taking for years. It kills the wolf and eventually the breed."

"Of course it does," she snapped. "We have the antidote to reverse it. So as we take our place –"

"You'll control thousands of wolves by having the medication or solution to them living longer."

"Don't ever interrupt me again," she snarled.

"I apologize." If they were going to allow him to leave, he wanted to take as much information as she would share with him.

After a brief silence, she spoke. "It's millions, not thousands."

He frowned but remained silent. Millions what?

She must have read the confusion on his face. "Millions of half-breeds have been documented as receiving this shot for five years or more. All it takes is twelve months of steady consumption and the wolf begins to deteriorate. It's slow, which suits our purpose. But now…now we are at the precipice of change. Things are in place."

"Place?"

"Pity they killed Robbie. To be fair, he was supposed to kill La Patron, to get him out of the way…" She sighed as though it hurt to think of her deceased relative.

"He was your son?"

"Yes. Alfred as well. But their father is human."

Alfred? Why did that name sound familiar?

He heard the scraping of the chair. "I just wanted to talk to Marsha's boy, I always liked her. She had a good heart and believed in the cause. She kept her oath and I believe she would be proud of you."

Jennings swallowed hard. He hadn't thought of his mother in years. She hadn't been a nurturing parent, but she'd done her best he supposed. "Thank you," he said into the silence.

"Mother, are you ready?"

Jennings froze. He knew that voice. He hated the fogginess still muffling his senses.

"Yes, dear." She paused and he knew she was looking at him. "It was nice seeing you again after so many years."

He didn't respond as he heard the steps grow distant. Who was her son? He focused on that mystery instead of wondering why she sounded as if she would never see him again. He lay in the dim room for what seemed like hours. Muted clicking sounds and the release of pressure on his legs and wrists signaled he could move his limbs. Slowly he drew his legs up and his arms down. Tingles of pain filled him as circulation returned.

Rolling to his side, he stopped himself from falling off the narrow cot with his hand and pushed up. Pain sliced into his skull as the room swam before him. He remained still and counted to ten. Inching forward, his head pounded ferociously, so he counted to ten again. This time slower. He placed his barefoot on the floor. It was cold and hard, like concrete. He placed the other foot next to the first and scooted forward, testing his weight. His knees buckled. He grabbed the bed and waited a few moments. When he stood the next time, his body cooperated and he walked in the direction he had heard the footsteps leave.

It took a while, but eventually, he tumbled outside into the scorching mid-day heat. Leaning against the wall he sucked in gulps of air to clear his head and calm his heated body. Fire burned in his chest from his heart slamming repeatedly against it. Something was wrong with him but he had no idea what. Again he reached for his wolf. Internal sounds of whimpering and a weak whine were the response. Jennings gritted his teeth in frustration; those bastards had done something to his wolf.

Blurry eyed, he gazed out at the area in front of him. A white Volvo sat off to the side beneath a tree. He shook his head and stared at the vehicle. It took a few minutes for it to dawn on him that the Volvo was his car. Pushing off the wall, he moved slowly to the automobile, opened the door, and sat down, the keys were in the ignition. A thousand things were wrong with this picture, this entire situation in fact. But sitting in the driver's seat of his car helped him return to a normalcy that he desperately needed.

He sought his wolf and felt his beast stir. "Thank you, Goddess," he whispered. He leaned his forehead against the steering wheel and breathed. His wolf was going crazy, growling and snapping. He knew he needed to drive away while he could, but the urge to be one with his wolf pushed him to shift.

Opening the car door, the interior light illuminated the folder on his front seat and that's when it came rushing back to him. "Merriweather, that son of a bitch," he murmured. That was the voice that sounded so familiar. The Merriweather's were at the root of tampering with breeds to displace La Patron and all full-bloods. He shook his head and closed the door, searching the car for his phone.

When he couldn't find it, he inhaled deeply, trusting his wolf to alert him to any additional danger. He started the car and drove down the broken path away from the house. When he reached the main road, he stopped and got out of the car to look around for some type of marker so he could return with La Patron's security to investigate the house. Without his phone, he couldn't take a picture. Even with his enhanced vision, there was nothing to distinguish this dirt road from any other. Unzipping his pants, he pissed on the bushes on both sides of the entrance knowing he could find his scent. Finished, he returned to the car and drove off. Five minutes later and a few miles down the road, a loud explosion tore through the silence of the day.

Jennings pulled over to the side and stared back at the burning building. In his gut, he knew it was the place where he had been held captive. It seems he didn't need to mark the location after all. He called out to Froggy through their link and this time he received an answer.

"Where've you been?" the gruff voice asked without a salutation. Jennings told him what happened. That information he wanted to tell La Patron.

"You headed home?"

"Yeah. I need to clean up and then I'll report in."

"Station or here?"

"Wherever La Patron wants me for debriefing. The old woman, Griggs, she's planning a takeover with half-breeds. Something about having the antidote for them to live. It's kind of foggy but I'll tell him what I remember. You'll tell him what happened, right?"

"Yes. Be safe."

"Will do. Changed my mind, I'm on my way to the station to check in with the Captain. I can't find my phone. After that, I'll be heading home to shower, grab a bite to eat, and then head back to work."

"Expect La Patron to contact you, he was worried when he got word you were missing last night."

Knowing somebody was concerned watered the dry areas in his life. He had always lived alone and never seriously dated. Being part of a pack completed him. *"I look forward to it."* Traffic into town was backed up due to road work crews. After taking a few detours, he pulled into a parking spot in the back of the police station, turned the car off, and headed into the building to report in. He hoped the captain was in his office and in a good mood because once he explained what happened, Jennings intended to arrest Merriweather and his mother.

"One moment," the security guard said as Jennings entered the building. "We have a new procedure and I need you to walk through this device."

Jennings nodded. "This is pretty far from the main building is there a reason for that?"

"Yes." The man didn't elaborate and Jennings didn't care enough to push. He placed the contents of his pocket into a small container for separate scanning and stepped into the small gateway. Immediately red lights flashed, the bars in front and behind him lowered, trapping him.

He gazed at the security guards, who backed up, and two men wearing hazmat suits headed in his direction. A siren went off, hurting his ears.

"Remain still, we are going to try to shrink it." The men pressed some buttons, there was a whirring sound. The sirens were loud in the background, making him dizzy. He placed his palms over his ears.

"Sir, return your arms to your side and remain still," one of the men said as the other backed off.

"*Jennings?*" Silas called out to him.

The background noise was so loud he could barely hear him. "*Sir...it hurts. The noise hurts.*"

"I know. Listen to me." There was a pause. "Jennings?"

Jennings closed his eyes to stop the pain. It got worse. He lurched forward and threw up. The sirens seemed closer as if they were in his skull.

"*Jennings?*" Someone yelled his name.

"*Hurts*," he murmured, squeezing his eyes tight.

"Listen to my voice...it'll make it easier for you. Just listen to my voice..."

Jennings tilted his head to follow the calm sound. There was an audible clicking inside his head, and then nothing.

Chapter 11

SILAS YELLED JENNINGS NAME again as he heard the explosion in his head. The following silence cut into him like a sharp knife. Disbelief that someone had gotten to Jennings that quickly ripped through him. How was that possible? Stumped, Silas sat on the step leading into the gym. He couldn't believe or accept Jennings had just exploded at the police station.

"Silas?"

He swallowed back the bitter taste of defeat and looked up at the beams in the ceiling to gather his thoughts. He had not been able to save one of his own. His enemies had taken Jennings, locked him down, and loaded him with a bomb intending to send him back into the public. What if he had been at the park where there were no detectors?

"Silas?"

Or the grocery store? How much longer before his people realized he was a failure, that he could not protect them from their enemies.

"Dammit Silas, thinking like that won't help, answer me," Jasmine shouted through their link.

"Yes?"

"Where are you?"

"I want to be alone right now."

"No. Where are you?"

"I have to go to the police station. Jennings just exploded. Part of the police station's destroyed, some deaths, some injuries. I...I need to go assess the damage."

"Okay."

He turned toward the entrance. She stood framed in the arched entryway.

Overhead lights created a soft glow behind her making her appear angelic in a light pink dress that fitted her curves. For a moment he stared at her image wondering how she could appear so clean when the world had turned so dark, so dirty. His chest burned with anguish over the loss of innocent lives. Good men and women died needlessly. Today was a dim mark for his people.

She moved toward him and wrapped her arms around him. Inhaling deeply, the scent of gardenias mixed with her natural scent and filled him. He closed his eyes as she pulled him close and pressed the side of his face against her breast. The solid thump of her heart anchored him as he struggled to maintain his composure. Her warmth seeped into his skin, chasing away the cold that started the moment he heard the echo of the explosion through the link. Flashbacks from the previous month ran in a continuous loop in his mind, the deafening sound, the shaking of the ground, the bloody aftermath.

"We're losing," he said, his throat so tight the words sounded garbled.

"We're just starting," she countered, drawing her fingers through his hair. The steady strokes on his scalp soothed and steadied him.

Releasing a long-held breath he spoke. "They have weapons we can't match."

"We have weapons they don't have."

He glanced up at her. "Like what?"

Their gazes met and for a second he thought she wasn't going to answer.

"Wolves, baby. We have wolves and all that goes with that… they use wolves. There is a big difference. I bet a wolf would've smelled those bombs a mile away. Why not have security work in teams. One in wolf form and the other inhuman. Allow the wolves to scent what a bomb smells like, have them patrol public areas."

Silas stared at Jasmine for a few moments, stunned by the simplicity of her suggestion. The top minds in his nation worked on a solution and he had overlooked something as basic as this. When in wolf form, their senses were much stronger than when human.

"What about the humans? What will they think when they see wolves on leashes?" It could work.

She waved it off. "They live in our back yard, chances are they've seen wolves already, if not they'll get used to seeing them do security work, like police dogs, only bigger."

He scowled at the reference.

She smiled and threw up her hand. "Just saying."

"It could work, I'll have Froggy look into it." He pulled her close and hugged her tight. "Thank you."

"You hurt, I hurt. You're blaming yourself, and I can't let you go through this by yourself. How could I not come to you?" Leaning back, she cupped his face in her hands. "No matter how hard this gets, we are going to beat this thing. You are La Patron." She nodded, emphasizing her point. "A Goddess-given position. We both have your back."

He nodded slowly. "You're right." Losing, being at a disadvantage was new for him. The technology, implants, humans invading his world to such a degree… mind-boggling. But Jasmine was right, he had been so intent on fighting his enemies on human terms he all but neutered his wolf. It was time for him to use the innate talents of the wolf and have the scientists create weapons that complemented their natural abilities.

"I wonder…"

He looked at her when she remained silent. "What?"

"Why Jennings? I mean he was a cop, so that gets the police involved. But obviously, they're not worried about that, so why Jennings? Why blow up the police station? Was there someone locked up they wanted taken out?"

Silas grabbed onto her words with the tenacity of a lifeline. He needed to channel his thoughts into a more productive arena. "They could've found an easier way to take out one or two people in prison. I think this was more…Jennings had left to go see Merriweather—"

"Merriweather?" She stared at him.

He nodded slowly. "Yeah. The guy whose brother or son was in the cave, he's been pestering me for a meeting. I told Jennings to close the case."

"I talked to him. Rose wasn't feeling good, remember?"

Silas turned to face her fully, remembering she had shut him out of an exchange that upset her. "Rone had the shot, go on."

She repeated the conversation she had with Merriweather for him. "What do you think?"

"I agree with you, he's crazy. But he did say talking to you confirmed the timing or something, next thing I know Jennings is taken and a bomb placed inside him."

"Are you going to pick up Merriweather?"

"I bet he would love that. No doubt he's locked and loaded as well. I can't chance anyone getting close to him. Not right now anyway. But he will be dealt with, that's for sure."

"What if you sent in a team?"

Silas shook his head. Jennings' death was too fresh to contemplate allowing any wolves to go after the man. "Too dangerous. I need Jacques here now; we need a new set of eyes on the information." He stood and assisted her up.

"He's on his way," she said, looking around the empty gym.

"I know. But with Rose taking care of Rone, and Tyrese coordinating security, I'm shorthanded."

"I'll work the office."

His head snapped up and he narrowed his eyes. What was she up to? She never worked in his office before. He asked the only thing he could think of without sounding suspicious. "Who will watch the babies?"

"Their nurses." She waved him down as she moved away. "I'll handle the office and keep things running smoothly here while you take care of the town. Once you leave, I'm locking the place down, so let your people know."

Stunned into silence, he couldn't think of a solid reason to say no. He stared at her back as she moved with purposeful strides toward the elevator. "Yes, Ma'am," he teased, ignoring her mocking frown and balled fist.

Chapter 12

"I WILL HAVE HIM call you, Jayden. If he isn't answering his link it's because he's in a situation where he can't. But I can assure you he is well." Jasmine wrote the message on the notepad. In the past three hours, forty-nine Alphas called, almost frantic because they couldn't reach Silas through their links. Once they heard her voice they calmed somewhat but were concerned over the bombing incident.

"Thank you, Madam Jasmine. I received my first shipment of detectors this morning. My people are busy installing them now. If La Patron requires anything from me, he only has to ask."

Jasmine nodded. Every Alpha had offered a similar remark. "We know you will, Alpha Jayden, and appreciate it. Thank you for your offer and the call. Warm wishes to Maureen and Callum." She wasn't pushing him off, but she was tired of saying the same thing repeatedly. She had complained about not talking or interacting with other adults, and now that she was in a position to do that, she wanted the simplicity of the nursery. In the back of her mind, she heard her sister mocking her with a 'be careful what you wish for' comment.

Once she clicked off, she called the nursery. Missing her babies, while being happy for the break, worked her nerves. Guilt and pleasure ate at her. She asked the nurse who answered, "What are they up to?"

"They're resting. They ate all of their food and fell asleep."

Jasmine glanced at the clock and stifled a groan. It was nap time. She had been so busy she hadn't noticed. "Alright, call me when they wake. I want to come over and spend some time with them."

"Yes, Mistress."

Grimacing at the name, Jasmine hung up and went to grab something to drink from the refrigerator when the phone rang.

"Hold on," she said, placing the bottled water on the desk before replacing the earpiece. "La Patron's office."

"Jas? Jasmine?"

"Mom?" Frowning, she straightened.

"Yes. We're at the airport. But I don't see you or the boys."

What? Her mom wasn't supposed to be here until tomorrow. "What airport?" She turned to look out the window, wondering how she got the dates wrong.

"Yeager. What happened, you forgot we were coming?"

Jasmine frowned. "No, you and Renee were arriving tomorrow morning, at least that's what you said when the three of us were on the phone a week ago."

"Oh... I must've gotten my dates mixed up. You want us to stay at a hotel and come tomorrow?"

Jasmine shook her head at her mother's antics. There was no way she would allow her mom to stay in a hotel. "No. Give me a minute and I'll get someone out there to pick you and Mark up... he is with you, right?"

"Yes, he's waiting for our luggage. Give me a call and let me know what to do."

"Okay." Jasmine clicked off, wondering who was available. She made another call. It was answered on the first ring.

"Mom?"

"Hi, Rese. Sorry to bother you." She explained the situation. "I need someone to pick them up."

"Alright, let me get cleaned up a bit and then I'll head over there. I'm going to take a couple of guys with me for this pickup. Security is tight and Nana could be targeted as the mother-in-law of La Patron."

Jasmine groaned. With the bombing, the timing sucked. "Security is in place for tomorrow, when she was supposed to arrive."

"I know. I'll call the airport and have them ushered to a secure location until we arrive. Tell her I'll be there in an hour, give or take fifteen minutes for traffic."

She bit her lip, wondering if his leaving was the best course of action. "Is this going to cause a problem with Silas, he said he was short-handed."

"I finished the job he had me doing and was on my way back to shower. I'll let him know, but other than pulling Rone out of bed, I'm the only other person who can pick them up."

"I hadn't thought of Rone. Do you think he can ride with Rose? Or would that be too much?"

"I can do this, plus it'll be easier with me scanning them. Rone might not be up to taking them through the paces."

"Okay, thanks, honey." Relieved to know he was going with security to pick up her mom, she breathed long and deep. "How are you feeling?" She had stopped asking every day about the aftereffects of the kidnapping when he told her in clear terms he was fine. It had been difficult not to hover when he returned from being taken, but Silas had insisted she give Tyrese space to cope with the changes to his body.

"I'm good. No problems."

"Have you seen Asia?" She changed the subject since his tone didn't encourage more discussion. Jasmine really liked the young girl and wished Tyrese took more of an interest.

"Yes, I have. But nothing is gonna come from it. I don't like her that way. She's good people, been through a lot, and will be a great catch for someone. Just not me, so please...just stop. Please."

Had she been pushing? Hearing the sincerity in his voice gave her pause. "You aren't interested?"

"She's a friend, maybe someone to work with on a team, nothing more."

"Okay, I'll leave it alone. Plan to have dinner with us tonight. Your aunt is going to want to see you before the christening, so plan to also spend some time with her after she arrives tomorrow."

"Will do, looking forward to it. I hate Mandy couldn't come. Maybe next time. So...Nana's married again?"

"Yes. I think so. Mark's with her at the airport. Silas has a file on him somewhere if you're interested in some lighthearted reading."

Tyrese chuckled. "I don't blame him. There's some crazy stuff going on." He paused, she heard someone talking in the background before he returned to the phone. "I just cleared the gate. I need to pull a team together and call the airport. Tell her I'll be there soon and until I arrive, someone will be coming to take them to a secure place to wait."

"Okay. I'll let Silas know they're here."

"Good idea, he didn't answer me a moment ago. I know he's busy in town."

Exhaling, she disconnected, and then called her mom.

"Jasmine?"

"Yes. Tyrese is coming to pick you up. He should be there in an hour or an hour and a half, depending on traffic. Someone at the airport is going to take you to a waiting area so you're comfortable." She hoped her mom didn't balk, this was the best she could do on short notice.

"You're not coming?"

"No, the babies just went down for a nap. I'll see you when you get here... we have to talk."

Her mom released a long sigh. "I know. I know. I'll see you soon."

Closing her eyes, she argued in her mind whether or not to tell Silas now or wait until later. He was adamant about doing deep scans on Mark and the minister. Her mom and sister he was willing to give a pass, well, he had scanned Renee when he met her in the hospital. Now that she thought about it he hadn't said he wouldn't do a personal scan on her mom.

They were a team. Releasing a pent-up breath, she reached for him. "*Silas.*"

"*Yes.*" He responded immediately, which lightened her spirits and bolstered her courage.

"*Mom and Mark arrived a day early; she got her dates mixed up. They're at Yeager, and Tyrese is taking a team to pick them up. I just wanted to let you know,*" she added when he didn't say anything.

"*They need to be sequestered until Rese gets there. I'll have security cover them until then. Is everything alright at the compound?*"

"*Yes, all forty-nine Alphas have called and offered assistance, the phone lines have been busy dealing with them. The kids are all asleep, it doesn't seem as though they missed me today.*" She pushed away that sobering thought. The fact that it bothered her became the deciding factor for continuing to take her medication. Now was not the time for a relapse. "*I plan to check on Rone before Mama gets here. I haven't seen Cameron or Lilly, they with you?*"

"*Yes. I'll send them back if you need them.*"

"*No. No, I was just doing a mental roll call, that's all. You okay?*"

It took him a moment to respond and she sat heavily in the chair, tempted to delve deeper into their bond to see what he experienced. Last night she explained she didn't want to do that. She wanted him to talk with her instead.

"*I will be better when I am with you,*" he finally said in a heavy tone. "*I need to be here, people are looking for answers and confirmation that everything is okay.*" He paused, "*I've implied the situation was contained without scaring everyone with the truth.*" His anger slammed through their connection.

Her heart wept for him.

He continued before she could say anything. "*I implemented the wolves on leashes program, which has sped up things. Everyone has been accounted for. The damage was contained to the back of the building, unfortunately, t the mechanical rooms were housed there.*"

She closed her eyes at the extent of the damage, "*How long to get the bomb detectors replaced?*"

"*The replacements are on the way from Arizona. Four days is what's quoted. The brick masons feel they can have the walls rebuilt in ten. We'll see.*"

"*That will be great if they can work that fast.*" She hoped it could be done for the morale boost alone.

"*I will return shortly.*" Silence filled their connection.

Jasmine sat slumped in the leather chair, her thoughts on Silas. These violent outbursts hit him hard. She was sure Merriweather was involved in some way but how? Was there a message behind Jennings' death? What did they hope to gain? Unanswered questions raced through her mind until she gave up. Placing a call to housekeeping, she made sure the rooms for her mom and Renee were ready and checked on dinner for tonight. "Place a bowl of fruit in my mother's room and some chocolates, she likes those."

"Yes, Ma'am."

"Thanks," Jasmine said and clicked off. Pesky thoughts that she had missed something continued knocking at her. Finally, she turned the phone to voice mail, locked the office, and headed for the labs. A few minutes later, she walked up behind Matt and tapped him on his shoulder. He had been so engrossed in reading some paperwork that he jumped at her touch.

"Jasmine," he squeaked, jumping away from her. His face reddened until it blended with his red hairline.

"Hey, Matt." She looked around at all the activity. Silas would be pleased. "I want to talk to Asia."

His eyes widened. "Asia? Why?"

"I have a couple of questions I want to ask her. Some things have been on my mind and she might be able to clear them up for me."

His eyes darted around the room, no doubt searching for Silas. She smothered a grin at his nervous reaction.

"Okay…wait a minute." His eyes narrowed. "I thought there wasn't a door here that you could not open," he said, repeating a statement Silas had made to him last month. "Why are you asking me if you can talk to Asia?"

This time she frowned. "I wasn't asking, I was telling you that's where I'll be for a few moments. That's the protocol when Silas or I am in the lab."

His face colored more as he fumbled. "That's right…it's just you never come alone, so it threw me for a loop. Sorry…sorry about that. I'll make a note." He stepped away but didn't move too far off. Jarcee, her security guard, stood near the door watching like a ghost. He walked with her to Asia's room, and then stopped outside the door. This was the tricky part. Silas did not want her alone with Asia; he had been very clear about that. She knew Jarcee was aware of this restriction.

"Stand near the door."

"I will stand inside so I can protect you if there is a threat."

Shock that he'd countered her directions raced through her. She thought of defying him, but then he would call Silas. With all her mate had on his plate, she would not add to them. She nodded. "Okay"

They entered the darkened room. Asia lay curled in a ball on her bed. Her head rose slightly as she inhaled. One moment she was on the bed, the next she was on the floor on her knees, head bowed. "Madam."

Jasmine shook her head at the speed at which Asia moved. Even blind, there were no wasted movements. Plus, didn't that hurt falling onto her knees from the height of the bed? "Please return to your bed, I want to talk about something that's bothering me. I think you can help me think it through." She took the only upholstered chair in the room while Asia moved back to the bed.

"I am honored that you would discuss your concerns with me. If I can help, I will."

Jasmine repeated her conversation with Merriweather and then the situation with Jennings. She figured she had another thirty minutes before the kids woke and then another hour after that before her mom and Mark arrived. Hopefully, she and Asia could work through the Merriweather puzzle to give Silas new information for his offensive. The idea of being more helpful brightened her day.

"La Patron and I talked earlier. We both agree there are two groups at work here; their goals are diametrically opposed to each other although they are using similar tactics. One group wants to preserve the breeds; I'd say that was Merriweather and his people. Why they destroyed Detective Jennings, who was a breed, is a mystery. The other group, the one that sent me, doesn't do bombs. Too much collateral damage and draws attention from the outside. They also want to manipulate La Patron, not kill him, so they can control the Wolf Nation."

Jasmine mulled over what she'd been told. "So Merriweather's group is the one who wants to get rid of Silas. He was communicating with Jennings when it went off."

"He must've been the trigger."

"What?" Jasmine looked at Asia. "How? Silas was in the compound, Jennings at the police station."

"Which means this was a test of sorts to see if the trigger would work through a telepathic connection. Someone, somewhere, watched and documented everything that happened." Asia sounded so sure, that Jasmine agreed.

"They will do this again, won't they?"

"I'm sure they will," Asia said softly. Jasmine heard the sadness in the younger woman's voice.

Suddenly nauseous, Jasmine placed her hand on her stomach and closed her eyes. Instead of finding something to help Silas, she discovered things were worse than they thought. "This whole thing sucks. I don't know why Merriweather is fixated on breeders, we're not wolves, just people like everyone else."

"No, not quite. The ability to give birth to another species is unique. The original group was certain they had a God-given assignment to merge the races if I recall. It's been so long since I had any interaction with them." Asia paused, her face scrunched. "They were evangelistic in that regard, telling anyone who would listen that the new world order was not the way the Bible or Koran predicted. Yeah, they are fanatical in their beliefs, you cannot reason with them."

"He sounded weird on the phone –"

Asia snapped her fingers. "Another thing. I had forgotten about them it's been so long. But they intend to take the breeds public. That was a big difference between the old group and the new. The newer group thrives off secrecy. They do not want the world to know or believe in wolves."

"Take them public…whoa. They can't…that's just crazy," Jasmine said, her gaze swinging from Asia to Jarcee and back to Asia. "Why?"

"Because they believe humans and wolves are supposed to co-exist on earth, as one large race. Eventually, the breeds will out-number the full-bloods and humans." Asia paused. "They have always believed that was their mandate."

Goosebumps prickled across Jasmine's arm followed by a tremor that raced through her. This was not the information she'd expected to hear. Later tonight, she and Silas would have a long discussion regarding this situation. But first, she needed to get through dinner with her mom and her new husband. "You've given me a lot to think about, thanks, Asia. Do you have everything you need?" She stood in preparation to leave.

"Yes, Ma'am. They're taking good care of me. How's… how's Tyrese?"

Jasmine's eyes slid to Jarcee, who faced the opposite wall. "He's good, no lasting effects."

"Good. But tell him not to be so sure about the effects. When you think it's all clear, something weird happens. I told Dr. Passen and I think he plans to have him come in for quarterly tests as a precaution."

Jasmine's heart jumped against her chest at the thought of Tyrese having additional side effects but she refused to react in a manner that would offend the young woman. "Thanks, I appreciate that." Swallowing down her fear, she walked to the door and looked over her shoulder. Asia remained seated on the bed, legs crossed beneath her, mask locked in place across her eyes, and her long braids draped across her shoulder. Jasmine marveled at the sense of alertness in Asia's erect posture and the irony that she was the one person, though blinded, who could see what was happening around them.

Stepping through the doorway, Jasmine glanced at the clock. The discussion, while fruitful, had taken longer than she anticipated. She had about thirty minutes to prepare. "We're going to stop by Rone and Rose's and then the nursery," she told Jarcee as they headed for the elevators.

Chapter 13

JASMINE, TYRONE, AND ROSE stood in the hallway leading to the west wing. Although her mom and sister would be staying in the north wing during their visit, dinner and socializing would take place here. Jasmine had taken her meds and felt more in charge of her emotions. One of the reasons she detested taking the meds was the few occasions when she felt nothing. It was as if her emotions left for the Himalayas on holiday. Tonight wouldn't be too bad, but she would need to work on keeping her anger in check. She had noticed a recent penchant to become upset over things that never bothered her before, and she didn't like that.

Earlier she had changed, and now wore a v-neck pale yellow dress with cap sleeves that fell mid-thigh, along with black and yellow low-heeled sandals. Since the removal of her braids, she wore her hair down or up in a ponytail. Today, she had it pulled back from her face with a yellow and black polka dot band which allowed it to fall down her back.

She glanced up at Tyrone. He was dressed in fitted jeans and a nice printed short-sleeve cotton shirt. His hair had grown out a bit and curled against his collar. His caramel-colored complexion glowed, which was a dramatic change from the other day. "You look much better, Rone." She smiled at Rose as a feeling of genuine warmth surged through her for the young woman. "You take great care of him."

Rose's face reddened. "He's a big baby, but I'm glad he's doing better." Tyrone gazed at his wife before placing a kiss on her forehead. The top of her head reached her mate's chest.

"Thanks, Ma. I feel better." He paused. "Rese says they just cleared security and are on the way up. He sent their luggage to their rooms. He wanted to know if Silas was here yet, I told him no." He gazed at her for confirmation.

Jasmine nodded and turned toward the elevator. Silas had not returned, but then she hadn't expected him. Today had been the worst day for a surprise visit from her mother. She still couldn't understand how they had gotten the days mixed up.

"Jasmine," her mother said, moving quickly toward her with outstretched arms. Jasmine met the smaller woman midway and they embraced. The smell of lavender and something else tickled her nose. Soft strands of reddish-brown hair brushed against her cheek. The strength and length of her mother's embrace surprised her. Eventually, Jasmine pulled back and met her mother's dark gaze. Perhaps it was the knowledge of breeding wolves or living with Silas, but she recognized uncertainty, fear, and yes, secrets, in her mother's stare.

"I'm so glad you could make it, Mom," Jasmine said when the silence stretched a bit long.

"Oh, I'm glad to be here." Her mom looked over Jasmine's shoulder. "Oh…Rone. My baby, look at you. How are you feeling? Better I can tell." She moved past Jasmine and took Tyrone in her arms. Seeing her mother rise on tip-toes to cuddle her grandson brought a smile to Jasmine's face.

"This is my wife, Rose," Tyrone said, with a large grin as he introduced his mate.

"Wife? I missed the wedding?" Her warm tone changed into one of surprise.

"No, we just went to the courthouse. No wedding," he said, still smiling.

"Oh… I've done that a few times myself." She hugged Rose. "Welcome to the family, call me Nana like my boys do. I'm happy to have another grandchild." She turned and waved toward the handsome tanned male who stood near Tyrese. He appeared to be Indian or someone with Middle East ties with his olive complexion, dark hair, and eyes. Right now, his eyes were focused on her mom. Jasmine's spirits lightened as her mom accepted the tight embrace and kiss from her man.

"I want you all to meet Mark, he and I will be getting married next month in Aruba."

Jasmine hid her surprise. She thought her mom had already tied the knot with this one. "Hi, Mark." Jasmine shook his outstretched hand, keeping her distance.

"Hello Jasmine, I have heard great things about you and Renee. Victoria is the best thing to happen to me. She's the light of my life." His gaze left her mother and met hers. "I'm honored to be a part of your family's event." His warm smile lit up his face, making him appear more handsome. Jasmine understood why her mom claimed he was the one. Then she remembered her mom had made that pronouncement a few times before. She hoped for her mom's sake that Mark would be the last man in her life for a while.

Jasmine nodded and stepped back so Tyrone and Rose could greet him. She caught her mother's eye. Was she gloating? The look seemed a bit off. Her mother's smile grew wider as Mark returned to her side.

"Come on inside, let's talk, catch up. Dinner will be ready in about thirty minutes," Jasmine said, still puzzled by her mom's attitude. Granted, Mark was handsome with hazel eyes, she put him around 45 years of age, much younger than her mom's 60. The scar on his chin made his face interesting. He wore a thin gold necklace, but no other jewelry. Jasmine liked a man who toned down on accessories. He was shorter than both her sons, so that would put him under six feet with what appeared to be a nice firm body. For some reason, her mother acted as though she had hit the jackpot, and that was a surprise. Normally her mother took her lovers in stride like you'd take a bus. If you miss one, there would be another shortly.

"Good. I'd like a glass of chardonnay if you have it," her mother said, holding onto Mark's arm as they moved into the living room.

Jasmine glanced at Rose and smiled. Tyrone and Tyrese exchanged glances as they followed behind her mom and Mark.

"How was Florida?" Jasmine asked after they all took seats in the living area. She went to the mini-refrigerator and pulled out a bottle of Chardonnay, as well as a Moscato for herself.

"It was hot, humid, and lovely," her mother said, patting her face with a handkerchief. "I had a great time. We're thinking of relocating there." Her gaze slid from Jasmine to Mark with predatory intent.

"I want to go to Orlando, see Disney," Rose said, breaking the silence. Jasmine handed her mom and Mark each a glass of wine.

He raised his hand. "No thank you. Water or a soft drink for me, please." Heat exploded in Jasmine's cheeks as she realized she hadn't asked him what he wanted. Instead, she had assumed he wanted what her mother did.

"Okay. Rese could you get him a bottle of water please?" She placed the wineglass on the table and took a seat across from her mom.

"Where is your... boyfriend?"

Jasmine choked and started coughing at the idea of Silas being called a boy or anything in that arena. Heat flared in her cheeks and she tamped down the snappy comment that rose to her lips.

Rose and Tyrone snickered.

Tyrese shook his head and looked away.

Once Jasmine got her breathing under control, she eyed her mother to see if that had been a deliberate dig. The pleasant smile plastered on the older woman's face left Jasmine unsure, but she needed to correct this now before Silas arrived.

"My fiancé is working a little late. He'll be here for dinner. And Mama..."

"Yes?"

"Don't ever call him a boy. There is nothing remotely boyish about

Silas."

Her mother blinked repeatedly but didn't speak.

"Victoria didn't—"

"Seriously." Jasmine cut Mark off, her gaze still on her mother. "This is his home and I will not allow you to disrespect him, not even as a joke." This time she sharpened her words so that everyone in the room knew she was not teasing.

"I didn't mean it as disrespect. I'd forgotten he was your fiancé. Sorry about that."

Jasmine held onto her mother's gaze a moment longer, reading her sincerity. "Okay." How her mother could have forgotten was beyond her. She had told Renee and her mother a few weeks ago that she and Silas were engaged. It was the best cover she could come up with to explain her current living situation without getting too deep. The conversation had veered into a possible engagement party, and then a wedding at the christening, both of which Jasmine promptly vetoed.

As La Patron, a formal mating was a huge deal which would take months to prepare. She and Silas planned to have that ceremony once the threats were neutralized.

"Where are the babies?" her mother asked as she looked around the room.

"In the nursery, we'll see them after dinner," Jasmine said, using her no-nonsense voice again. Silas had been adamant that he scan Mark before the man was allowed near his children and she would honor that.

"Nana, Rose, and I are thinking of buying a vacation house in Colorado, have you spent much time near the Rockies?" Tyrone asked, drawing his grandmother's attention.

Mark glanced at Jasmine before turning his interest to Tyrone. He continued rubbing her mother's back, something he had been doing since they sat on the loveseat together. Jasmine's opinion of him rose a notch.

Silas arrived at the compound. Butterflies filled her belly as she sat still on the long sofa, pretending the discussion on vacation homes was of interest.

"Hello, beautiful." His voice had taken on a dark, wicked cadence that had her creaming in her panties. It didn't make sense that he could still do this to her, from a distance no less.

"Wolfie," she purred through their link, making sure he heard her desire for him. After dealing with his duties at the police station she felt his sharp need for her. It was a pulsating live wire through their link.

He chuckled. The intimate husky sound was refined fire. Her hand flew to her throat. Her breath hitched as molten heat raced through her.

"You okay?" her mother asked, causing the conversation in the room to stop and all eyes to fall on her.

Jasmine cleared her throat. "Yeah…um hmm, I'm fine."

"That's true," Silas said smugly.

Jasmine didn't know what happened to change Silas's attitude from earlier today, but she was glad. He hadn't teased her like this in… months, now that she thought about it.

Silas stepped into the room and immediately met Jasmine's gaze. She was gorgeous in that dress. He wanted to peel it off and sent her an image of him doing exactly that. The scent of her lust punched him in the gut. Sitting on the chair, with her hands folded in her lap, she presented a prim picture while sizzling decadent thoughts danced through her mind. Some centered on sexual aerobics which made him hot and hard. She wanted him and it didn't matter who knew.

"Hello there."

The loud spoken words reminded him that there was mixed company in the room. After another glance at his mate, he strode forward, nodding at the twins and Rose. He stopped next to Jasmine, his hand unerringly touching her back before cupping the back of her head. Their gazes merged and he bent down to accept the invitation of her kiss. Soft sweetness assailed him as the kiss deepened.

His wolf growled.

The sound rolled from his throat as he pulled her up and wrapped his arms around her waist. The day had been long and brutal. Returning to her had been the one thing that kept it from being a total loss. Heat poured from him as he fed on the love she freely gave, allowing it to strengthen and renew him.

"Mom?"

Silas felt Jasmine push against him and tightened his hold. Neither he nor his wolf was ready for her to move. His wolf howled, demanding to be one with his mate.

"Silas," Jasmine whispered, her voice sending sparks of need through him. He sought her mouth again as his skin prickled. His gums itched and he knew his eyes had changed colors. Reminders of the blood and loss of life he'd witnessed earlier flew across his mind. It was her calm, her beauty, that kept his wolf leashed all day, and now being so close to her, his beast refused to be denied.

"Silas." She turned her face aside. His lips grazed her jaw as he fought to bring his wolf under control. This was one part of living with humans he didn't understand. In a den, loving your mate was seen as a natural, beautiful occurrence. It showed love and commitment to the Pack as well as his pups. Jasmine had been horrified at the idea of him loving her wherever. When he realized it was a real problem, he relented. But damn, he didn't like it. Her hand rubbed his back in understanding. *"We have company,"* she reminded him through their link.

He blew out a frustrated breath and gave her some space without releasing her. *"I need you."*

She nodded and looked up at him. *"Likewise. But first…"* She took a step back. His arm tightened around her waist, he refused to let go. That, he would not change, especially with an unknown male in the room.

"Silas, meet my Mom, Victoria Channing, and her fiancé Mark..." She looked at Mark for him to supply his last name. He stood and stepped forward with his hand outstretched. Silas stepped in front of Jasmine to make sure the man did not come too close to his mate.

"Mark Fulnory." He shook Silas' hand. The two men stared at each other for a moment and then Silas released him. Mark returned to his seat and retook Victoria's hand.

"Well, after that greeting I can see why you took offense earlier, Jasmine," her mother said, chuckling. Silas nodded but remained silent. From his peripheral view, he noticed Tyrone and Tyrese were seated a small distance from their grandmother. He didn't know much about family dynamics, but he thought they'd be sitting closer.

"Everything okay?" he asked the twins through their links.

"Yeah, it's good. I thought Nana was married, I'm surprised mom made a mistake like that," Tyrese said.

"Also, Nana forgot that you and mom were engaged, that's not like her. I thought they didn't age."

Silas redirected his attention to Victoria. The older woman could have passed for Jasmine's sister. She was shorter and a shade or two lighter, but she appeared to be in good health. He released Jasmine and stepped forward. He took Victoria's hand, held onto it for a scan, and then kissed the back of it.

"It's a pleasure to meet the woman who delivered my Jasmine. She is my world." He turned and met Mark's gaze. "And I take everything regarding her seriously." He faced Victoria again. "You are welcome in my home for as long as my lady would like."

He stepped back and took Jasmine's hand.

"It's time to eat," Jasmine said. They stepped back while waiting for Mark to assist Victoria. Tyrone and Rose stood. Tyrese would bring up the rear. When they stepped into the hall, Cameron and Lilly were there waiting for them.

"Hi Cameron, Lilly," Jasmine said as she disengaged from Silas to wrap Lilly and then Cameron in a hug. Silas tugged on his black trousers to give his hard erection some ease. It didn't help much. He caught Mark's commiserating glance and nodded. The man wasn't in much better shape as he stood behind Victoria for cover. Her wide smile directed over her shoulder was in approval to her lover.

After greetings and introductions were done, they moved to the large formal dining room. They took their seats and prepared for what Jasmine told him would be a home-cooked meal. Over the past year, Jasmine had changed the taste and variety of meals served from Silas' kitchen. The chef embraced her love of soul food, often surprising her with added touches. He smiled at her constant attempts to domesticate him, to teach him about family living. He glanced around the table at his godson speaking softly with his mate. Rose and Tyrone chatted with Mark, while his mate sat at his right hand, speaking with her mother. Tyrese watched his Nana silently. Silas gave his mate high marks for the effort she put into turning his compound into a home.

"So Silas, what is it that you do?" Victoria asked.

Jasmine frowned. *"I told her you were a corporate tycoon, owning a lot of businesses. Why is she so forgetful? This isn't like her."* He picked up on her concern that her mother might be ill.

He rubbed her hand to soothe her. "I own a company that buys, sells, and manages other companies. Jasmine should have told you this." He wanted to see Victoria's response.

"I did. Don't you remember, Mom?" Her voice rose at the end.

"Careful sweet. You don't want to offend her," he cautioned.

Victoria frowned. "I don't know what's going on with me. Seems I'm forgetting a lot of things, not the most important stuff…" She gazed at Mark, obviously not realizing she had just inferred the things she discussed with her daughters were not that important. Silas took Jasmine's hand as the hurt flowed through their link.

Mark reddened. "Sometimes things slip her mind. But that doesn't happen often," he rushed to say. "When we met, she talked about her grandsons all the time. She said you both joined the military and did really well." He looked between Victoria and the twins. Silas thought better of the man for protecting his woman. He hadn't been able to get as good a read on Mark as he would have liked. Scanning humans were hit and miss sometimes.

Tyrone glanced at Jasmine before answering. "Yes, we did. It was an interesting experience. I got out last year. What about you? Where are you from?"

Mark smiled and Silas noticed it reached his eyes, another good thing in the man's favor. "I'm from Miami, but my family is from Egypt. My parents came to America before I was born, and lived in Homestead, which's closer to Key West than Miami. They were farmers until we sold the land twenty years ago. It's now a large subdivision." He chuckled.

"You met Nana in Miami?" Tyrone asked. Silas wasn't sure if the young wolf was interested or just stepping forward to do the interrogation. Hands down, Tyrone excelled at that particular skill.

"We met online and then she came for a visit." The man smiled so wide it was no wonder he missed the horror that flashed across Jasmine's face.

"Mom said the two of you met on a cruise," Jasmine said, slowly watching her mother.

Victoria's brow furrowed. "We did. I took a cruise with my girlfriend Cathy to Mexico. That's where I met you, Mark. On the ship."

His smile dimmed. "That wasn't me, Victoria. The only cruise I have ever been on was the one we took together last month."

The room went silent.

"Well that's awkward," Victoria murmured, although her eyes flashed with what Silas recognized as fear. It bothered her to get her facts wrong on something she deemed important.

Mark held her hand but remained silent. Silas had no doubt the younger man was thinking about the mental capacity of his older lover. According to Arianna, breeders remained young. But in the end, she had gone off the deep end, attacking his Alphas and using his godson as cannon fodder. There was still a lot he didn't know about breeders.

Jasmine squeezed his hand. *"She's embarrassed, what should I do?"*

Silas slid back in his chair, there was only so much family drama he could stomach. He had met his quota for today. "Cameron, I need to talk to you and the twins. Follow me."

He felt his mate's glare on his back as he and the men, minus Mark, escaped.

Chapter 14

"WELL, THAT WAS EMBARRASSING," Victoria said to Jasmine, Lilly, and Rose as she poured some lotion on her hands and massaged them. Mark had excused himself a few moments after Silas escaped with the boys. One of Silas's security team members escorted him to the room he and her mom would be sharing for the next few days.

"How long has this been going on? You forgetting things?" Jasmine asked. Was this another unknown hiccup with breeders? Thinking back, neither Siseria nor Julie suffered memory lapses. If anything, their memories were *too* good. They'd played their roles to perfection until they were caught on the cams. Afterward, Jasmine had Siseria sent to the basement to keep her from corrupting Julie with her ideas. The plan backfired once they discovered Siseria was locked and loaded with an internal bomb. She'd died on the operating table when they tried to diffuse the device. Julie had sunk into depression and barely ate or spoke these days.

"I guess before I met Mark." She shook her head. "Strange, some things are perfectly clear, like you, Renee, the twins, Mark, even the exes. But my short-term memory acts up on me at times." Her gaze slid over Lilly and Rose before landing on Jasmine. "Have you heard anything about that happening?"

Jasmine picked up the reference to their previous conversation almost a year ago in which she had told her mom the twins had learned something about breeders. That was the first time her mother had admitted to being raped as well as being a breeder.

"No. Nothing like that," she said. "But I'll check into it." She would talk to Julie, maybe the woman would rouse herself from her self-induced stupor for another breeder.

Silas and the other men entered the room. He winked.

She shook her head at his antics. He was a handful but she wouldn't have him any other way.

"Mark left?"

Jasmine gave him credit for acting as if he cared when she knew he didn't.

"Yes, he was…tired and went to lie down. I'll be joining him shortly." Victoria stood, looked at everyone, and spoke. "It was nice seeing you boys again, we'll spend more time together before I leave." She nodded at Tyrone and Tyrese, who tried unsuccessfully to hide their winces at being called boys.

Jasmine, Rose, and Lilly grinned at their discomfort.

"Night, Nana," Tyrese said, placing a kiss on her cheek. Tyrone and Rose followed suit. Cameron and Lilly remained seated on the sofa holding hands in a rare show of solidarity.

Victoria stepped forward, placed a kiss on Jasmine's cheek. "We'll talk more tomorrow when I'm more rested."

Jasmine nodded. "Okay. Renee gets in before ten tomorrow morning. We can get together for lunch and catch up if that's good for you."

Victoria nodded, although her gaze slid up, watching Silas. "That's fine. Silas, thanks for your hospitality and for making my baby happy. That last man gave her two sons and left her heart-broken. I don't see that trait in you. Something tells me you are exactly the man she needs, and that makes *me* happy."

Jasmine felt Silas preen and knew he would repeat her mother's words soon.

"You are right. I am the only man for Jasmine."

Jasmine rolled her eyes while everyone else coughed to cover their laughs.

"I think my daughter agrees with you." She patted his cheek and glanced at Cameron and Lilly. "Congratulations you two. You make a lovely couple." She looked at each one of them again with a large smile. "This is a wonderful family you have, Jasmine. Just wonderful." With that declaration, she turned and left the room.

"Hold up, Nana. I need to show you where you're staying," Tyrese said, moving quickly to catch up to his grandmother. Once he left the living room, Silas slid into the seat next to Jasmine and pulled her close. Inhaling, she relaxed against him while waiting for his verdict. She didn't have to wait long.

"I couldn't get a good read on Mark or your mother either. Sometimes it's like that with humans. He seems to care deeply for her." She gazed up at him and relaxed. That declaration was about as good as she was gonna get from him.

"He acted like he was really into her," Tyrone said, frowning. "But I don't understand why she's forgetting stuff. Arianna was crazy at the end, but when we met her in Mexico she had perfect recall. I verified most of her information and she had been on the money."

"That bothers me that she's forgetting stuff," Jasmine said, concerned.

Silas pulled her close. "I'll ask Matt if he heard anything about that and you can ask Julie. She's been refusing to speak, but maybe she'll tell you something."

"Why are you keeping her around?" Cameron asked, gazing at Silas. "I mean she refuses to cooperate, she's mean and nasty to Jasmine." He glanced at Jasmine as if to confirm, and then back to Silas. "I'm just curious why you continue to take care of her when she is no longer an asset."

"You think they should release her?" Lilly asked from her perched position next to him on the sofa.

Cameron blinked and then smiled. His large grin made him appear more boyish instead of the fifty-year-old man Jasmine knew him to be. "Yeah. Maybe we can turn the tables on them. Install a bug up her…somewhere on her," he amended, grinning sheepishly at Jasmine.

Silas nodded slowly. She could hear the wheels turning in her mate's head. "That might work."

"It could at least lead us to the local contacts. Maybe even the people behind the deal with Jennings," Tyrone said, his voice softening at the end. Every wolf in the compound who'd met Jennings while he trained at the complex had felt the impact of his demise intensely. Jasmine had sensed the increased testosterone levels all day. The wolves wanted to fight, someone, anyone, over the situation. Not only did Silas deal with the humans today, but he had to combat the natural aggression of a lot of wolves.

Silas's grin turned feral. She saw his wolf behind his eyes and exhaled. It was going to be a long night. Vengeance took careful planning. Jasmine tried to feel sorry for Julie and simply could not. The woman had rebuffed her numerous times and had resorted to offensive name-calling. She'd even spat in Jasmine's direction once. That had been her final trip to the cell. "Should I ask about the memory thing first?"

No one spoke for a moment or two. Rose broke the silence. "I think so. I mean she is probably ready to hear a voice right about now after all this time in solitary."

Silas had wanted to kill Julie when he heard she had spit at Jasmine and she didn't doubt he would have if the woman had made her target. Jasmine had pleaded long and hard for Julie's life. Silas didn't kill the woman, but he'd stripped her of every comfort, including light and company. The only thing she received was a weekly shower and two meals a day. It was the most Silas would give and Jasmine had been glad another death had not been added to her conscience.

Silas looked down at her, no doubt remembering what happened on her last trip. "You and I will go and ask her tomorrow. If she does not respond, I will ransack her memories to see if there is an answer to your questions." The look he gave said 'I won't be too gentle either.'

"Okay, tomorrow." Jasmine knew when to drop a subject and Julie was one. The older woman was on her mate's shit list.

"I'll talk to Passen to get his take on this." Silas rubbed his hands together, obviously pleased with the idea.

Jasmine squeezed her thighs together to quell the ache that had been on a slow burn since her mate arrived earlier that evening. She glanced at the clock and was surprised at how late it had become. Standing, she tried to control her irritation of being left alone again tonight while Silas took care of Pack's business. She hated her conflicting emotions. A part of her was uber proud of her mate's status of being the top man. The other part, her more womanly side, wanted all of his attention on just the two of them. Finding a balance was becoming harder and harder because he spent so much time at work.

Inhaling, she glanced at her son and then Cameron. "I'm headed to the nursery to check on the kids. Make sure each of you stops by at least once a day to check on them. It's important to me that they know and recognize you. Rose and Lilly are already doing that…" She let the sentence hang.

"Will do," Cameron said, meeting her gaze. "I apologize that you had to even remind me of that. I promise to do better."

Touched by the sincerity she read in his gaze, Jasmine nodded.

"I was sick, but that's no real excuse I suppose," Tyrone said with a grin and chuckle.

Rose smacked him on the shoulder. "No, it's not."

Jasmine shook her head and turned to leave.

"Hold on," Silas said, taking her hand and stopping her. "I'll walk with you." He stood. "Cameron, Tyrone, go find Dr. Passen and Matt, tell them what we discussed, and get their feedback. It was a good idea, so follow up on it. Rose will schedule a meeting for all of us to discuss it tomorrow."

For a moment, Cameron's eyes widened and then he smiled. Tyrone sat forward in his seat as he listened intently. Rose and Lilly both preened at the important assignment Silas gave their mates. Jasmine hoped they didn't mess up or it would be a long time before her mate ever again followed her advice to delegate.

"You want me to give you an update later?" Cameron asked as if he couldn't believe Silas would wait until morning.

"No. I'm spending time with my mate and pups. I prefer not to be disturbed." On that note, he ushered a happy Jasmine out the door.

Chapter 15

"WELL, I'LL BE DAMNED," Renee said as she gazed at the artwork and furniture in the hall leading to the suite assigned to her. "Who knew a man could have a body like that and be loaded...no, I take that back. This is beyond loaded." She laughed. "Only you could meet a rich guy while sitting next to your son on his death bed."

"I know, right?" Jasmine joined in the laughter. Having her sister here felt good. The two of them had always been close, even as young girls. When Renee realized she was interested in women, she had called Jasmine crying that she would never have children. Jasmine had been surprised at her sister's leanings, but as a mother of twin boys and an absent husband, she'd allowed her sister to experience motherhood through her. It worked. While the boys grew, Renee had always been a phone call away. She had spent vacations and every major holiday with them.

They hooked each other arms and Renee spoke candidly in a soft voice. "He any good in bed? Did you at least get off?"

Jasmine's cheeks burned at the intimate question, but that had always been her sister's way. Nosy.

Renee stopped, grimacing as she stared into Jasmine's face. "Oh no, Jas. Not again. I don't give a damn how much money he has, if he's not getting you off, leave his ass."

Jasmine's head jerked as if slapped. She had no idea what her sister saw just now but she quickly straightened the matter. "What are you talking about? I can't halfway walk now because of the loving he laid on me last night. Trust me, Silas handles his business." That was as much as she was comfortable saying.

Last night her lover had been insatiable. They made love in the living area of the suite, against the wall in the bedroom as if the bed weren't a few steps away, and then he took her again in the shower. Goosebumps flew over her skin just thinking about it. By the time they fell asleep, her voice was hoarse from all the screams that were ripped from her throat with each orgasm. And there had been plenty. A tremor ran through her at the thought of the last one when they lay in bed whispering their love to each other. It had been…magical. She never knew it could be this good.

"Um-hmm, I was wondering what was with the cowboy walk and all that…"

Jasmine laughed so hard at her sister's wild comment that a couple of staff members stopped and looked at her. When she could speak, she hugged Renee. "Girl, I miss your crazy. I'm glad you're here. I had them bring lunch to this room. Mama's going to join us in a few."

"Sounds good, and I'm glad to see you finally happy, even if it's with a man."

Jasmine shook her head at her sister's jibe. When she had been miserable over Davian's treatment, Renee had advised her to give up men and go the lesbian route. And since Renee and her lover, Mandy, were happy avoiding male drama, they assumed she might be interested in giving up hard chests, hairy faces, and permanently attached penises. A few choice words had corrected the matter and now her sister openly teased her about men but never suggested she give women a chance again.

"Hey, he made you look…more than once."

Renee stared at her and laughed. "You're right he did and I did. There is something…primitive about that man." She eyed Jasmine, whose face was on fire. "He won't be a pushover, that's for sure."

Pushover was not a word you would use to describe Silas Knight, although she usually got her way in most matters. Jasmine hugged his love close to her heart as she thought of all the concessions Silas made to make her happy. Walking into the suite set aside for her sister's use, Jasmine pointed to a door on the far wall. "They put your luggage in there, that's the bed and bathroom."

"Okay." Renee sat on the love seat and gazed at her. "What do you think of Mom's new man? I only ask because she's taking it further with him." She paused, shook her head, and then spoke as if the words were stuck in her throat. "She is thinking of starting over, having a baby with this guy."

Jasmine's jaw unhinged. "You're kidding me?" Her thoughts rushed back to last night. Mark was attentive, loving… but no more than the other men her mom had dated and later married. Over the years, her mom had been adamant about not having any children. "Something weird is going on."

"What?"

Jasmine bit her lip trying to decide how much to say. This morning's discussion with Julie had been a dismal failure. The woman refused to look up at her, let alone speak. Silas had rifled through Julie's memories and came up blank, well almost blank. There was a name that kept resurfacing, Corrina Griggs. Silas had Tyrone researching for information on the woman.

"Remember when I had you and mom on the phone and we talked about my engagement?"

Renee nodded.

"She forgot all of that. She called Silas my boyfriend."

Renee's brow furrowed.

"I apologized, but I see you still hold grudges," her mom said, strolling into the room wearing a white sundress that showed her curvy figure. She looked well-rested and much younger than her sixty years.

Jasmine felt ten years old again beneath the rebuke. They had been common when she was much younger. Remembering her journey to adulthood and life's lessons, her chin raised a notch. "Yes, you did. I was just bringing Renee up to date."

Renee rose when their mom walked in and held onto the woman with an extended embrace. Jasmine wondered if her mom held Renee with the same tenacity as she'd held her the day before. When Renee and her mother broke apart, her mom placed a kiss on her cheek, grabbed her hand, and squeezed.

Concerned, Jasmine stared at her mom for another minute, and just as she thought to ask questions, the food arrived.

"Did you and Silas enjoy your evening?" her mom asked as they ate grilled salmon on top of a salad of fresh greens.

Her throat and face caught fire in remembrance of the loving Silas threw down last night. Her man had been relentless, taking her to the edge and then drawing back. She had become a babbling idiot begging him to stop so she could gain her release. After teasing her mercilessly, he'd slammed into her with such fervor the heavy, solid wood bed danced as it bumped against the wall. She withheld her dreamy sigh...last night had been the best since the babies were born. He didn't stop loving her until the wee hours of the morning when she simply gave out.

"That sappy look on her face says she more than enjoyed it," Renee said with a smirk.

"You should have seen them last night; I thought he was going to pull her dress up right there. I mean the room got hot." Victoria fanned herself. "Temperature-wise it was like somebody turned on the heat."

Embarrassed, she placed a fork full of lettuce in her mouth. Silas had wanted to take her right then. If somebody hadn't spoken to break their concentration, who knows what would have happened.

"I hear your fella's pretty hot, too." Renee winked at Jasmine, letting her know the conversation had been veering into muddy waters.

Victoria's face reddened as a huge smile rose on her face. "Yes...yes he is." She looked up and met Jasmine's gaze. "I love him. Mark is wonderful. So smart, handsome... but I'm scared."

In her entire life, Jasmine had only heard her mother admit her fear twice. The first time was when her daddy died and the second had been when she returned from a trip overseas. Both times her mom refused to discuss the basis for her fears, she simply admitted to them and dropped the subject.

"Why?" Renee asked.

Her mother turned slowly as if she had forgotten Renee was in the room. "I'm going to share some things with you girls…no, not girls." Her lip curled in a smile that didn't reach her eyes. "Women." She exhaled.

Butterflies filled Jasmine's stomach. This nervousness was so out of character for her mom.

Renee sat forward and placed her hand over her mom's. "Go ahead, Mama. Talk to us."

Victoria nodded. "I was raped after you were born and got pregnant with Jasmine and Jacris, her twin. Jacris had some horrible birth defects and died. That was the main reason I refused to have any more children. George…" She looked at a wide-eyed, Renee and patted her leg this time. "Your dad never knew about the rape, never questioned why you and Jasmine looked so different. Not once. He accepted you." She pointed at Jasmine. "As his baby, his daughter, and loved you."

The fierce look of devotion to a man who'd died a decade and a half ago surprised Jasmine. "I know, Mama. I know daddy loved me."

Her mom nodded and exhaled.

"Raped? You were raped and never told anybody?" Renee asked, her voice rising with each word.

"I told one person. But that's not what I want to talk about right now. I was scared and didn't want any more children. The thought of another child struggling to live and not making it would make me sick to my stomach. Plus, I never had the love and support of another man like your father." She shook her head. "None of my exes came close to George." She inhaled and then released it slowly.

Jasmine's heart raced as she realized where her mom was going with all of this.

"Until now," her mom whispered into the quiet of the room.

"Mark?" Renee said in a remarkably calm voice that Jasmine envied since she couldn't think of a single thing to say.

"Yes, Mark."

Jasmine cleared her throat, wondering what to say. "So why are you scared? You love him, he seems to love you."

"Something is wrong with me," her mother said softly.

"What?" Renee asked, eyeing Jasmine. "What's wrong with you?"

Her mother raked her fingers through her perfectly styled hair. "I don't know…I just forget things, like an old woman. I am not old," her mother snapped when Jasmine and Renee remained silent.

"No…no, you're not old," Jasmine agreed.

"Not at all, Mom. You're just getting into your stride. I hope I look as good as you when I'm your age."

Her mother's face fell at Renee's comment. Jasmine's heart dropped with the realization that Renee would age and die before her or her mother.

"He asked me to marry him, but he wants children, at least one," her mom continued, and Jasmine was glad the dark moment regarding her sister's mortality had passed.

"And that makes you afraid?" Renee asked, sounding confused.

Jasmine flicked her eyes over her mother, wondering how she intended to navigate the choppy waters of this discussion. The plea for help she read in Victoria's eyes went unanswered. The reason Jasmine had never told her sister the truth about Silas before was that there is no going halfway with Renee. She wouldn't stop asking questions until she got all the crumbs as well as the main scoop. Her mother must have forgotten.

"I'm sixty-years-old, damn it."

Jasmine turned away to hide her grin at her mom's response. It was a stall tactic, but she knew Renee wouldn't be deterred.

"Does he know the truth? About your age I mean," Renee asked without missing a beat.

"He knows I can still have children, thanks to my monthly. I'm not sure he knows my true age."

"Tell him how you feel. Please do not marry or date anyone you cannot be open and honest with, it never works out in the end." Renee glanced at Jasmine before returning her attention to their mom.

"I did. But he says we can do it together. Having a child means a lot to him."

"What about you? What about you're not wanting to go through this again? Does that mean anything to him?" Renee snapped.

"Tone. Watch it," their mother reprimanded with a pointed finger at Renee.

"Sorry, but please don't do this," Renee continued in an unapologetic tone. "Don't marry this man, have a baby, and be miserable, Mom. Just don't. Think about yourself for once."

"I did, and for years I denied the man I loved the family he wanted. He died and I can never prove to him how much he meant to me." Victoria's chin dropped to her chest at her outburst. "The feelings I have for Mark are the closest I have ever come to loving anyone like I loved George. I don't want to mess this up."

Renee stood, knelt in front of their mother, and took her hands. "I know you love Mark. But he's not dad. Having a baby for him won't make you feel any better. A man who loves you won't push you to do something like that. He would respect your decisions." She looked at Jasmine and tipped her head a couple of times.

"She's right, Mom. As much as you love each other, things will go sour pretty quickly if you have a child just because he wants one. You need to want to give birth and then be prepared to raise the child. Think about that before you jump into this marriage," Jasmine said, watching her mom struggle to remain dry-eyed.

"I'm tired of being alone," she whispered brokenly. "I want this to work, it may be my last chance."

Concern ripped through Jasmine. This was not how her mother talked, at least she had never heard or seen her mom this defeated. And over a man…never happened before.

"What's going on, Mama," Renee said softly. "This isn't like you. Has something happened we should know about?"

Jasmine nodded her agreement, glad Renee spoke what was on her mind.

Her mom rested her forehead in her palm. "Some days are so dark…I have a tough time getting out of bed. It's unbelievable what getting old will do to you." She snorted. "No matter how desperately I cling to the days of yesterday, they still slip through my fingers. What can I say, I'm getting older, just can't do the things I used to do."

"Mom, you're only sixty. Old is another twenty-five years. Stop talking like this, you're scaring me," Renee said, grabbing her mom's hand, tethering them together.

Her mom's gaze flicked over at her and then returned to Renee. "I'm having a bad day, that's all. It'll get better…just as soon as I see my grandbabies." She smiled brightly as if the gloomy discussion never occurred.

Jasmine eyed the older woman a second longer, honestly debating if she should take her around the kids. Something was off but she couldn't put her finger on it.

"You didn't see the kids last night?" Renee sounded surprised.

"No." She glanced at Jasmine.

Exhaling, Jasmine explained what'd happened and ended the story with Mark leaving after her mom's slip up.

"You told me the same thing, that you met him on the cruise. What's Cathy's phone number?" Renee asked, standing.

"I don't know it."

Renee and Jasmine stared at their mom. "She's been your best friend for the past 20 years, how can you not know her phone number?" Jasmine asked.

"I don't know. We haven't talked in months." Victoria frowned. "I'm not sure why."

"Um-hmm…what does she think about Mark?" Jasmine asked, her opinion of Mark taking a turn.

"She likes him. We've had dinner together with her and Grant a few times. But she's been busy with her new grandkids and hasn't had a lot of free time."

Renee had been fiddling around with her cell and yelled. "Got it." She pressed a button and eased back onto the sofa while keeping her eyes on mama. She smiled. "Hello, Cathy? This is Renee."

Jasmine watched her mom as Renee talked with Cathy. Her mom appeared interested but it wasn't as if the conversation mattered, which again was strange. Renee's face changed from being happy to one of boredom. Cathy could talk the length of a movie without breaking for air.

"Okay, Cathy, I'll tell mom when I see her. Bye." Renee shook her head when she disconnected and placed her finger in her ear, jiggling it a bit. "She said you told her you met him online and flew to Miami to meet with him. She didn't remember meeting him on the cruise. She thinks he's great, yadda, yadda. She was his cheerleader."

They had finished eating when there was a knock on the door. Surprised the staff would return for the tray without her call, Jasmine stood and went to open it. When she saw who was on the other side, her eyes widened before she screamed.

"Jacques." She launched herself into his arms and hugged him tightly. He stood shorter than Silas, with a round barrel chest, and thick arms. It took a moment before he returned her embrace. "I am so happy to see you. When did you get here?"

She stepped back to look him over. The last time she had seen him, he had been sick and on bed rest. Long, thick wavy brown hair shining with health touched his wide shoulders. Sharp, milk chocolate brown eyes beneath bushy brows returned her inspection.

"An hour ago or so, Madam. I was with Silas and he suggested I come greet you. How have you been?"

"I am good. Come, meet my mom and sister. We just finished a late lunch, but I can have another plate brought for you." Holding his hand she pulled him into the suite.

"No, I ate with Patron, the twins, and Cameron. I just came to say hello."

"And you will as soon as you speak to my sister and mom. Stop dawdling," she said, laughing at his reddened cheeks.

"Mom, Renee…this is Jacques, Silas' administrator. They go way back. We named Jackie after him."

Renee nodded. "Pleased to meet you. They named the other girl after me." She laughed.

"I guess Victoria is too old-fashioned," her mom said in a petulant tone.

"Victoria is a beautiful name for a beautiful woman," Jacques said, taking the seat near her mother. Jasmine grinned at the older man's antics. Her mom glanced at him and then looked away, but not before Jasmine saw the pleased smile on her face.

Maybe Jacques would be what the doctor should have ordered but didn't.

Chapter 16

SILAS SAT AT THE conference table waiting for Dr. Passen to enter information into his computer regarding the device he and Matt confirmed could be placed in Julie with little effort. The plan was to put her asleep, insert the device, and return her to her cell without her realizing what had been done. Leonidas and Tyrese would then take her to the hospital. She had lost weight after refusing all food and water for the past two days. Silas hoped she would escape from the hospital and return to her group. Although his mate never said, he knew it bothered her to see the woman in her present state of decline. Last night, when he went over this plan with her, she'd disagreed. Jasmine believed Julie was willing herself to die.

"Julie will never leave the hospital. She is done," Jasmine had argued. But they both agreed the woman needed medical care, so regardless of whether she became his unwilling pawn or not, she would be leaving the compound as soon as the doctor could set things up.

"Here it is," Dr. Passen said, his voice rising in gleeful satisfaction as it always did when he discovered something new.

Silas glanced at the paper the doctor took from the printer. "Good news?"

"Yes, Sir. Most definitely. I found the device to fit. The military has been using this for years with its operatives. It has great range and is precise in terms of locating its subject. I just special ordered it, should be here within three hours via special courier."

"Good," Silas said nodding, pleased with the progress. "Will it require a lengthy surgery?"

Dr. Passen shook his head while pushing his glasses further up the bridge of his nose. "It can be done in less than an hour and she should be fine within five hours max. The surgery is not too invasive, I will go in through her nose to place it and then secure it. After the anesthesia wears off she may be groggy for another hour or so. Five hours gives me a cushion."

"So she can leave sometime tomorrow?" Silas asked, calculating the time in his mind. The christening was the day after tomorrow and he would be busy with that a large portion of the day. His jaw clenched as he thought of what bad timing it was to have house guests and an event. Despite this being a small family gathering, Silas was still uneasy. Jennings was a cop who had been taken and then used to destroy others. It was a slap in his face that his enemies had pulled it off right beneath his nose. When Jasmine's Mom flew in early with no security, he feared someone might grab the woman to use as leverage against him. There was no doubt in his mind that his mate would do whatever was necessary to ensure her mother's safety. The twins would walk through fire and brimstone for Jasmine, so it must be a family trait.

"Yes, Sir. I would say in the afternoon. Have you made arrangements with the hospital?"

Silas nodded. "Rose will set it up as soon as I tell her a date."

"Good. I will schedule the surgery later today."

After standing, Silas looked in the direction of Asia's room. "We making any progress with the information from Asia?"

Dr. Passen's lips tightened slightly. "Yes and no. We have the information, she has been extremely helpful in that, but it's disjointed, hard to understand. I have sent everything to you in a file. Maybe Tyrese or Tyrone can connect the dots so we can move forward and catch those assholes so that young woman can have some peace. I don't know if we can fix her, the other alternative is to get rid of the threat."

"I agree, Doc. But let's keep looking for a way to rid her of those devices; it'd be good to have her in the field working on my side."

"I understand, Sir."

Silas heard the disappointment in the doctor's voice. "You misunderstand. I respect the bitch and value her service. But she is a warrior and will never be content outside of the action. It's who she is, a warrior bitch. Never forget that."

"I understand. It's just...she's been through so much. She's been used and it's not right. When does she get the chance to have her life back, to be normal, to smell flowers, and tend a garden, if that is her desire? She has never had a chance to make choices regarding her future. I don't think that's right."

Silas thought of his mate and wondered what she would say of the doctor's defense of Asia. Did Jasmine have a choice? Did he choose to have half-bred pups? Higher powers had chosen them to be mates. Asia's choices had been taken from her, but did that invalidate the life she had lived? Not necessarily. She was one of the most powerful bitches alive, with knowledge most could only dream of. Did the end justify her painful journey? Most would say no. But he was not sure Asia would agree.

"We will ask Asia what she wants to do when she is free of the technology that imprisons her, and I will make sure she receives whatever that is. That will be the beginning of her life of making choices. Thanks for reminding me of that, Doctor." Silas nodded and left the room smiling at the stunned look on the good doctor's face.

As he headed down the corridor he contacted Jacques. The man should be in the office by now. Silas couldn't imagine his friend spending more than few minutes with Jasmine and her family. He had not been able to do more than greet his friend with a slap on the back before his meeting with Matt and the doctor. Now he needed to get Jacques started on the file Passen had sent him with all the information Asia provided. The man was a genius when it came to putting abstract information together to make a cohesive whole.

"*Jacques, meet me in my office.*" He sent the message as he stepped into the elevator.

"*Yes, Sir.*"

Silas frowned at the strange sound of reluctance in Jacque's voice. "*Jacques?*"

"*Yes, Sir?*" There it was again. The man sounded strained as if he were being pulled in two directions.

"*All is well?*"

"*Yes, Sir.*"

"*My office.*" Confused, Silas stepped out of the elevator wondering what the hell was going on. Jasmine had not contacted him, so he knew she was okay. But Jacques did not sound at all like himself.

"*Yes, Sir.*"

Silas nodded at Rose. "Make an appointment for Julie at the hospital tomorrow after two pm. Talk to Doctor Kelly, he is expecting her."

"Yes, Sir," Rose said as Jacques walked in.

Silas frowned at the silly grin plastered across his friend's face. Jacques strode past him into the inner office, waited for Silas to enter, and then closed the door behind him.

"What?" Silas demanded when Jacques stood mute in front of him, smiling.

"Good news… I have found my mate." Jacques raked his fingers through his hair and yanked before releasing it. "I cannot believe….after all this time…" he murmured, and then his gaze snapped to Silas.

"You… you my friend have done this." He grabbed Silas's hand, pulled him close, and embraced him. "Thank you, La Patron. Thank you."

Silas's mind spun. Who was Jacques talking about? If it was one of Jasmine's family members, his friend was in for a world of pain. He pushed back and eyed Jacques. "Congratulations, who is the fortunate person?" He tried to inject happiness in his tone but knew he failed when Jacques eyed him before laughing.

"Oh...you will not deter me. I know what you are thinking. You think after that bitch Arianna I cannot make a correct assessment. But you are wrong, this woman, this wonderful...beautiful...magnificent..."

"I get it," Silas said. "She's wonderful, but who is she?"

Jacque's smile dipped a bit. "Victoria of course. You did not know?"

"No. I just met her last night for the first time. And why would I know who your mate is, you told me Jasmine and I were mates, remember?"

Jacques waved him down. "You knew she was your mate, you simply refused to accept it. Today, the moment I entered the room, my senses sharpened. It was as if a string that had been afloat for centuries finally found its anchor. The air in the room changed and I was smitten by her beauty."

Silas fought against rolling his eyes at the flowery words. "She's engaged to marry another."

Jacques rolled his eyes and waved his hand. "I heard some other believe she is his destiny. They are mistaken. I am her mate. I will claim her before I leave."

Hearing Jacques talk of leaving reminded Silas of the job he needed his friend to work on. "We can discuss that later, right now I need you to focus on this file." Silas sat at his desk and pulled up the file on the computer. "What station are you using?" He glanced up. Jacques remained in the same spot, except he was gazing out the window and smiling. Silas released a breath to reign in his aggravation.

"Jacques, have a seat."

"Oh...okay."

Silas leaned back in his chair and decided to bring his former assistant current. After telling Jacques in explicit details about the bombs, about Jennings and Asia, he was pleased the goofy smile had been replaced with the sharp thoughtful expression he had counted on in past decades.

"Bastards," Jacques hissed. "I will pull open the file and begin at once, Sir. We will beat the insolent bastards at their own game. My Victoria cannot leave, Sir. I understand this is not the best time for a family visit. But she is my mate and I cannot stay if she leaves."

Silas nodded in understanding. "I am aware of how mates work. But if she rejects you, I cannot allow you to make her life more difficult. She is human and does not know who or what we are. Be mindful of her human lover, they plan to wed. To us that means little. But my mate disagrees with me on that, it's very important to them."

"But it can be easily broken," Jacques said, standing.

"Yes. I know. It's not mating, my friend. It's marriage." Silas watched as Jacques left his office with a befuddled look on his face. "Welcome to the world of living with a breeder," he murmured, knowing the confusion his friend now faced was the tip of the iceberg.

"Silas?"

He smiled at the purring Jasmine put in her voice. *"Yes?"*

"We are going to the nursery; mom wants to see the kids."

"I will meet you. Do not go in without me...please," he added.

"You need to be there when we arrive; I'm not going to hang outside the door like I cannot go in to see my children."

He heard the bite in her voice as he headed for the door, *"Give me a head start. I'll meet you in five, make that ten minutes."*

"Okay. Love you," she said, adding that purring sound that went straight to his groin.

"Keep that up and I'll have you up against the wall like I did last night, and it won't matter who's around." He waved at Jacques to follow him.

"We're going to the nursery," he called out over his shoulder to Rose as Jacques fell in beside him.

"Will it be possible for me to speak directly with Asia, to get some context and nuances," Jacques asked as they reached the elevator.

"Yes. I would be interested in your opinion of her."

"Thank you, Sir. We are going to see my Jacqueline?"

"Yes. Jasmine's family didn't get to see the pups last night, and her sister just got in this morning. I have to be in the room whenever strangers are present." If it bothered Jacques to be considered a stranger, he never said. Silas strode down the hall in silence, his mind on the various projects in the works. He stopped in front of the nursery door, glanced over his shoulder at Jacques, and then stepped inside.

All four pups had his inky black hair, the girls had his eyes, while the boys' eyes were various shades of brown, like Jasmine's.

Adam and David were playing a game on the floor with a ball. Silas's chest expanded with pride every time he watched his pups interact. When one was upset or distressed, the others would attempt to soothe or calm that one. He had witnessed them crawling or scooting close and huddling into a puppy pile until the pup calmed. Despite their human side, their wolves made them operate on instinct. Jackie worked on her puzzles and Renee used a crayon to draw on a piece of paper, but the moment they saw him they stopped.

Grinning over the "Da's" that were coming fast as well as the raised arms, Silas stooped and picked up the girls first. "This young lady is our artist, Renee." He placed a kiss on her forehead. "And this one, who loves to figure out puzzles, is our future strategist, Jacqueline."

"They are both beautiful, Sir," Jacques said with genuine awe in his voice. His fingertip touched Renee's cheek and then Jackie's. Jacqueline reached for him and after Silas nodded, Jacques took his namesake into his arms.

Silas shook his head at the instant connection and headed to his sons. David had stopped playing and now watched Silas. When he placed Renee on the floor next to Adam, Silas picked up David and hugged him tightly. "So serious all the time," he murmured.

"Sir?" Jacques said from behind Silas.

"This is my son, David. David, this is my friend Jacques."

Jacque's brow rose at the introduction. "Hello, David."

David stared at Jacques in silence. When Jacques reached forward to touch David's face as he had done with each girl, David pulled back out of his reach. Silas was surprised. He had never seen his son react like that with anyone.

"Sorry," he said to Jacques as he placed David next to Renee and picked up Adam. "This is Adam, he was the first of the litter."

Adam wrapped his arms around Silas' neck but peeked at Jacques. When Jacques touched his cheek, Adam laughed in delight. Jasmine, her mother, sister, and Mark entered the nursery. Renee crawled as fast as she could toward Jasmine, squealing and talking gibberish. Jasmine lifted her from the floor and swung the small child around, placing kisses on her cheek.

"And who is this tiny fellow? I bet you're David. I've seen your pictures," Victoria asked, looking at David. He stared at her a moment and then lifted his arms. "Oh my... how handsome and strong you are." She placed a kiss on his cheek. David said a few words of gibberish but stopped when Mark came close.

"Honey, this is my grandson, David. David, this is Mark, your future grandfather." The words fell flat and Silas didn't need to glance at his friend to know he was unhappy. Mark took David from Victoria. David stared at the man for a moment and then screamed his displeasure. Adam, Renee, and Jackie stopped, turned, and tried to get to David. Silas handed Jacques a squirming Adam and went to get his son, but Jasmine got there before him.

"Sometimes he takes longer to warm up to people," she said, comforting his son. Renee held her namesake, laughing and teasing the child. Silas turned and saw that Mark now held Adam and Victoria held Jackie. Jacques stood to the side taking it all in.

"We have a problem," Silas said over their link.

"David will be fine, he doesn't like many people." Silas watched from across the room as she changed David's shirt.

"Jacques believes your mother is his mate." He grinned as Jasmine stopped mid-motion and turned toward him, wide-eyed. He sensed her disbelief through their link. *"Oh yeah, this christening has just gotten interesting, don't you think?"*

"But...but...she's with Mark. How can... oh my God, is he sure? I mean after the deal with Arianna, how can he be sure?"

"Well, he didn't pick Renee."

Chapter 17

"TAKE THE BREEDER STRAIGHT to the hospital and then remain in the observation room," Silas said. "Security is in place, and the doctor will check her out and try to find out what's wrong with her. If your mom is right and she's willing herself to die, then there may not be anything that can be done to save her." He didn't care one way or the other, but his mate did, so he would at least make an effort to help the woman.

Tyrese put on his sunglasses and pushed them up the bridge of his nose. "Mom has a sense about these things, she's usually right. The human body fights death tooth and nail, so I'm surprised Julie's shutting it down through sheer will."

"That's one of the things Matt will be looking into once the preliminary work is done at the hospital. There may be more going on than we know." Silas glanced at Leonidas, one of his newer security workers, as he approached. He and Tyrese would handle this job.

"Sir," Leonidas said when he came to a stop behind Tyrese. With hooded light brown eyes and his tawny head lowered slightly, he appeared the essence of calm. But boiling energy rolled off the young wolf. Silas wondered how the young man stood so still. Every once in a while, one of Leon's shoulders quivered. Silas made a mental note to plan a run for the younger wolves before tempers exploded and fights broke out.

Silas greeted Leonidas with a nod. "I just went over the instructions with Rese. I expect to hear from you once she is delivered to the hospital. I don't think she will attempt to leave today, but I want round-the-clock surveillance." He had instructed Tyrese to use the small room in the hospital he had used before.

"Yes, Sir." Tyrese turned to leave as Tyrone walked up. The twins nodded to each other but didn't speak. Silas suspected they were having a private conversation and waited a moment or two for them to finish.

"I have the report on Corrina Griggs," Tyrone said, handing Silas a disk, "She's Arianna on steroids. I think she's top dog for the breeders and running the show. She's old, older than Arianna, and hates full-bloods."

Silas took the disk with a shrug. "Hating full-bloods seems to be the new thing these days."

Tyrone chuckled and walked beside him toward a vacant conference room. "Her name has changed three times over the past two hundred years. I think she came from Europe and was one of the early settlers. Her family name was Graves." He glanced at Silas. "Ring a bell?"

"No, should it?"

Tyrone shrugged before continuing. "Just asking. Amanda Graves settled in Virginia near Jamestown. Her family had money, owned a large plantation with lots of slaves. She married young, I think in her late teens, sixteen or eighteen."

"That was not young back then," Silas said, remembering that era fondly as he entered the room. He hadn't been a farmer. Instead, he'd financed many ventures and dealt in commerce, staying ahead of the action. The women had been lovely and specialized in playing a nice game of 'come and get me.'

"Yeah? Hmm, glad I missed that time period then. But she was active in the community, quite the organizer. She had two daughters. They died at childbirth. Then she had a son, he lived until he was forty-five, and died right after her staged death. She then changed her name to Virginia and reappeared in Georgia posing as a relative of her Virginian family. She married a Henry Cochran, no children with him. She 'died' at the age of forty-eight, leaving him free to remarry, which he did. His new, young wife promptly provided him with four children. Her current name is Corrina Griggs."

"Okay, so she learned early how not to conceive. What made her want to destroy me personally?"

"Other than the rape?"

Silas's gaze returned to the screen, to read the file. "What rape?"

"Yeah... she was raped and had to marry some poor sap. People handled things differently back then. She was *not* treated as the victim," Tyrone said grimly.

Silas read the report but did not need it to know what happened to an unwed mother back then. He had seen the outcasts, the labeling, and the shame firsthand. It made him glad he was wolf. "Same question, I did not rape her, so why hate me?" He glanced at Tyrone, interested in his take on the matter.

For a moment Tyrone didn't respond, finally, he shrugged. "I don't know for sure, we won't know until we talk with her, but I think it has something to do with the rape. Somehow she blames you for it."

"That doesn't make sense. A full-blood wolf did not start this madness of blood mixing." He looked at the data again. There were too many holes, too many unanswered questions. "You did a good job of tracking her through the years. The rest of the information will come from her. Have someone bring her in for questioning. Make sure you run a full scan and cross scan on her, make sure she's safe, and then take her to the basement of the condo building. If she's this old, she should know who started the cross-breeding and why." He scrolled through the report, taking in dates and events in Corrina Griggs' life. "Also, send this list of possible locations of sanctuaries to the Alphas. They are not to engage the occupants, but if it is a confirmed sanctuary I want the people watched. I don't know how far Griggs has gone to carry out her plot, but the more we can contain them, the better."

"Yes, Sir."

"Silas?"

"*Yes?*"

"*Do something about Jacques! He and Mark almost came to blows a few minutes ago. Renee may think his love-sick expressions over mom are funny. But mom is taking Mark's side against Jacques, and he's having a hard time controlling his wolf.*"

"Has he told her she was his mate yet?"

"I don't think so. She thinks he's crazy."

"A stubborn mate will do that to you," he murmured.

"*I heard that. Just come get your boy,*" she snapped.

Silas looked at Tyrone as he stood. "Let me know when you hear something regarding Griggs. I agree with you, we are on to something with her."

Tyrone nodded as he stood. "Yes, Sir," he said as he left the room.

Silas pinched the bridge of his nose and inhaled. "*Jacques, I am in the lower labs, meet me here.*" He steeled his voice into a command.

"*Yes, Sir.*" Silas shielded himself against the angst in Jacque's voice. Human laws and accounting systems made things more difficult. Gone were the days when a wolf could simply steal away with his mate, Silas thought wistfully. And then he choked on the possible reaction of his mate had he attempted to take her away from her sons and family against her will. Jasmine would have castrated him in his sleep, and that would probably have been the least of his worries.

As much as he empathized with his friend, he could not allow him to disrupt his household. He knew Jacques could not leave Victoria, his wolf would never allow it. But the man had to use wisdom and bide his time.

Jacques strolled into the conference room with a sheepish yet stubborn look on his face. Silas knew he had to tread carefully, when it came to mates, a wolf would defy the Goddess if she interfered.

"Yes, Sir?" Jacques' rigid posture screamed 'I will take whatever you mete out but I will not stop.'

"I want to talk to Asia. Do you have any questions prepared for her?"

Jacque's eyes widened as his shoulders relaxed a bit. "Asia, the bitch that was experimented on?"

Silas nodded, unsure if he spoke, that his words would lack a sarcastic element.

Jacques pointed to the chair at the table. "May I sit, Sir?"

Silas's brow rose at the extreme courtesy, realizing Jacques had not relaxed his guard fully. "Yes."

Jacques took the seat, leaned forward with his hands clasped on the table. "I have read through the notes and have a few points I plan to submit to you later after verifying a few items. This woman...Asia, she is remarkable and not of common stock. Few wolves can withstand the type of altering that she has. A titanium leg, arm?" He scoffed. "Who is she really? Was she born or created? If she was created, for what purpose? Is she the Eve in this drama? If so, who is her Adam?" He paused.

Silas could not utter a word, the questions Jacques voiced had never entered his mind, yet they made sense in a warped way.

Jacques leaned back in his chair. "She is a huge part of the mystery and the success of your enemies' plans. Yet she helps you, why? To what purpose? I am not sure she is a wolf. I am not sure she is not a red herring or sleeper. If she is gathering intel on your operation, the best way to do it is to gain your trust, to feed us bits of information difficult to confirm. And if we use her data, it may be a setup to lead us into a trap." Jacques exhaled. "So, to answer your question, I have questions but they are not very nice. I have never met her but I do not trust her. She is a weapon, no question. But for who?"

Silas closed his eyes and mulled over everything he just heard. When he opened them, he met Jacque's gaze. "You lost control last year."

Jacques flinched but remained silent.

"Arianna rolled your mind, had you acting out of character, doing things to those you love while hating it, so I know you have an inside track of what Asia may be going through. When we meet with her in a few minutes, I want you to search for signs of that. Once again I find your thoughts invaluable, they have walked a path I had not noticed despite my dealings with Arianna. But hold them close to your chest, I don't want her to think I am considering she may not be as she appears." He paused, unsure if he should share this bit of information. "I spared her life at the request of the Goddess."

Jacque's head snapped up and met his gaze. Silas tried to read the emotion in them, but couldn't settle on fear or disappointment.

"I have not conferred with her in two months. I have been lax in my duties. I will remedy that today, perhaps that will allow me to make the connections clearer without bringing in my personal experiences."

"Jacques." Silas had not meant his comment as a slight, but he wanted, no needed, his friend to listen to Asia with an open mind uncolored with his past experiences.

Jacques held up his hand as he glanced away. "I am much better these days. Although there are still moments... when I have these flashes." He inhaled and then released it. "I would like to speak with Asia, Sir."

Silas gazed at the man who had been his friend for two centuries. They had seen and been through much together. The experience with Arianna changed Jacques, as it would any wolf. The woman captured Jacques' wolf and turned it against his humanity. The wounds beneath the scars still festered, yet the man offered his assistance knowing Asia's condition resembled his nightmare.

Unable to think of a way to gracefully refuse without causing more damage, Silas nodded, pushed back the chair, and stood. "This way."

It did not take long to reach Asia's cell. After typing in the code, Silas waited a moment for her to scent them and become presentable. Opening the door, he noticed her head bent, kneeling on the floor. He ushered Jacques in, allowing him a moment to take in the scene before speaking.

"Hello, Asia. I have a friend of mine with me today. Jacques, this is Asia, Asia...Jacques. As usual, I want to talk, see if we can discover anything new."

"Yes, Sir," she said without raising her head.

Silas sat in the chair. Jacques leaned against the wall, watching intently. "Please take a seat, Asia."

"Yes, Sir." She moved fluidly from the floor to the top of her bed, folded her legs beneath her, and sat with her hands in her lap. Even with the locked blindfold, she appeared the picture of serenity.

"I am going to scan you. I want to check the devices in your head to make sure there has been no change."

"Thank you, Sir."

Silas glanced at Jacques to gauge his reaction. After Arianna had left Jacques almost comatose, Silas had entered his mind as well. There had been a few lesions but nothing that should have been permanent. He and Jacques had never talked about it.

With the conversation fresh in his mind regarding her humanity, Silas searched her cranial cavity with a sharper eye. He looked for anything that might suggest Asia was not as she appeared. The vein joining the eye camera and the small device attached to her brain looked the same. He would let the doctor know so they could alter their treatments. This time he took a little longer, poked around a bit for additional abnormalities. Everything in him said the brain was human tissue, but he had been fooled before. He radiated energy, sending waves of healing through her body. His wolf recognized an answering response in her wolf. She was lonely. This separation from all others was hard on her wolf, she needed Pack. Silas stroked the beast, allowed her to make the connection with him. He would talk to Tyrese, someone had to spend quality time with Asia or she could lose it.

When he pulled out, she was wiping moisture from her face. "Thank you, Sir. Thank you so much."

Touched that such a simple thing as stroking her wolf evoked such a response, Silas released his breath. He had been remiss in his duties, Asia was a wolf and under his protection. He would find a way for her to exercise her beast and remain safe.

"I am your Alpha, it's my job to make sure you have what you need. I will inform Dr. Passen of the scan. Have you thought of anything else that might help me win this war?"

She shook her head and stopped midway. "When you were in my mind a moment ago, you did something different before you dealt with my wolf. It seemed familiar. There was warmth and a moment of clarity, like a sunrise. I saw a warehouse with a long corridor with doors on both sides. Some glass as well." She stopped. "It didn't hurt." She laughed. "I said warehouse and it didn't hurt." She covered her mouth with her hands. "Sir, can you do that again, whatever you did?"

"Yes." Silas entered her mind, focused on her and who he was to all wolves, and then released healing energy. He remained longer this time, hoping to counteract whatever had been done to her. He heard a pop but continued the stream. There was a slight hissing sound and another popping noise.

"Sir."

Silas heard Jacques and started to pull back when he noticed the small device detached from her brain. Quickly he surrounded it and tugged on the cord leading to the camera. It wouldn't break free so he left it, and pushed the other device through her system.

When he exited, Asia lay on her side on the floor with blood trickling from her nose. Jacques knelt in front of her with two fingers on her neck. "She passed out."

"I see that," Silas said, watching from his chair. "Step back, I am going to call her wolf." Jacques stood and moved away as Asia flowed into her wolf.

"Hard to believe she has metal inside when she changes so smoothly," Jacques said.

Silas watched the wolf stand shakily with her head lowered before walking around the small space. "Sit for a while, Asia. Your body is healing. The small device that was attached to your brain is gone. The camera is still in place and I don't know how it transmits, so the blindfold will remain. But if that device blocked your memories, they should come back to you soon."

Asia released a howl and then another.

Silas laughed.

Jacques smiled.

"Be easy, young bitch. I want you healed and whole. Then you can decide what you want to do with your life."

Asia stopped howling and sat on the floor. Silas had no idea what she was thinking over his announcement. The room remained silent. He met Jacques' quizzical gaze with a shrug. Asia shifted.

"I will decide what I will do or where I will go?" Her voice held a measure of uncertainty.

Silas silently thanked the good doctor. "Yes. You're here for two reasons. One, you are not well. Two, there are those who would capture or kill you if they could. I don't believe either of those situations will last forever. Perhaps after a few more healing sessions, the camera behind your eyes will clear up, who knows? I plan to win this war, so those who would harm you will be defeated and you can live free from fear, or at the very least be in a position to defend yourself against your enemies."

Jacques nodded at him.

Asia may not push the envelope as hard for others, but the promise of freedom was an intoxicating nugget. One he intended to dangle in front of her at every opportunity. He was convinced the secrets to defeating his enemy were stored in her mind; they needed her cooperation to access them.

"Thank you, Sir. You have given me a lot to think about. And for the first time since…well I cannot remember when thinking is not painful. Passen gave me a recorder to use as my memories return. I will continue to use it and push harder to wade through the sluggishness of my mind. It always seems as if something important is just on the other side, close but out of reach. As we speak, there are tingles in my head, not unpleasant but different. I hope this is a good sign."

Silas recognized the statement for what it was, a need for reassurance. "It is a good sign; your brain is making repairs. The healing energy followed by your shift helped." Silas stood. "Don't push it, let your memories return naturally, use the recorder. You should be fine. But if you have any discomfort, shift and call out to me. Your wolf will start healing immediately, but I want to know if there are any adverse effects from removing the device."

"Yes, Sir."

Silas and Jacques left the room, both quiet and locked in their thoughts. "She was willing to die," Jacques said softly as they stood in front of the elevator.

Silas glanced at him. "What?"

"When you were in her mind healing her. Blood ran down her nose and I called you because she fell over onto the bed. She stopped me from calling you. Her words exactly, 'he is Patron and knows what he's doing.'" He paused and gazed at the concrete wall.

"I asked if she were dying, just to gauge her response. She grimaced and said yes. It was obvious she was in a lot of pain but she would not allow me to stop you. That scared me." Jacques licked his lips. "It was too close to how I felt…with you know."

Silas wasn't sure if being compared to Arianna, the crazy bitch, was a fitting example, but Jacques was talking and that was something he had not been willing to do in a long time.

"She trusts you implicitly…I do as well…but it was difficult to see. I apologize if the comparison to that woman offends you, I merely used it as a point of reference." He glanced at Silas, who remained silent.

Jacques continued. "I am over that, at least I believe I am over the incident. And now… now that the Goddess has allowed me to find my mate, I know it is just a matter of time before that period of my life is a distant memory." They entered the elevator and Jacques turned to Silas. "I know I am being a nuisance with Victoria. In my defense, I will say I do not trust this Mark fellow. He is always looking around and smiling too big. He acts as though Victoria will disappear if he takes a step back so she can breathe, it's rather infuriating how he tries to control her every move."

Silas hid his smile and nodded.

"I merely suggested that he take himself for a walk if he wanted to see the gardens, Victoria had already complained of a headache. He took offense and for some reason, she did as well. Your mate ushered them into the nursery and I came here." He glanced at Silas and then looked away. "I'm making a mess of this aren't I?"

"Yes, my friend you are. If Mark is an ass, he will be found out, but you cannot be the one to point it out. That's like saying she cannot choose a good man. I have every confidence that my mate's mother is as smart as she and will eventually notice you are the better man. But…" He put up a finger when Jacques started to speak.

"But you have to back off. Let her see you without anger clouding her vision. Be close but not too close. I know you can woo her from a distance, the trick is this…don't make her so angry she will deny you even if she wants you."

Jacque's cheeks turned a light shade of red as his eyes widened. "She would do that? But…but we are mated," he stammered.

"And she is human."

Chapter 18

TYRESE AND LEONIDAS SAT in the small room on the top floor of the hospital, monitoring the halls leading to Julie's room. So far, a barrage of doctors and nurses had done tests, taken blood, and many other things to the woman. Through it all, she remained in a state of near stasis. She answered no questions, and if it were not for the blinking of her eyes, Tyrese would think she was dead.

He hoped this plan worked.

"How much more blood will they take from her?" Leonidas asked, watching as a male nurse stuck a needle into Julie's arm.

"I don't know, but I doubt she can take much more." Tyrese watched the nurse secure the blood, but instead of placing the tube with the others on the tray, he stuck it in his pocket. Tyrese jumped up and headed for the door. *"Keep watching, open our links,"* he yelled at Leon over his shoulder as he headed to Julie's room. The distance between the surveillance room and her room was the one set-back in the plan. He had to maneuver around slow-moving gurneys and sick people to reach the stairwell. He hopped over the railing twice down to her floor.

"Where is the nurse?" he asked Leon through their link.

"He is headed down on the elevator."

Tyrese raced down the stairs to the first floor and looked around. *"I don't see him, did he get off?"*

"He's changed. He's wearing black pants and a dark shirt. I don't see him either."

"Damn."

"See if you can scent her blood."

Inhaling, the faint scent of Julie hit him. He turned and ran toward the parking lot on the other side of the building. He saw a man headed at a fast clip toward a large navy blue suburban and ran after him. The man looked over his shoulder and ran to the truck. Two men, much larger than the nurse, stepped out of the truck from the back seat and ran toward Tyrese as if they were linebackers protecting the quarterback.

"*I can be there in a flash,*" Leon said. Adrenaline pumped through Tyrese, preparing him for the confrontation. He had forgotten the other man was still monitoring the cameras.

"*Still need to keep eyes on her in case this is a distraction. Get the license plate number,*" Tyrese said as the truck drove off and the first man reached him. Without slowing down, he cocked his fist and slammed it into the oncoming man's chest with as much force as he could before pulling it back. His fist throbbed at the impact and he stumbled slightly. A loud crack accompanied the punch as the man flew past his companion and bounced on the ground, his hand holding his chest. Tyrese barely had time to catch his breath before the other guy closed in. Inhaling, he watched.

The other assailant pulled out a gun, aimed, and fired. Tyrese jumped up and flipped forward as the bullet whizzed beneath him. His opponent's eyes followed him and tried to get off another shot. But Tyrese landed to the side, his foot shot out, and kicked the hand holding the weapon, sending the gun to land a few feet away. Disarmed, the man charged. If the fight wasn't so public, Tyrese may have engaged the guy a little longer. It had been a while since he'd sparred with anyone other than his brother. But with one man on the ground, possibly dead, and cameras on the parking lot, he decided to end this immediately. When his assailant closed in, he punched him in the stomach, face, and then got behind the man who was too weak to do anything. Tyrese placed his arms around the man's neck and twisted.

"*I can't believe you killed them on hospital grounds,*" Leon said.

"*I have a cleanup crew on the way. Any activity in her room?*"

"*No, it's quiet. No one's been in since he left. Any idea who that was?*"

"*More than an idea. I know exactly who it was. I've got to call this in to La Patron. Hold down the fort until I can get back there,*" Tyrese said before he bent to check the pockets of the dead men.

"*Roger that.*"

Tyrese checked each man with methodical precision, falling back on his military training. Just as he finished, a large white van pulled up and Froggy stepped out.

"Wot you got 'ere?"

"Two dead pawns whose job it was to keep me from reaching their boss. He got away in a large navy blue suburban a few minutes ago."

Froggy nodded and then threw the first man over his shoulder, walked to the back of the van, and tossed him in.

Tyrese watched to make sure there were no problems before he contacted

Silas. After tossing in the second body, Froggy saluted him and drove off. Returning to the surveillance room, Tyrese went over everything that happened, checking to see if there was anything he could have done differently to change the result. Once he entered the hospital he reached out to Silas.

"*La Patron?*"

"*Tyrese.*"

"*Merriweather was here, dressed as a nurse, and took at least one vial of blood from Julie.*"

"*Continue.*"

Tyrese went on to give Silas a full accounting, including the removal of the dead bodies.

"*Have the doctors check to see if he administered anything to her as well. I don't think you can get another angle in that room but have Leon check. I will contact the police captain. I'm sure he will want to see the tapes, so make him a copy.*"

"*Yes, Sir.*" Tyrese relaxed a bit.

"*One of you can stand by her door. According to the doctor, she is too weak to attempt to escape. I want all activity in her room monitored, they may send someone again.*" He paused. "*I see Leon sent the plate information on the truck, I'll pass that on to the captain as well. Good job, Rese.*"

"*Thank you, Sir.*" Tyrese's spirit lightened as he reached the top floor near the surveillance room.

"*Leon, La Patron wants one of us at her door to monitor traffic in and out of her room.*"

Leon stood and placed his cell phone in his pocket.

"*I'll contact the administrator so they understand what you're doing and don't interfere. I'll have them give you a list of personnel who can enter her room.*" Tyrese pulled out his cell to make the calls.

"*I'm on it,*" Leon said as he left.

Tyrese returned to his seat and watched the monitors. Silas had been right; there was only one camera angle in that room. He couldn't tell if Merriweather had done anything other than taking blood. He split the view and watched Leon peek inside the room before resuming his new post next to the door.

The line to the administrator went to voice mail and Tyrese hung up. He called again a few more times but received the same result. Tyrese was observing Julie when she jerked and flailed on her bed. Lights and bells went off as nurses ran by a startled Leon into her room.

"*What the fuck?*" Leon said through their link as he was pushed out of the way by a nurse bringing in a cart with a large defibrillator. Dread filled Tyrese's gut as the nurse placed the paddles on Julie's chest two more times. She never recovered.

Tyrese stared as the room cleared, leaving Julie just as alone in death as she had been the past few weeks. He zoned out Leon's questions as he continued to stare at the still woman lying on the bed. There was no question in his mind that the woman had been murdered. Matt would handle the autopsy to see if there was any trace of whatever Merriweather had given her.

Could I have done something differently? Nothing came to mind, his instructions had been to monitor from afar and that'd kept him from being close enough to grab the bastard.

He slammed his palm against the desk and turned away from the sight. "*La Patron.*"

"*Tyrese,*" Silas answered through their link.

"She's dead. Julie. They tried to revive her and failed. She's lying in her room alone. You will probably receive a call soon. I'm sorry, Sir."

"*No. You did your job, you both did. There was always a chance of this happening. With the camera footage, an eyewitness, and now her death, the human police can legitimately pick Merriweather up for questioning. This is not the way I planned things, but the result is the same, along with a huge bonus.*"

Tyrese faced the bank of monitors again. Leon remained at his post. The corridor traffic remained the same. Life went on even amid death.

"Bonus?"

"*Yes. The van belongs to Virginia Cochran, one of Corrina Griggs' former names. The police can pick her up as well. Rone was preparing to search for her and now we will work with the authorities to bring them both in.*"

Tyrese whistled. "They're fat cats in the state, why would they risk something like this? They knew we were watching; I can't believe they took that kind of chance."

"*Eh...who knows? I want to talk to both of them. If one of them placed the bomb in Jennings, they will pay through wolf justice. Not human prisons.*"

Tyrese heard the judgment in Silas's voice and knew he planned to handle it personally.

"What would you like me to do now, Sir?"

"*I'll update the captain, and a detective should be there within the hour. You'll be his point of contact. Tell him what happened, show him the video in the hospital, and a portion of the parking lot action. There's no need for him to see the destruction of the two men who disappeared. The captain is aware of this but let's not broadcast the information. The hospital security cams have already been altered.*"

Tyrese should not have been surprised at how fast Silas worked but he was. "Yes, Sir."

"*How is Leonidas working out?*"

Tyrese watched the big man on the monitor. "He has not moved from his post and has been steady. He wanted to fight...he needs to run. We all do." Silas had restricted all of them from running in the forest, and the gym track just wasn't the same. Although they all understood his reasoning, it had been too long since he felt the ground beneath his paws or pulled down prey. His wolf needed to be free and become one with the earth.

"*Yes, when you come in tonight, the six of you should run.*"

"*Six?*"

"*The two of you, Rone, Rose, Cameron, and Lilly. I want you calm for the christening tomorrow. Be careful that Renee, Mark, and Victoria don't catch sight of you. Maybe after dinner, you can run.*"

"*Dinner?*"

"*Yes. My mate expects all of you here for dinner tonight and tomorrow night. I do not want her disappointed.*"

"*You don't want to be at the table alone with them is what you mean,*" Tyrese said, *chuckling*.

"*Exactly.*"

Chapter 19

SILAS WALKED INTO THE silent dining area. Mark and Jacques were alone in the room, staring at each other. Silas had to give it to Mark for standing up to a much larger Jacques, even though in the end it wouldn't matter. Jacques had waited centuries for his mate and would never back off now. Mark seemed just as determined to stand his ground.

"The minister has arrived. Jasmine and her mother are meeting him now to show him where to refresh himself." Silas filled his plate with steak and eggs from the side buffet before turning toward the table. Neither man spoke.

He placed his plate on the table and glanced at Mark, who made no pretense of eating and then at Jacques, who leaned back in his chair glaring at Mark.

"Victoria told me," Mark said in a smug tone. "We will prepare for the christening after she returns."

Silas heard the low rumble in Jacque's throat. Where were the twins, he wondered? Renee walked into the dining room. She stopped, looked at Jacques and Mark.

"Morning, everyone." The twinkle in her eyes warned Silas her addition to breakfast would liven things up a bit.

"Morning, Renee," Silas said, watching Jacques.

"Hello, dear Renee," Jacques said, smiling at the woman.

Mark frowned.

Silas wondered if Jacques had found a champion in Jasmine's sister.

"Morning, Renee," Mark said as she sat across the table from Silas and winked at him.

"Where's everybody?" she asked before taking a sip of her grapefruit juice.

"Jasmine and Victoria are meeting with the minister, he arrived a short while ago. They will show him the small cathedral where the christening of my Jacqueline will take place," Jacques said with smug satisfaction.

"And my Renee," she said, smiling at Jacques. "It's a hoot having the kids named after us isn't it?"

"Hoot?" Jacques laughed.

Frowning, Silas sputtered.

Mark smiled.

"An honor for sure," Jacques said in a somber tone. "Such beautiful babies, healthy and strong. It is an honor to stand for them, one I pledge my life to uphold."

"Thank you," Silas said as he received the tribute from his oldest friend.

"They are beautiful, kinda big for their ages though." She gazed at Silas.

He shrugged. "I'm big."

Her brows furrowed as she looked him over with a doubtful expression. "Mandy didn't believe me when I said they were crawling and scooting. She said they were too young to be doing that."

Silas had no idea what Jasmine planned to tell her sister, so he shrugged and remained silent.

"I brought gratitude stones for each of my nieces and nephews," Renee said in between bites. "I chose each one based on the characteristics Jas told me." She looked at Silas. "It's hard to believe each one is so different. Renee's an artist. She showed me her coloring pages and already she's mixing colors and making beautiful abstracts."

Silas laughed. Only a doting relative would call the coloring over previous colors on paper, abstract art. "She is talented."

"My Jacqueline is a strategist. She sees patterns and creates from the obscure. It is a great gift to have. You have been blessed."

Silas glanced at Jacques and realized the man was serious. Jackie worked puzzles and was pretty good at it. But so did the others. Granted they didn't work on them all day as she did, but he had attributed it to her liking the texture and feel of the pieces.

"Adam...now that one right there. You're going to have to watch him. He's going to be a ladies' man straight up. Jasmine will rein him in some. She did that with the twins. Kept them out of trouble when trouble in a skirt came looking for them." Chuckling, she shook her head. "He reminds me of Rone. Charming, but slick." Staring at Silas, she pointed her fork. "My sister can and will handle them all, but she shouldn't have to. Adam is going to be the break wild child in that bunch and he will need a firm hand."

"Adam is ... playful," Silas said, agreeing with her assessment.

"David has alpha male written all over him, which is creepy in a way because he's so young," Renee said. "I mean that's not a bad thing, but he's so serious. And the way he watches everything and everybody..." She gazed at Jacques, who shrugged.

"Oh come on, don't tell me you haven't noticed. He's younger than Adam, but he has this look he gives his brother." She made a face Silas thought mimicked his son perfectly. "And Adam backs up. It's like they listen to him or something. It's cool, just weird."

"My son is not weird," Silas said with a grin to soften the impact. No need to alienate his mate's sister. "He is smart to watch his surroundings and people in them. Children can sense a person's true nature, and danger as well. I think all of my...children are special and wise."

Renee clapped as she laughed. "Spoken like a proud papa."

Silas nodded. "I am."

"Well, David wouldn't have anything to do with me yesterday, but the others did. I hope to win his trust in time," Jacques said.

Mark snorted before taking a sip from his cup.

Renee glanced in Mark's direction. "You're not the only one, Jacques. He wouldn't let Mark hold him either."

Mark looked up with a smirk. "I don't think Adam is the only ladies' man, Renee. David only allowed the women to hold him." He glanced at Silas. "Other than you of course."

Silas hadn't thought about it but Mark was right. David made allowances for the twins but had little to do with Cameron or Hank, the head of security. He would talk to Jasmine about that.

"Smart boy," Renee smirked.

Jacques laughed.

Mark's smile appeared forced. "Not everyone hates men you know. Victoria and I have gone to the homes of my lesbian friends for meals and we all have a great time. Just because you prefer women does not mean you have to dog men."

"Uh… yeah it does." She held her hand up, cutting Mark off, before pointing her finger at him. "Not because some of you guys aren't cool. I like and respect a few guys. But for the most part, I dislike you guys on general principle. Most men haven't got a clue how to treat a woman, let alone respect her. You give women what you think they need and usually that falls way short of what's necessary. And then you fall back on fragile egos, guilting her into taking watered-down affection that masquerades as a relationship.

"Most men are still little boys stomping their feet in a pseudo temper tantrum trying to get their way. They need to grow the hell up and recognize women bring just as much to the proverbial table. Sperm alone has no creative ability; likewise, an unfertilized egg is a life of sterility. It takes two working in tandem with each other in appreciation and respect of who they are at the core to make a decent relationship. Everything else makes it better. Most men have no idea who their woman is at her core level and that…" She tapped the table with her finger. "That's the reason I dislike men. They want fast food style relationships instead of using a crockpot to allow the flavors of individuality time to develop."

No one spoke.

"I believe Jasmine said you taught at a college," Jacques said into the quiet. "Your students are well served by your brilliance. You have given me pause. I heard everything you said and as I examine my past actions, fear you are correct. I will remember your wise words in the future."

"Suck up," Mark whispered.

Silas heard and could tell by Jacques' reddening face that he had as well. "That was an interesting point of view, Renee," Silas spoke to ease the rising tension in the room. "Does Jasmine believe the same as you?"

Renee's cheeks pinkened. "Some. She is utterly heterosexual." She glanced at Jacques. "Like Mom."

Silas's brow rose as she sidestepped his question regarding how women see men. He would discuss it with his mate later.

"Why did you look at him when you said that?" Mark asked in an angry tone.

Renee glanced at him with a bored expression. "What do you mean? I was making conversation."

"Silas, you may not be aware of this, but your friend here has been making inappropriate remarks and attempting to get my fiancé alone. We are invited guests in your home and I would appreciate it if you would ask him to stop pursuing my future wife."

Silas heard the growl low in Jacque's throat and whipped out a command through the link. *"Cease."* The sound stopped.

"You are right, my fiancé invited her family to the christening of our children and I apologize if you feel uncomfortable for any reason. I will talk with Jacques. I promised my lady nothing would interfere with this day. I want her happy." He glanced at Jacques, who got the message. But just in case he did not, Silas sent a more direct one through their link.

"Do not make me ban you from the compound. I will not have anyone mess up this day for my family and that includes my mate's mother. Can you back off?"

Jacques was silent.

"I will only ask once again. Can you back off?" Giving Jacques a choice was a boon and they both knew it.

"Yes, Sir. It is killing me seeing her with him. My wolf goes wild at her scent and to smell him on her...it is hard not to kill him."

"Thank you, Silas. Victoria was becoming upset at his pursuit." Mark stood. "I'm going to the room to wait for Victoria. I'll see you all at the christening." He turned and left.

"I don't like him," Jacques said after a moment or two.

"Why?" Renee asked, gazing at the man. "I mean I get that you like Mom and all, but she likes this guy. So other than being jealous that he's with the woman you want, why don't you like him?"

Jacques shook his head. "I don't know. I just don't."

Silas watched Jacques struggle to bring his wolf under control. He wondered how he would have handled meeting Jasmine when she had been married to Davian. A streak of anger sliced through him. His wolf growled low in his belly at the thought of his mate with anyone else. No doubt he would have recognized her as his mate and his animal instincts would have taken over. She would have had him arrested or worst. It would not have been pretty.

"I understand," he said, meeting Jacques' sad gaze. The wolf wants what the wolf needs. His friend had to be patient. Human relationships were fragile things, easily broken. Silas would work behind the scenes to expedite that conclusion.

Renee stood. "I do too. Good luck with Mom. She needs a steady mature man on her arm. I think you fit the bill." She winked at Jacques. "I'm going to call Mandy and then get ready for the christening, I'll see you guys there." She waved as she left the room.

Silas stood as well. "I know you think I don't understand what you're going through, I do. Remember, Jasmine is still married. Her husband is below ground with his mate. Fortunately for us all, he is mated or things would be really bad. I cannot allow myself to think about it without a red mist of anger. So I do understand. It will happen. I promise you that one day you and Victoria will be mated, but she cannot think you are mentally deficient. She needs to see you as a man worthy of her love. Back up but don't disappear. Remain busy but always be available. Be charming but not a suck-up." He chuckled at the glare Jacques sent him. "Some of the stuff you said sounded like you were trying to get on Renee's good side, which was unnecessary by the way. I picked up that you were her favorite as soon as she came into the room."

Jacques grinned. "I like her. She's got spunk. Pity she only likes women, she's a fine bitch." He glanced at Silas. "Who does Jasmine prefer?"

"Ask her." Silas left the dining room.

＊＊

Jasmine couldn't stop grinning. The christening had been perfect. The children behaved admirably, allowing Minister Jones to make a cross with his oiled finger on their forehead. David balked initially but calmed after Silas gave him a look. They just finished dinner and retired to the living room for the presentations of gifts. The minister was on his way back home. The twins, Rose, Cameron, and Lilly rounded out the small gathering.

"Mark and I have checks for each of my grandbabies," Victoria said, handing Jasmine four envelopes. "It's the same as I did for the twins, no need in breaking tradition."

"Thanks, Mama," Jasmine said, quieting David, who sat on her lap.

Tyrone held Adam, while Renee and Jacques held their namesakes. She didn't miss the glance her mom sent Jacques before settling back next to Mark in their seat.

Jacques stood and handed Jacqueline to Victoria. Mark's lips tightened but he remained quiet. "I have four deeds of land in four different countries, one for each child." He handed Silas a brown envelope before looking at the children. "May you always own a piece of earth to call your special place. A place to reflect on the challenges of life and living. You are blessed children of a phenomenal couple who I am honored to call friends." He bowed and then reclaimed Jacqueline, who nestled quite contently against him.

"Wow, that was beautiful, Jacques. I hate to come behind you," Renee said, rising. She handed little Renee to Tyrese and then picked up a box. "Okay, I have a titanium necklace containing a gratitude stone for each of you." She placed the first one on little Renee. It was a highly polished mahogany-colored granite stone. "My hope is that each day you rise, you will find at least one thing to be grateful for." She placed a silver stone around Jacqueline. "And as you realize how special each day is, you will speak words of gratitude aloud." She placed a blue stone around Adam. "And as your positive words enter the atmosphere, they will attract good and positive things to you." She placed an onyx stone around David. Instead of allowing it to rest on his chest as the others did, he held the stone and rubbed it for a moment before releasing it. "My gift to you is a stone to remind you that every day is a gift and you should always be grateful."

Jasmine smiled at the beautiful sentiment.

"Thank you, Renee," Silas spoke before Jasmine could. "Those are indeed precious gifts."

Renee took little Renee from Tyrese.

"I want to hold a baby," Victoria said, pouting. Tyrone handed her Adam.

Jasmine took Silas's hand and squeezed. She hoped he understood what having her family here today meant to her. David stroked his stone as he looked around the room quietly. Adam played with Mark and her mom now held Jackie again.

"*Happy?*"

"Yes, thank you for not fighting me on this," she said, pouring love down their link. "*I know you have a lot going on with…work. So thanks for stopping to do this.*"

"*You and my pups are my world, Jasmine. This pleases me to see them honored from the heart of those we know. It is a good tradition.*"

She hugged his compliment tight. It was rare that he saw anything good in human events, and that he liked the christening pleased her greatly.

Chapter 20

"I WANT THEM OUT of here," Silas yelled.

Jasmine closed her eyes as splotches of heat danced across her skin. Counting to ten, she looked at his clenched jaw and red face, and counted silently again. Her anger took on a life of its own, rising to the top like cream.

When she could speak in a calm voice, she opened her eyes. "I am not going to accuse my mom or sister of making the kids sick. They have a fever, kids get fevers. It's not uncommon."

His scowl deepened. "With the exception of David, my pups have never been sick, not one day, until your family entered my compound." His nostrils flared as he stepped closer and leaned forward. "Tell them to leave," he growled.

Jasmine ground her teeth as her patience snapped. "No. I will not. Do you think Rese or Rone would allow their mates to tell *me* to leave their homes because their children were sick? Worse, do you think they would suspect I was the problem?" They both knew her sons would never do that.

"No. They know better. You're twisting this around."

"That's my mama you're accusing, damn it. *I* know better than to accuse her of making my children sick." She inhaled and pointed at him. "They stay and you will not say one fucking word to them or I will leave with them. Don't test me in this, Silas. That's my mama, my sister. They had nothing to do with our kids having temperatures and I will not accuse them of anything."

"Did I say accuse them? I said tell them to leave, give them any damn reason you want, just get them the hell out of this compound and don't you dare threaten to leave me woman, I won't have you giving me ultimatums."

She crossed her arms and tapped her foot. "Ultimatum?" she scoffed.

"That was a damned promise. I'm not your servant. I am your mate, an equal partner. You don't get to treat me as some ignorant bitch who you give commands to…no sir. This is not going to work like that." She tilted her chin up meeting his icy glare. "Is this my home?"

"What?" He eyed her suspiciously.

"Answer me. Is this my home or not?"

"Yes, it's your home, you know that. But our children are in danger. It's my job to protect them."

"And I don't want to protect them?" She exhaled. "Look Silas, if I thought for one moment that my family had anything to do with the kids getting sick, I'd be on their asses so fast you couldn't blink. But I don't. I'm asking you to trust me on this."

Silas met her gaze for another moment. They were getting nowhere fast. His wolf howled with the knowledge that someone had gotten to his pups beneath his nose. She had no idea what that did to him. His failure to protect his den, his pups, ate at his very essence. It tap-danced on who he was, what he did, and he was within his rights to expel everyone new to his domain.

He could not agree to this.

The one thing his wolf knew was that one of the five new people who'd entered his compound within the past two days was guilty of harming his pups and Jasmine was too close to sense it. Without another word he turned and left their suites, heading for his pups.

"I'm changing your assignment," he said to Jarcee, who stood outside their suite. His primary responsibility had been to shadow Jasmine, to keep her safe. "Follow me," Silas said without looking back. His mind flew in a whirlwind of anger, pain, shame and embarrassment that his sanctuary had once again been violated he strode to the nursery. "Wait here," he said as he walked inside.

Matt and his assistants were taking blood samples and his pups were not happy at being poked with needles. "Almost done," Matt said, returning Renee to her bed. "David's temperature has normalized, but the other three, theirs is still high and rising. What did the doctor say?"

Silas stroked Jacqueline's warm cheek. It pained him to see her lying listless in her crib making pitiful small noises. "He's baffled. He ran some tests, gave them something to bring the temperatures down, but nothing has worked. That was eight hours ago, which is why I wanted you to run some tests to see if there's something more going on. Too many damn strangers around my pups," he growled as he stroked Renee's cheek.

"I understand. I'll get started on this right away." Matt paused. "You have a beautiful litter, Sir."

Silas glanced up at him and nodded before turning to Adam, who whimpered while turning on his side. Silas picked him up and rubbed his back. Jasmine entered the room and checked the babies without speaking to him. He was in no mood to argue with her and moved away.

She picked up David and kissed his cheek. Silas turned and walked a few feet away as he sent healing energy into Adam.

Renee whimpered.

He twisted slightly and watched as Jasmine picked up the child. She rocked her on the balls of her feet until the babe quieted a bit. Adam had fallen asleep on his shoulder and he returned his son to the crib. Next he picked up Jacqueline and sent healing energy into her body. Once she fell asleep, he laid her down. Renee still whimpered, and he touched the child's back before lifting her.

"I've got her." Jasmine tightened her hold.

He didn't speak as he took his daughter, stepped aside, and sent healing energy through her body. He had done this exact thing four hours ago. It brought his pups' temporary relief, but eventually they woke screaming with high temperatures.

"Why was Matt in here?" Jasmine asked to his back.

Without turning he answered. "I want him to run some tests to see if there is anything else going on."

"They have temperatures, could be teething or allergies, Silas. It happens with babies."

He glanced at her. She had been wrong with her own diagnosis. If he had listened to her then she'd probably still be lying in bed. "If that's the case, no problem. But my wolf says you're wrong, so I'm going to go with my gut on this one. No one is allowed in the nursery other than me, you, or the twins. Security will enforce my decree. Tell your family whatever you want, but they will not be allowed in here."

"Jacques too? You suspect Jacques?" she asked incredulously.

"No. But he is one of the five new people to interact with my pups in the last two days."

"This is…I cannot believe you're doing this." She released a breath. "Okay, if this is how you want to do it, fine."

He nodded and left. Jarcee stood in the same position as before. Silas explained his new duties and left for his office. Dark coldness burned his gut. Somehow his enemies had crossed into his den and affected his pups. The thought slammed against his mind. For that they would pay the highest price. His wolf pressed against him, the desire to shift and destroy his enemies had never been stronger. He stopped, leaned against the wall and took in gulps of air. His wolf howled for freedom. It was all he could do not to join his beast right then. Moving toward the stairs he ran down to the basement level to the gym. Once there, he ran to the door, sending a message to security to open it before he reached it. The slight burn that flowed through his limbs as they stretched and reconfigured melted the whips of ice buffeting him. Shifting complete, he took off for the woods.

"*Sir?*" Tyrese called to him but he refused to answer. His wolf had to release some energy so he could think. Over grassy mounds of dirt his beast ran. The dirt beneath the pads of his paws eased his spirit. Crisp mountain air cleansed his nostril. The warmth of the mid-day sun warmed his back and hindquarters. It came as no surprise when the twins and Cameron caught up and ran behind him. In silence, they ran until they reached the edge of the forest.

Silas slowed and then stopped. His wolf had calmed but the underlying current of anger remained. He nosed the ground, clearing his scent as he searched the area for prey. A sound caught his attention and he took off tearing through the woods. The footfalls of his pack were behind him as he sighted the small wild boar. He scented the air for the sounder, or group of pigs, and picked up nothing. This boor had somehow become separated. Silas doubted the animal would survive alone, but he would not be the one to kill the animal. With a howl, he took off running toward the compound. There was work to be done.

"Sir?" Tyrone said once they sat in the office after the run. "I missed one of Corrina Griggs marriages, possibly because it wasn't recorded through proper channels." He waved his hand dismissively. "She married Cornell Merriweather, they had two sons—"

"Robert, who died in the cave, and Alfred, the one who has been a pain in the ass. That explains a piece of the puzzle. Since the truck was registered to one of her past names it's safe to say she is either running the shots or is heavily vested in this scheme of a breeder world."

"Yes," Tyrone said.

"How are we coming in the search for the Merriweathers?" Silas asked, although his thoughts were on his pups. They should be resting. In a few hours he would return to the nursery to give them more relief. His stomach clenched in disgust with the knowledge that he could heal other wolves and not his own pups. The deficiency galled him.

"The cops are searching, as well as our network. They went to ground. When they resurface, and I think they are somewhere nearby regrouping, there's no telling what new toys they will bring to the party," Tyrone said.

"That's the problem," Cameron said. "We have no idea which group has what toys. I thought the group who sent Asia was behind the bombings, but it was Merriweather's group, right?" He gazed at Tyrone.

"It looks that way. Asia's peeps deal with body modification. They used the serums to make changes and surgical reconstruction. Merriweather has found a way to insert explosives quickly. Remember Jennings had only been missing for a day. According to the lab, the triggers are imprinted in the bomb, not in or on the person."

"Merriweather's group is also responsible for the serum to kill wolves. Which makes no sense considering they claim that we will all live together in harmony one day," Tyrese said.

"Crazy is as crazy does," Tyrone murmured.

Silas shook his head. "Crazy they may be, but the body count is growing and I want it stopped."

"Asia give us any more info to help find the labs?" Tyrese asked.

Silas brought them current on Asia's situation. "In the next day or so, Dr. Passen will take her through some tests to see how much of her memory is intact. Anything she tells us from this point on must be verified."

Cameron nodded. "She shouldn't be under their control any longer. I hope she has coordinates. I'd love to pay that lab a visit." He looked at Tyrese. "I saw the feed from the parking lot fight, were those amped up humans or breeds?"

"Humans. That's why I had to clear the grounds quickly."

"Mom said the babies have a cold with a temperature," Tyrese said into the quiet.

Silas met Tyrese' gaze. "I don't know what's wrong, the doctor is looking into it."

"Is that why Jarcee is standing guard at the nursery?" Tyrone asked.

"Until I know why my pups are sick for the first time, yes."

Cameron's gaze swung between the twins before settling on Silas. "No way. You think someone did something to your pups?"

Silas released a stream of air as he looked at each of them. "Yes."

"They've never been sick before, the timing is suspect," Tyrone said slowly. "Mom's probably freaking that you suspect one of our fam, but I see your point."

Tyrese nodded slowly. "It's the way I would call it."

"You would prevent your mother from seeing your pups?" Cameron asked the twins, his voice doubtful.

"Hell no." Tyrone shook his head. "Mom would never do anything to hurt me or Rese. And never our kids. I'm just saying I understand the rationale behind not wanting anyone around now who wasn't around before the kids got sick."

Tyrese shook his head. "Nope, I'd never stop mom from hanging with my kids. I can't even imagine that."

"What if she wasn't being herself? Had some challenges?" Cameron asked.

Tyrese eyed him. "Like Nana?"

Cameron shrugged.

Silas waited to hear the twin's opinion. According to Jasmine, Victoria has not been her normal self. What if his enemies had gotten to her? It was a sobering thought.

"She's been forgetting stuff. It's not like her, but we don't really have much of a guide book on breeders. This could be normal. Her body could be handling everything differently. Julie willed herself to die and walked that path. Arianna used her breeding abilities to her advantage and caused some serious damage. Breeders have powers that we know very little about. Even mom doesn't fully understand her capabilities." Tyrone paused. "I said all of that to say this, I don't know if Nana could be used as a Trojan horse in this instance. It's possible."

"What about the necklaces? Could they be having a reaction?" Cameron asked.

"Those were the first things I took off," Silas said, remembering David's outrage. His son had screamed until he'd placed the black stone back into his hand. "Still no change."

Cameron scooted further in his chair. "What if they were activated when the pups touched them?"

"Or some chemical in the oil the priest used?" Tyrese added.

"I provided the oil," Silas said. He had refused to allow anyone put something on his pups he hadn't checked. The minister had been surprised but went along with Jasmine's request. "I gave it to him as he started the long prayer."

"Okay, so the only thing that touched the babies were the stones, damn…" Tyrese said softly.

"Aunty is going to be hurt behind this. Let me say this for the record. Although I understand why you have the ban in place, I don't believe my aunt or nana has anything to do with my brothers and sisters being sick. I hope it's a cold like mom thinks but…the timing is suspect," Tyrone said, his voice trailing off.

"Right now it's the only anomaly I have. I take this strike personally and will not be swayed by hurt feelings. This is my den and those are my pups. I will do whatever necessary to protect them."

"Mom by herself is a handful, add aunty and nana…" Tyrone shook his head. "Let's just say I'm glad I live in another wing."

Chapter 21

TWO DAYS LATER, THE children's fever's spiked up to one hundred and ten degrees, well over the norm of one hundred and two for pups. The mewling sounds of their discomfort tore at Jasmine's heart. Her eyes itched with unshed tears as she silently agreed with Silas that there was more at work here than a cold.

Yesterday, the doctor hooked them up to IV's to insure they received medication, nutrients and remained hydrated. She and Silas had moved into the nursery. He was constantly in and out during the day, changing diapers, wiping sweat covered brows, and holding a babe when the pain was too much. They spoke little to each other and that was fine with her. His sadness, tinged with anger, was palpable. Guilt ate at her that he had been right and she had unwittingly put her children in danger. She couldn't fathom how it was accomplished but the devastating results spoke for themselves.

After the first day, Silas taught her how to tap into her energy and feed it to the babes, which provided them some relief. She even suggested he feed them drops of his blood since it had helped David. Nothing worked. Watching her babies suffer cut her deeply. Every agonized cry peeled a strip off of her heart. Her limbs ached with fatigue, yet she refused to take a break. Rose sent food and exchanged her worn clothes with clean ones through the doorway.

The day after the christening when she didn't appear for lunch, her mom found her in the nursery. When she stepped out to explain, her mother accepted her story about the cold and cause for isolation. She and Mark acted as though they were on vacation at a five star hotel, frequenting the pools and sunbathing on the private deck outside their suite. Mark was generous with his time and affection with her mother. Jasmine couldn't remember seeing her mom so happy.

Renee wasn't so easily dissuaded. Initially she'd offered to assist Jasmine with the children, and it had been difficult to look her sister in the eyes and say no. But she had. Couple that with her spending all her time with her babies, it came as no real surprise when Tyrone entered the nursery that morning with the news.

"Mom, Aunty wanted me to tell you she's leaving today." He raked his fingers through his scalp while looking at the babies and the equipment. "She said more…but she's hurt and no doubt will talk to you again. One day. Probably not this week, but give her some time."

Jasmine slumped in the chair. Her bones ached. Her heart was torn. She had made a mess of things. Now she would have to find a way to placate her sister. That was a muddle she wasn't ready to tackle. Once the kids were better, she'd work on that relationship.

Most of all, she missed Silas. He was her rock, her solace, and he had left her to find her own way and she didn't like it. It didn't matter that he gave her what she asked for. She didn't like the results and knew she would have to make the first move to change things.

She offered Tyrone a smile, knowing he was uncomfortable being the bearer of such news. "I know she's pissed, not that I blame her. I didn't have a chance to explain the wolf culture thing to her, so she has no way of understanding what's happening." She released a breath. "This sucks."

Tyrone nodded but remained silent.

* * *

Silas strode into his office and closed the door. He slumped into his chair and placed his head in his hands. With the exception of David, his pups had not made any improvements. David had responded well to the meds after the first day. But Jackie, Adam, and Renee had slipped deeper into whatever gripped them. Once he dismissed the nurses, speculation ran rampant through the compound regarding the pups, but he didn't care.

There was a knock at his door. He turned in his chair and studied the door as if he could tell who was on the other side simply by looking. It was a wasted effort, he knew it was Rose.

"Enter."

Rose stepped in, her eyes downcast. "These came in for you today. I postponed your weekly Alpha meeting until next week."

"Thank you." He nodded as she laid the envelopes on his desk and then left him in peace. Tyrone had told him of Renee's departure this morning and he wondered how Jasmine handled her sister's abandonment. Not that Jasmine had spent any time with her family since the christening, but still… there was a protocol in place for what they were going through.

He opened the letter on top and read the contents.

La Patron,

It has come to my attention that Cameron Knight is your choice for the Alpha position in West Virginia. Previous reports had been of a different challenger. Cameron is a full-blood whom I respect and believe will fulfill the position of Alpha admirably. I humbly withdraw my challenge.

At your service,
Serrano Knight

Silas read the short missive twice. Bigotry still flowed through his ranks. Cameron's full-blood status did not make him Silas' first choice, and the back-handed compliment from Serrano rankled Silas. The wolf should never have challenged Silas' pick regardless. He placed a call.

"La Patron, Sir," Jayden answered.

"Serrano ceded the Alpha position to Cameron, he thought he would be fighting a breed but since it's a full-blood wanting the spot…well, there's no challenge, smug bastard. I should make him fight Tyrone just to teach him a lesson."

Jayden chuckled. "True. There was never a doubt in my mind who would have won that battle. Rone would've wiped the floor with him. The only other person I would've considered was Rese, but he's not interested in sitting behind a desk or using tact. He's enforcer material."

Silas wasn't surprised with Jayden's assessment of the twins, they were both deadly. Tyrone merely appeared more amicable than Tyrese, who refused to make an effort. "I agree. I leave it to you to handle the dismantling of the event."

Jayden remained quiet for a bit longer. "Perhaps we can use this as a drawing card."

Interested, Silas sat up. "What do you have in mind?"

"Word has gone out about the challenge already. We muffle Serrano so he doesn't let on about the cancellation and use the event to set a trap."

"No more deaths. And that's how those assholes play. They kill innocents. Think of a way to set a trap and I'll listen, but I want to know every angle including possible death counts."

"Yes, Sir."

Silas debated whether or not to tell Cameron. He thought about the earlier discussion he'd had with Cameron and the twins. Although neither twin let on, Silas knew Cameron's suspicions regarding Victoria and Renee struck a nerve. The last thing he needed was problems with his core group. Perhaps a visit to the Alpha house would do Cameron, Lilly, and Thorne, Lilly's teenaged brother, some good.

"Cameron," Silas called through their link. Moments later Cameron and

Lilly entered his office. Once they sat in front of his desk, he handed Cameron the note from Serrano. To his credit, Cameron frowned before passing it to his mate.

"That's no reason to give up a challenge. He would have a better shot at the alpha position by fighting me than with Rone."

Lilly's brow rose at his comment.

Cameron laughed and tapped the tip of her nose. "I've fought Rone before, he is skilled and a better fighter than most alphas. I'm not ashamed to admit he's better at fighting than I am. Even when we practice I have no qualms asking him pointers. I will get better, but right now he is better. Deal with it." He laughed at her frown. Seconds later she laughed as well.

"You are such a goof," she said, taking his hand.

Silas watched in amazement at the evidence of the transition in their relationship. The easy-going bickering and laid-back camaraderie pleased him greatly. This is what he wanted for his godson, and for his pups one day as well.

"You should go to the Alpha house, look things over, become acclimated. It's been vacant for over a year. Let Rose know if you need anything. She will help until you hire your own staff."

Lilly and Cameron stared at him as though he spoke Latin. "Now?" Cameron asked.

Silas shrugged. "Why not? Just don't advertise you're moving in or that you have the position yet. Jayden is working on a scheme to use the Challenge event as a trap. But other than that, go and see your new home."

Cameron stood, pulling his mate with him. "Thank you, Sir. We'll do that." The two left his office grinning. At least he had made someone happy. Silas thought of his mate and wondered what she was doing, if she had eaten or taken a break. He glanced at the time, it had been a couple of hours since he'd relieved her.

"Tell Jacques and Dr. Passen I want to meet with them in an hour. Tell Matt to get me some answers. I'm headed to the nursery, have you already sent lunch for Jasmine?" he asked Rose as he left his office.

"Yes, Sir. And I'll get those messages out."

"Also, I need Serrano's contact info, send it through the link."

"Yes, Sir," Rose said.

He strode around the corner, and ran into Victoria, who looked really nice in her two-piece bathing suit. "Were you lost?" he asked politely. There was no reason for her to be in this part of the building.

"I'm looking for Jasmine and Renee, I wanted us to have lunch, just the girls again. Have you seen them?"

Silas took her by the hand and completed a scan while he answered her questions. "Renee returned home to St. Louis this morning and Jasmine is in the nursery in the other wing with the babies, they are sick."

"Oh no, what's wrong with them?" Her brow creased as she met his gaze.

"Really bad cold. They are in isolation."

"For a cold?" She looked up at him with a confused expression.

"A bad cold," Silas emphasized.

"Oh…okay. Tell Jasmine to find me later, we can eat dinner together," she said as Silas escorted her to the elevator and walked inside with her.

"Where is Mark? Why are you alone and way over here?"

"I left him at the pool. I had to go to the bathroom or my room for something." She shook her head as if to clear it. "We're at the pool. This place is so big I must've gotten lost."

"Yes, that's it." The door opened and they stepped out. In silence he walked her to the door leading to the pool. Silas scented Mark before he saw the man lying on the lounger near the pool.

"Thanks, Silas," Victoria said, waving as she headed toward her lover. The man sat up, grabbed her close, and the sight of the two of them cuddling on the lounger was the last one he saw before walking off. The woman had been genuinely confused with her whereabouts and even the babies' sickness. Jasmine was right to be concerned about her mother's mental health.

Chapter 22

THE NEXT DAY, JACQUES sat at the long table with stacks of paper covering the surface. When the pups became ill, he'd doubled down to find answers. He knew better than most that Silas walked a thin line and it wouldn't take much for him to explode as he had before during the debacle with Arianna. He tapped the document in front of him. "You slimy bastard, you're here, I feel you."

After reading through a few more of Asia's reports, he had an idea of the location of the lab. He wrote that down and set it aside for Silas. He needed to talk to the young bitch to clear up a few gray areas.

"Sir?" He searched for Silas through their link as his thoughts drifted to Victoria. The scent of Mark on her skin made him physically ill, which helped him keep his distance. It amazed him that such a smart, beautiful woman didn't see past Mark's smarmy personality.

"Jacques?"

"I have a possible location for the warehouse. Also, I need to talk to Asia again to clear up some other information."

"Thanks. Go to the lab, I'll meet you there." Silas' excitement sizzled through their connection. Jacques stood with his tablet in hand, and left the conference room he had commandeered as his work area. After locking the door, he left for the basement. Her scent slammed into him before he saw her.

"Victoria? What are you doing over here?" he asked, taking her arm and leading her to the elevator. Silas was on edge as it was, no need to push things with him discovering her near his office.

"I wanted to talk to Jasmine, where is she?" She gazed up at him and his heart lurched in his chest.

"You are so beautiful."

She stilled. A smile slowly appeared on her face. "You think so?" she asked hesitantly.

"I know so. You have no idea how you affect me. I adore you."

He smiled as her cheeks colored and she placed her palm against her face. The ring on her left hand flashed, reminding him that for the moment she belonged to someone else. "Thanks, I'm sure this is improper...yes, you shouldn't say those kinds of things to me."

He took her hand and kissed the back of it. "Yes, I should. But you need to go to your floor. Jasmine is unavailable until she comes to you. He guided her into the elevator and pressed the button for her floor. The rapid beats of her heart filled his ear. She wasn't unaffected by him and that knowledge filled him with hope. When the elevator door opened on her floor, he walked her to the hall leading to her suite.

"Thanks, I appreciate your help," she murmured before moving down the hall. He waited until she entered her rooms before leaving. When he reached the labs, Silas sat in the conference room with the twins.

Silas watched Jacques enter. Victoria's scent tickled his nostrils. Based on the smile his friend wore, something good had happened. "What do you have?" Silas asked regarding the location of the warehouse.

Jacques took a seat, and connected his tablet to the screen in the room. Silas turned and waited.

"Asia has consistently talked about an area similar to these locations. Leonidas' reports support two of the four. So for now we focus on these two. If you notice her descriptions, which are written in the sidebar, it could be either of these buildings. But this building has the starburst that she mentioned twice."

"Starburst?" Tyrone asked.

"My take on it is fireworks. Twice a year the town of Youngstown has fireworks displays. July Fourth and November 20th, some type of founder's day event. The town is within fifteen miles of this warehouse and more importantly, you can see fireworks in the sky from here." Various pictures of an abandoned warehouse and the small rural town filled the screen.

"How long has the building been abandoned? The grass and trees have almost taken it over," Tyrone said.

"Which means there is another way inside," Silas said, gazing at the pictures intently. "No doubt security is tight, but no reason to expend energy on the outside if everything is done below." He looked at Jacques. "Any underground activity?"

"The warehouse is on the north side of Highway 80 in Pennsylvania, you see the Susquehanna River here?"

"Yeah," Tyrese said.

"The warehouse is here in the valley."

Silas studied the area. "How do we get inside?"

"There are no utility bills," Jacques said into the quiet. "However, I pulled this satellite image of a propane delivery five miles from the warehouse. Considering there were no other deliveries within miles of this place and the large quantity of propane delivered, I'd say this might be a good starting point." An image of a propane fuel bill appeared on the screen. "I hit a dead end trying to locate the people who ordered the propane…which plays to my hunch that this is the right place. And that it's occupied or at least it was…" He zoomed in on the date on the invoice. "Two weeks ago."

A surge of satisfaction swept through Silas. "So we start at the drop point and work our way in. There has to be some form of ductwork to exchange oxygen and to release vapors and fumes from below. That would give us some sort of idea what we're looking at." Silas' gaze swept those in the room. "Keep this quiet for now. I need to contact Alpha Samuel in Pennsylvania, let him know what's going on. His people will assist on this. Let's use them to do a lot of the groundwork before we head out there."

"Sounds good," Tyrese said.

"Rone, I want you to work point with Samuel and Jacques. See if there are any places the Merriweather group overlaps with the Pennsylvania group."

"Yes, Sir."

"Rese, I want you and Leon to pick up Corrina Griggs. Some information came in on her current location. I had her file sent to you. Read everything before you meet her, use anything in the file to gather more information. We think she's behind the breeders organizing."

Tyrese nodded.

"When can I speak with Asia?" Jacques asked Silas.

"I want to sit in on the discussion, so give me fifteen minutes to take care of some things."

Jacques nodded and sat with Tyrone going over the information.

"You smell like nana," Tyrone said to him after a few minutes.

"Really?"

"Yeah, good for you," Tyrone said before leaving the room.

Silas smiled as he finished his discussion with Jayden and Samuel regarding the joint take-down of the warehouse. "Ready?" he asked Jacques, who sat staring at the door the twins had walked out of.

Jacques glanced at him and stood. "Yes."

When Silas entered Asia's room, she fell to the floor on her knees. "Rise, Asia," he said, waiting for her to stand and return to her bed. After she was situated he spoke. "My assistant, Jacques, was here with me before."

"Yes, he is the one who wiped the blood from my nose."

Silas had forgot about the bleeding. "Yes, he has some questions for you, answer him honestly and completely."

"Yes, Sir."

Jacques stepped from the door and told Asia about the children's sickness. Stunned, Silas tamped down the anger choking him at the frank discussion. What was Jacques up to? He glanced at his friend, their eyes met for a moment before Jacques asked Asia a question.

"Have you heard of anything like this happening before?"

"No... no, I have not. I wonder how the transmission was made."

Silas spoke up. "Transmission?"

She nodded. "It sounds like poison. Poison administered in a way that you wouldn't notice, something commonplace. Also, why not David? Think back to the day before the illness, was his behavior different than the others? How? That will give you a clue how the poison was delivered. It has to be something so simple it was overlooked, that's how and why they have been so successful."

Silas thought back to the day of the christening, nothing jumped out at him. Jacques stepped back to the door and signaled he was done.

"Thanks, Asia. How are you feeling?"

She smiled and it was genuine. "Each day I remember more and more. Some things I hope to forget. I've done some really bad things to people." She paused. "Thank you for giving me my life back, Sir."

"You are welcome. Thank the Goddess as well," he said, leaving her space.

"Every day, Sir, I thank her."

When he stepped outside, Jacques motioned him closer. "David refused to allow me and Mark to hold him."

Silas stared at Jacques while trying to place the statement into some sort of context.

"Sir," Matt said, walking toward them at a fast clip. "La Patron, Sir, I must talk to you. It's extremely important." He stopped next to Jacques, breathing hard.

Silas pointed at Jacques and introduced the two men. "What is it?" He gazed at Matt but his mind was stuck on David not allowing himself to be held by the men.

"I found something in the blood work. It was so well hidden I missed it the first few times, but I knew it had to be there. This time I found it," Matt said in a rush.

"Asia?"

Matt frowned. "No, your pups. I found a trace of poison. Very subtle and disruptive over time. It wasn't administered directly on them, otherwise this conversation would be very different. They received traces or got it second-hand."

Silas' heart plummeted as his worse fears were confirmed. He moved the conversation to an empty room. "Slow down, Matt. Tell me exactly what you discovered and what you think happened."

"It's sneaky. The first set of tests did not show the poison, I can show them to you to prove it. We looked but it didn't show up."

"I'm not blaming you or your team of anything, Matt. Calm down and tell me what's going on with my pups."

Matt exhaled and swallowed. "I'll say this plain, without all the scientific jargon."

"I appreciate that," Silas said, wishing the man would just get on with it.

"The poison entered the bloodstream through the skin. I don't think it'd work if it was ingested, but we are working on duplicating the formula so we can test it and create an antidote." He waved his hand. "I'm getting ahead of myself. Bottom line, your pups were poisoned through touch. Someone had something on their hands and then held your pups. There was transference at that point. It's slow-acting and not meant to be noticed immediately. It's a great way to destroy someone slowly and from a distance."

"Not so great," Silas growled, thinking of the suffering his pups were going through.

"I apologize, Sir," Matt stammered.

Silas waved him off. "Lotions, creams, perfume, cologne, aftershave, soap...could the poison have been in any of those?"

"Yes, Sir. To affect your pups, they would have come in direct contact with the affected area. Perfume, cologne, or creams on the face, hands, neck or legs would allow for a transfer of the chemical."

"What...what other side effects would this poison have?" Jacques asked slowly, a frown marring his brow. "I mean if an adult took it over time?"

Matt released a breath and squinted. "Our testing is not complete yet, but we have identified two of the toxins used. Nausea, fevers, chills, body shakes, aches, that type thing."

"Could it be fatal?" Silas asked.

"Yes, Sir. If taken in a high enough dose, death would occur. But I don't think you have to worry about that, Sir."

Silas gazed at the red-faced man. "Why not?"

"They would be dead already if the dose was high enough to kill. You shut down all contact which prevented additional exposure. If your pups had been in continued contact with the poison... we would be having a different conversation. The base poisons utilized were outlawed when certain third world countries used them in chemical warfare. Seeing the full impact of what this poison does is not pretty."

Silas jaw tightened. "The cure?"

"There is none, not yet. It's going to take some time, right now, all I can say is let it run its course. Your energy dilutes it but you can't over do it. You said you and the Mistress were feeding them healing energy every four hours, keep to that, if you do it more often it could have an adverse affect. We'll continue the research and eventually create an antidote for it." He paused, glanced at Silas and then gazed at a point over Silas' shoulder. "This... this is parallel to the bombs, Sir. Putting this poison in lotions and creams is a very subtle way of killing groups of people. That issue has to be addressed as well."

Silas had been thinking of that. "I thought the poison was outlawed, is it easy to get?"

Matt shook his head slowly. "It *is* very difficult to secure the components I've identified so far. I had to use my clearance just to get information and answer a lot of questions."

"So mass production isn't a real threat right now?"

Matt released a breath and met Silas' gaze. "You're right, Sir. The way the government doled out bits and pieces of information, I'd say only those able to pull some serious strings could access the poisons."

"Yet, the poisons are here in my den." Silas pressed his finger against his lip. "Is the person who transmitted the poison affected?"

"Yes, Sir. The poison is killing them," Matt said.

Puzzled, Silas gazed at Jacques. "No one in the five appeared to be dying."

"No, Sir," Jacques said quietly.

"This doesn't make sense," Silas said to no one in particular.

"No, Sir, it doesn't," Jacques said.

Chapter 23

"THIS IS THE PLACE?" Leon asked Tyrese as he pulled into the driveway of a large two-story home in a moderately priced subdivision.

Tyrese turned off the ignition and replaced his sunglasses on his face. "Yes." He pulled out two pistols. One held darts with a knockout drug and the other held bullets. Whichever he used would be up to Ms. Griggs. He glanced at Leon, who checked his ammunition as well.

"We go in, ask a few questions, and she leaves with us one way or the other."

"Aw man, don't tell me we have to play nice with the lady that killed Julie," Leon said with a feral grin.

"At first." Tyrese stepped out the car and inhaled. There were at least five bodies nearby, three humans, two breeds. Leon mimicked his actions and then grinned.

When they reached the door, it was opened by a large breed who had the appearance of a short Schwarzenegger. "May I help you?"

"Are you Corrina Griggs?" Tyrese asked, staring the man down.

"No."

"Well then..." Tyrese brushed the man aside and walked in. Leon entered behind him.

"Hey," the male who opened the door yelled as he ran behind them. "You can't just walk in here."

Tyrese looked around and then gazed at the young pup. "Corrina Griggs."

"She's not available."

"Yes, she is," Tyrese said. "Go tell her she has company."

The pup stared at him and growled.

Leon laughed at the puny sound. Tyrese shook his head.

"Did you hear that?" Leon asked while watching the pup turn red. "You sound like a wet cat, man. Seriously, you should get that checked."

The pup stepped up to Leon, who continued to smile. "Fuck you."

Leon reached out so fast it was a blur and caught the pup by the neck, lifting him from the floor. He shook the hapless male twice while the pup tried in vain to remove Leon's hand from his neck. "I don't play that way. But if you ask nicely, I'll consider ramming my cock up your ass."

He released the pup.

"Andrew, I told you not to engage them." A woman walked into the room and touched the young pup's throat. "Go into the kitchen, get some warm tea and ice for your throat. It'll be okay."

Tyrese watched the woman and knew she was not Corrina Griggs. He wasn't sure how he knew but he did. The brunette looked at Leon and then at Tyrese. "I'm Corrina, what can I do for you?"

Tyrese thought of all the problems Corrina Griggs had set loose on his family, the deaths and unnecessary heartache he'd read in her file, and decided to set the tone immediately. Without another word, he stepped up to the woman, grabbed the front of her dress and ripped it.

She screamed and tried to cover her naked flat chest.

"You're a man in women's clothing." Tyrese's hand circled the male's neck and pressed.

"Please..." the man whispered.

"Corrina Griggs?" Tyrese stared into the man's eyes and read fear. He squeezed tighter.

"Mistress?" the man whispered as water filled his eyes.

Tyrese smelled her before she appeared. Her scent had been on some of Jennings' belongings. He waited for his raging anger to abate.

"I'm Corrina Griggs, what do you want?" Her imperious tone grated on Tyrese' nerves. He was too close to the edge to play nice with the woman. But Silas knew that. If he'd wanted this woman treated kindly, he would've sent Tyrone. When she walked in, he activated his pocket scanner, she was clean.

Tyrese squeezed again and then threw the male backward. No one spoke at the loud crack that accompanied the impact of the hit to the wall. Tyrese turned to meet the woman who would kill his Alpha.

Her eyes widened as her gaze landed on his face and traveled the length of his body. She was taller than his mom, with a curvy figure that bordered on chubby. Her pale skin could use a day at the beach. Wintry blue eyes narrowed at him from a thin face. Life had not been kind to Ms. Griggs, if the pockmarks on her skin were any indication.

"What the hell did you kill him for?" she snapped.

"Why did you kill Lieutenant Jennings?" Tyrese asked, stepping closer to her.

She didn't bat an eye. "I do not know who you are talking about."

Tyrese spoke over his shoulder to Leon. "Bring somebody else out here."

She eyed him curiously before taking a seat on the couch. "You plan to kill all of them?"

"Before or after?"

Her brows furrowed. "Before or after?"

"Before or after I kill you?" Tyrese asked, staring down at her.

She waved him down. "Oh, you're not going to kill me, young Bennett. You want information, you think I'll talk, but I won't and then you'll tell that bastard you work for that you failed." She grinned. "He failed. At everything."

Tyrese stared at the woman and then grinned slowly. Silas had given him a prize. "Thank you," he whispered. He read her uncertainty before she masked it.

"De nada," she quipped. Her expression darkened as Leon brought in a large human dressed in a g-string. The man probably doubled as security as well as lover.

"Here's someone willing to die for the cause," Leon said right before he hit the man in the stomach. Corrina's hand flew to her mouth but her eyes gleamed in excitement. She got off on this stuff.

"*Throw him on top of her*," Tyrese told Leon. The next second the almost nude male sailed through the air and toppled over the sofa.

"Get off me, asshole." A loud smacking sound rent the air. "Get off me Biff, I mean it." Corrina yelled. There was no sound from Biff. "I need some help here." She sounded desperate, but no one would be assisting her today.

"*Go get someone else*," he told Leon. Grinning, Leon left the room. Tyrese crossed his arms, listening to her curse as she struggled to break free from the dead weight of her lover and the sofa.

"I am not going to talk to you. As a matter of fact, get the hell out of my house before I call the police. You murdered my servant… you're a murderer," she yelled.

"So are you. You murdered a cop… so go ahead, call the cops."

A moment later she pushed the sofa out of the way and stepped in front of it. Red-faced, with one hand on her hip, she pointed at him with the other. "I did no such thing. I told you I don't know the man. But I have witnesses of your murder."

"You're a liar."

She jerked as if slapped. "What did you call me?"

Tyrese was enjoying the game. "A liar. You Corrina Griggs are a murdering liar, just like your son Robert. He was a contract killer you sent to kill Silas Knight, and then cried like a baby when the bitch died on the job." He shrugged at her reddening face.

"You…you, asshole," she screamed as she lunged at him. Tyrese waited until she was close and stepped aside. She landed on the floor, jumped up and wiped the hair from her face.

"I am going to kill him for this, you hear me?"

Tyrese crossed his arms and watched her take in huge gulps of air. "You thought the bombs last month was something?" She threw her head back and laughed. It was a creepy, cackling sound that made Tyrese wonder if she were sane.

"For this...this coming into my home, threatening me and harming mine..." She trailed off as Leon brought in another struggling male, this one was a breed with a filthy vocabulary.

"Shut up," Tyrese yelled baring his fangs as he leaned toward the teenager.

The breed stopped cursing mid-stream and stared wide-eyed at him.

"I'm surprised you didn't shoot him," Tyrese said to Leon as he returned his attention to Griggs.

"I started to, but you said to bring out the next person."

Tyrese shrugged. "But he didn't have to be alive. If he starts talking that bullshit again, shoot him."

"Yes, Sir," Leon said as he pulled the young pup to an upright position.

Corrina turned and looked at Tyrese. "You think you can get away with killing all of us?"

Tyrese nodded. "Does it matter? You'll be dead." Maybe it was the absolute certainty in his voice or the fact he hadn't wavered. Whatever the reason, her next actions surprised him. He'd thought she would release her hormones like Arianna had. He and Leon had brought along masks for that possibility.

She shook her head. "That's... that's..." She sighed. "What do you want?"

"Did you kill Detective Jennings?" he asked, needing confirmation of her most recent flagrant attack.

"No. A bomb killed him." She eyed Tyrese and then sat on the loveseat. "But I ordered the installation of the bomb. So I guess in a way I did."

Leon pushed the young pup to the floor and left to get the male who'd answered the door.

"Why? Why did you kill him?" Tyrese had wondered about the randomness of the murder and couldn't put the matter to rest.

"He regained control of his wolf without assistance. For years, Jennings had been a poster child for the movement, when that changed so did his usefulness," she said in a cold calculating tone. "I could not allow others to see him in his new persona, could I?"

Sadness welled up in Tyrese. He and Jennings had hung out a few times, the man had been pack. "No, I guess you couldn't. Just like I had to kill Robert when he tried to carry out your instructions to kill my Alpha, we all do the things we feel are necessary."

She jumped up and ran at him. This time he called his wolf and shifted into his hybrid form. She slammed into the wall of his rough chest and fell backward a few feet.

"Ma'am," the young pup yelled while scooting over to the moaning woman. Leon walked in with the last occupant as Tyrese returned to normal.

"I caught this one trying to climb out a window on the top floor. They have quite a collection up there, want me to call it in?"

"Collection?"

"Lots of cages. I think they used this place as a holding place for breeds."

Fury ripped through Tyrese as he pulled out his gun. "Call it in," he growled as he shot the two breeds, one after the other, and then Corrina Griggs.

* * *

"You scanned her?" Silas asked as he walked into the bomb shelter where they held Corrina Griggs.

"Yes, Sir," Tyrese said. "Every test, including an x-ray, has been done on her. I think the blood samples we took from her made Matt's day. She's the oldest breeder to date, so he's running all kinds of tests. But unless there's something really weird going on that we don't know about, she's clean."

Tyrone entered the room and stared down at the woman under the influence of the anesthesia. "We verify she's Corrina Griggs?"

"Yeah, dental records, bloodwork, and fingerprints," Tyrese said. "Most of it you had in the file, the rest we pulled from the police and federal records."

Silas signaled the doctor in the other room. "Any chance she'll release hormones? Make everyone crazy?" He asked remembering Arianna's reign of terror and Jacques mental state from that time.

"Not that we are aware of," Matt said. "Not all breeders have the same abilities. Arianna was pregnant all the time; I think her mating scent was recycled a bit. But Griggs, she didn't have the pregnancies. I think it's a use it or lose it kind of thing. But I plan to do more research into that area."

Silas glanced at the woman again, hoping she could provide them with some answers. "Bring her out of it and let me know when she is lucid."

"Yes, Sir."

Silas and the twins stepped out of the bunker and headed to a secure room in a nearby section. After the door closed, Tyrese shared what'd happened when he picked up Griggs.

Silas snorted as he took a seat. "There is a freaked out pup who swears you were going to kill him and the Ma'am as well. He probably wet himself when he talked to Hank." Silas chuckled. "Good work by the way, the cops are all over that house and have a warrant for Griggs' arrest. They're looking for her son as well. Alfred's gone underground but he'll surface soon."

"Leon and I played it okay," Tyrese said in acknowledgment of the compliment.

Silas glanced at him. "When she wakes up, let's see if we can find out the root of this thing. Maybe she can explain how humans and wolves started mixing? Even though I'm experiencing it with my pups, I'm still baffled how it happened in the first place. It shouldn't." He glanced at them.

"Okay." Tyrese shrugged.

"Rone, you got point on this," Silas said. "I might kill her before we get any answers. I sent a list of questions to you. Get through as many of these as you can. We'll be recording so we can go over her responses again and again."

Tyrone looked at the file on his tablet and nodded. "Yes, Sir." He whistled. "You want to tie her and Arianna together?" He looked at Silas.

"Not unless they are somehow connected. Those questions are to close holes and fill in blanks. I need closure on some things, plus I want to know what she has planned."

Tyrese stood and stretched. "She knows she is going to die, she may not answer."

"I've got something to motivate her," Silas said as he typed on the keyboard. The young pup appeared on the screen. "This is her youngest son. Her legacy. She planned for him to take over, to rule by her side."

"Wonder what big brother Alfred thinks about that?" Tyrone said, chuckling.

"You think she'll cooperate to save his life?" Tyrese asked.

Silas shrugged. "I hope so. Leon said she caved when he brought this one into the room."

Tyrese nodded. "I had forgotten about that. He's right."

"Asia doesn't think Griggs is from the warehouse but I want you to take this…" Silas handed Tyrese the dress Griggs had been wearing, "…to her. Let her smell it, just in case."

Tyrese stared at him a moment before taking the material. "What's up?"

Silas respected Tyrese too much to mix words. "She's lonely and needs more contact with pack. There's no one else I trust to send. This way I accomplish both."

"You pimping him out?" Tyrone asked softly from across the table.

Silas met his serious gaze. "No. I'm sending him to complete a task. Allow her to scent the material. She needs pack other than the doctor and myself. Tyrese has already been intimate with her and understands. What he does is up to him."

No one spoke.

Tyrese fingered the material before he spoke. "Asia… being with her intimately feels wrong. It's like I'd betrayed the trust of someone important and I don't know who. I am attracted to her, who wouldn't… but she's mated and I know that person or will know them."

Silas sat forward. "Who is he?"

Tyrese shook his head and then shrugged. "I don't know specifically, just...it's a strong feeling that she's off limits. Can't explain it any other way."

Silas thought for a moment and then sat back. "Tell her that then, maybe it'll give her something to hold onto. I promised her freedom when this is over, she didn't seem too excited. But knowing there is someone looking for her might be just the thing."

"Okay. I'll be back." Tyrese left the room.

"Jacques thinks we can move on the warehouse in another week. He found more invoices for supplies delivered to the same place. Satellite surveillance showed vapor releases from areas within a five mile radius of the delivery point connecting to the abandoned warehouse. Alpha Samuel sent scouts to do a preliminary search. Everybody's anxious to shut that group down."

Silas nodded his agreement. "I don't think they are in one location...but we will hit them as we find them. That's one of the things Griggs can help us with if she actually split with them a while back. I wonder what happened to make her hate us?"

"Huh?" Tyrone looked up from his tablet.

"Think about it. She's been doing this for decades... she never had any pups until now. What is this really all about?" He tapped the desk with his fingertip.

"You don't have those questions on here, want me to add them?"

"See if you can work it in the conversation. I'd like to know the 'why' of all this. Granted it's not as important as what she has planned and how...but if you can find that out, I'd like to know."

"Will do."

The intercom beeped. "She's out of it, Sir, a bit dazed but she's alert."

"Thanks." Silas stood and reached out to Tyrese. "Griggs is up, Rone and I are headed over. Meet me in the observation room when you can."

"Yes, Sir."

Silas glanced at Tyrone as he opened the door. "Let's go." Dr. Passen and Matt met them in the corridor.

"I'd like to sit in on the questioning, Sir," Matt asked.

"So would I," Dr. Passen added.

"Okay," Silas agreed and continued to the small room next to the bunker. He grabbed a chair and sat near the two-way glass before giving Tyrone the go ahead.

For someone who had been under, Griggs appeared remarkably alert. Which served as a reminder that there was still so much to learn about breeders and their physiology.

"Hello, Ma'am," Tyrone said as he bowed his head in a formal greeting.

"Oh hell. Is this good cop versus bad cop? You're supposed to be the nice one who gets me to talk?" She snorted. "Hell, send in the other one, at least I knew he didn't give a damn. No games with that one."

Tyrone chuckled as he took a seat. "I won't play games either, but my mama raised me to be polite to my elders. If that bothers you, you'll have to blame her."

She eyed him with suspicion. "You Jasmine Bennett's other twin, eh? Two boys, so different."

"Not really all that different," Silas murmured.

Tyrone shrugged. "Your son is here."

"Alfred?"

"No. Tomas."

Her skin whitened. "He's not my son."

"Careful, he can hear you," Tyrone said kindly.

She swallowed hard while searching the room. "I don't believe you."

Tyrone shrugged. "That's within your rights. However, La Patron has instructed me to tell you the young man is here and the future of his mental health depends on you. We can mute the sound or keep it on. If you want your son to hear everything…"

"You mean my death?"

"No. I meant what I said. You have to understand, I'm fascinated with your history." Tyrone went on to repeat everything he had learned about her to this point. "You are a formidable woman, yet Tomas is the first breed you gave birth to since you killed the twins. Why?"

She met his eyes with gleaming pride. "One of the girls still lives, somewhere. The servant didn't kill her. Or she wouldn't die. I saw her once, or at least I think that was her. Anyway, it was time to meet my obligations. How could I be a part of the breed nation with human sons?" Her one hand, not in cuffs, rose and fell. "Optics. It was all about optics."

Silas was glad Tyrone didn't buy that.

"So you don't care about Tomas? It's okay if La Patron reprograms his wolf like he did Jennings?"

Visibly, she stiffened. Her face reddened. "No. Hell no, it is not okay. I don't want that bastard anywhere near my…Tomas. You keep that pedophile away from that boy. Silas Knight cannot be trusted," she screamed.

Stunned by the accusation, Silas leaned forward with his elbows on his knees as he searched his mind for anything that might have been mistaken for what she claimed. He came up empty. *"Ask her why or who I approached,"* he told Tyrone

"That's a serious accusation, Ma'am. Can you prove La Patron is a pedophile? I mean who did he violate?"

"What difference does it make? You won't believe me."

"Try me," Tyrone said in a strong tone. "I have younger siblings, so if you have proof that he violates young children I'd appreciate hearing it. And so you know, I have this weird gift of being able to detect lies."

Silas ignored the stares from the doctors and focused on the answer to

Tyrone's question.

"My girlfriend, Pammie Lee, was ten. One summer day I met her in groves midway between our plantations. We had just climbed the tree and settled down when she told me she met this man, only he wasn't a man. She swore he could change into animals, she'd seen him do it. I didn't believe her of course and she swore me to secrecy. I thought that was the end of it until I came across the biggest, blackest wolf I'd ever seen. His eyes were emerald green and he stared at me for a moment, sniffed, and then walked off. That's when I remembered Pammie Lee's description of her wolf. Pammie Lee was pregnant before she turned eleven and died during childbirth. I heard she had a son, but of course he died too."

"You assume that wolf was La Patron?"

Her eyes flashed as her chin tightened. "I know that bastard raped and impregnated my friend, and she was only ten, had just become a woman if you know what I mean."

Silas understood the inference. The woman had spoken the truth, as she knew it, regarding the incident. But he knew with certainty the green-eyed wolf wasn't him. When she lived in Virginia, he had been in the mid-west preparing for expansion. Plus, this had nothing to do with her rape, or did it? Had the green eyed wolf raped Corrina and not her friend? Is that why she had such recall? Was she hiding her own experiences behind an impenetrable wall of misery so that she could deal with her nightmare? Or was she just as crazy as Arianna had been? He didn't know and grew weary chasing shadows for answers.

"It wasn't me. Move on with the questions," he told Tyrone.

Tyrese stepped into the room and sat in the chair next to Silas. "She vaguely recognized the scent but said it was old. She's going to think on it."

Silas nodded but kept his gaze on Tyrone and Griggs. For the next hour and a half, Tyrone had an in-depth conversation with the woman, in which they laughed and chatted like old friends. Tyrone called her out on her lies three times before she settled into the cordial interrogation.

"Hungry?" Tyrone asked Griggs when he turned his tablet over.

She snorted. "My last meal?" There was a resigned note in her voice.

Tyrone shrugged. "You did try to kill La Patron. But I think he could forgive that if his mate and babies hadn't been nearby. That was poorly done, Ma'am."

"The bomb was for the caves. Jasmine refused to leave, that's the only reason Siseria didn't detonate then. Jasmine Bennett should never have been in danger. When she was, Julie's life was forfeit. She should have disposed of Siseria before the woman was taken."

"They were both knocked out, so that couldn't have happened," Tyrone said in a dry tone, he had carried the unconscious women back to the complex and knew they'd had no chance to do as this woman suggested.

Silas sat in disbelief at such poor planning. Lives had been lost unnecessarily because of miscommunication.

"Oh… too many mistakes, plus they never reported that." She nibbled on her bottom lip for a moment before looking at Tyrone. "I think I'll pass on the meal."

Silas sensed Jasmine's presence just as she entered the bunker and faced Griggs.

"What the hell?" he murmured as he shot to his feet.

"Back down Silas, I got this," she said through their link as she walked to the bed and sat at the foot.

"I'm Jasmine."

The woman's face brightened as a smile appeared on her face. "Hello Jasmine Bennett. It's nice to finally meet you."

"I have a question, well two, actually. First, my mom is a sixty-year-old breeder who seems to be forgetting things like she has Alzheimer's or something. Have you ever seen or heard of anything like this before?"

"Jasmine, do not discuss the pups with her, I have information regarding their illness that I will share with you. I do not know who is privy to her conversation," Silas said, struggling with his wolf to grant her request and not go racing into the room to protect her.

Griggs' brow furrowed. "No, I haven't. That's really odd because we get better with age as you will discover. I'm sorry to hear that about her, it's a first."

"Second, why do you think my babies will play a role in leading the wolves?"

Silas was surprised he had not thought to ask that question and waited for the answer.

"I don't think it. I know it. All of your pups will be special and probably already display aspects of their talents. Whatever they are now will be magnified tenfold. But one of them will have a bit of each and will rise to lead both full-bloods and breeds one day. He will be wise beyond his years; along with his mate, he will take the Wolf Nation into the next century."

"And you know this how?" Jasmine asked.

Griggs stared at his mate. "I was told this by the Goddess."

Chapter 24

"SHE'S LYING," MATT SAID.

"She wasn't lying," Tyrone said.

Silas agreed. "She believed everything she said."

Jasmine looked at the men in the room before speaking. "Tell me what you found out about my babies."

Silas nodded to Matt.

Jasmine listened in growing disbelief at the prospect that her children were deliberately poisoned by someone she'd allowed into the compound. Her head spun at the implication. Blindly she reached for a chair and sat down hard holding her forehead in her palm while struggling to bring the nausea rising in her throat under control. Silas had told her, had asked her to put off the christening, but she hadn't listened.

Heat filled her belly, chasing away the cold. Impotent rage at the circumstances whipped through her. Why would anyone hurt her babies? Her temper escalated, her sense of reasoning faltered beneath the onslaught of guilt.

"Jasmine."

She heard her name through a tunnel of sound but her focus, her intent, was on finding the perpetrators who'd harmed her children. Moving through the fog, she shook off the hand that would hold her back.

"Jasmine, you are hurting Rese and Rone. Stop this."

Rese? Rone? The words ricocheted through her mind before settling. "What?" she whispered, her throat bristly dry.

"Tamp down your anger, you've got everyone else in this room pinned to the wall. They cannot move and I suspect breathing is also a problem."

Exhaling, she counted to ten as she attempted to diffuse the flame in her core. It went down a notch, but still burned.

"Your eyes are translucent gold," Silas whispered near her ear as he wrapped his arms around her. His heat touched off a spark in her belly. She shuddered at the contact.

"Mom?" Tyrese said, standing a short distance.

She turned.

Tyrone stood next to Tyrese. They both wore stunned expressions. Matt and Dr. Passen remained near the wall. Silas dismissed both men before Jasmine spoke to her sons.

"Someone hurt my babies on purpose," she said. "I cannot allow that."

"Yeah, we got that, but when did you start…doing Silas?" Tyrone asked.

"Your energy was his but different," Tyrese said, gazing down at her as if he didn't recognize who she was.

"I don't know. It's been happening for a while, I've been working to control my anger but it just flares at times. And the only reason for it being like his… is because we're mates." She turned in his arms and held him tight. "I'm sorry. I should've listened." She placed a kiss on his chest before resting her head against him. The solid thump of his heartbeat helped calm the red flames of anger leaping inside her.

"We will discuss that later. In private." He sent her images of the things he intended to do to her. She shivered at the picture of him taking her over his lap and spanking her.

"Mmmm, okay."

"Well, now that mom's not on a killing rampage, what about the Goddess?" Tyrone asked. "Is she playing both sides against each other?"

"No. She is honorable and would not warn me against her own actions," Silas said.

"If history is any indication, she would do that in a heartbeat," Tyrone argued.

The discussion went back and forth for a few minutes until Jasmine spoke up from her chair. "How many Goddesses are there?"

Silas looked at her in surprise.

Tyrese pursed his lips in consideration.

Tyrone nodded as if he had come to that same conclusion.

"One?" Silas said with uncertain hesitation. "At least I have only heard of one."

"Ask Jacques," Jasmine suggested. "I bet we are talking about two or more gods here."

"That would certainly explain matters," Silas said.

Tyrese sat in the chair next to her. "You okay?"

She stroked his face and smiled. "I'm fine, sweetie. Just got to get a handle on this energy boost. Silas is going to work with me on it. Don't worry." It bothered her to see the concern in his eyes, and now she understood how he'd felt when she came to him after he had been altered.

"Mom, you and Silas didn't feel it. It happened so fast, I hit that wall so hard, if I wasn't a breed it would'a killed me. You were like Silas on steroids. Your eyes changed and you looked like you were walking on air. I mean you were on the ground but the wind tunnel around you made it look… I was scared for you." He grinned. "And proud at the same time. My mama can kick some serious ass. Knowing that changes how we'll handle your security. Let me know when you want to go shopping, I'll make it happen." He winked.

Ecstatic over the prospect of going to a store, she grabbed his face between her palms and kissed him. "Thanks baby."

"Hey, he beat me to saying it, but I should get a kiss too, I thought the same thing. Mama got skills and nobody better brush up against her," Tyrone said as he stooped in front of her. Laughing, she hugged him before placing a kiss on his forehead as well.

"I love you." She glanced at each of her sons. They were smart, handsome men who made her proud.

"We know. That's why Silas used us to bring you out. Smart man," Tyrone said as he stood.

"Yeah, even in anger, you did a three-sixty at the idea we were in danger. That's just one of the reasons we love you, Ma," Tyrese said as he stood.

Heat rushed to her cheek at the praise. She met Silas' gaze and melted at the love she read in them.

"Jacques says there are fake goddesses, but ours is the one true Goddess." Silas walked over to her, pulled her up, and then sat her on his lap.

"Everyone feels that way about the God they serve," Tyrone said.

"I know and that creates a problem," Jasmine said.

Chapter 25

THEY AGREED TO PUT the Goddess issue on the back burner and deal with the more pressing issue of who had touched their children with poison. After leaving the lab, they visited the nursery, where Silas accepted her apology for her role in their children's dilemma.

"I am so sorry, Silas. Honestly I had no idea." She opened herself wide open for him to search her motives if he chose.

Instead he sent waves of love and warmth, filling her to the brim. Her legs buckled beneath the onslaught. He caught her and together they sat in one of the rocking chairs in companionable silence.

***

Jasmine and Silas joined her mother, Jacques, and Mark for dinner. The twins were assigned clean up for Griggs and her son. After Silas pulled Tomas' wolf, Dr. Passen had been horrified at the condition of the animal. Tomas's wolf was immediately hooked up to medication to reverse the effect of the drugs he had been on since birth. Froggy would take on the job of strengthening the wolf once Tomas was strong enough. The nurses had returned to the nursery and security remained in place to keep everyone else out.

"Hello, sweetheart," Jasmine's mother said, reaching out for a hug.

Jasmine didn't hesitate as she took her mother in her arms and inhaled. "Hi mom. Sorry I've been busy the last few days. The kids had a really bad cold, but they are much better now." Which was a lie, their temperatures were still high, but she and Silas agreed that it would serve their purpose better if everyone believed otherwise.

"I'm so glad. I told Mark just this morning that they were doing better, didn't I, Mark?"

He came up behind Victoria and placed a kiss on her neck. "Yes sweetheart, you did." He gazed at Jasmine and then Silas with a warm smile. "I'm glad to hear they are well. I don't have any children...yet." He winked at Victoria, whose face lit up. "But I can only imagine how difficult it must be."

Jasmine liked Mark for her mom. He seemed a likable guy but he was a suspect, along with Jacques and Renee. She cringed with embarrassment over the conversation Silas'd had with her former pastor an hour ago. Although her mate stopped short of accusing the man of wrongdoing, she was certain her pastor never wanted to hear from either of them again. Silas had instructed Rose to send the church a large donation.

"Thanks, Mark."

She moved to Jacques, who had his back turned to everyone in the room. "Hey."

He glanced at her over his shoulder with a forced smile. "Hello." Her heart dropped. Jacques was one of her favorite people, and he was hurting. Worse, there was nothing she could do about it. Instead of speaking, she wrapped her arms around him from the back.

He held her arms on his chest a moment before releasing them. Turning, he looked over her shoulder. Certain he would ask a question about her mother, she waited. He frowned and then glanced down at her.

"Your mother just washed her hands and then lotioned them with a small bottle from her purse. Could you ask where she got the lotion? And perhaps have Matt take a look at it?"

Stunned by his remark, she looked over her shoulder and watched her mom talk to Mark while rubbing the cream into her skin. Prickles of unease assaulted her. Please God, not my mama, she offered in silent prayer. But the more she thought about it, the more it made sense. Victoria Channing would be the perfect Trojan horse. A gift of lotions and perfumes from a colleague or friend, and voila, it would be a done deal.

"I can and I will." She headed toward the table as the head server entered the room. Dinner was about to be served. Silas' brow rose as she approached.

"I see the light of battle in your eyes, what happened?"

"I know you scanned Mark again, anything?"

"No, his mind is clean. No more secrets, tell me what happened?"

"Mom washed her hands and then lotioned them. I'm going to ask her about it after dinner in private and then have Matt look examine the lotion."

Silas whistled. "That would ... definitely be hard to digest if she's been using the poison. On the other hand it might explain the memory lapses."

She hadn't thought of that. "Let's get through dinner so I can get her alone."

After dinner, Jasmine and her mom walked hand in hand through the gardens next to the patio. "It's so beautiful and restful here, Jasmine. Thanks for inviting us. We're going to leave day after tomorrow. Mark's family invited us to some type of gathering. I'm kind of nervous meeting them, but he assured me they will love me like he does."

Jasmine squeezed her mom tight as she sent the information to Silas. "You smell good. I noticed you put some lotion on before dinner, is that what that is?"

Victoria tittered and Jasmine bit back a groan at the sound. "It was an engagement gift from Elsie and John, we met them on one of our dates and we all became good friends." Victoria lifted her hand and inhaled. "It smells better when I first put it on, that's one of the reasons I go through my supply so quickly and have to order another bottle."

Jasmine took the bottle her mom handed her. "Order? You get this online?"

"Yes, it's from a perfume maker in Italy. A real classy place, it's expensive. You can have that one. I have more in my room. If you want I'll give you the internet address, they have other products. Use my code so you can get a discount, they don't have to know it's not me." She giggled and this time Jasmine kissed her mom on the cheek.

"Thanks, mom." She stuck the small bottle into her pants pocket.

"You're not going to try some now?" her mom asked, frowning.

Jasmine thought quickly. "I need to wash my hands first."

"Oh...okay. That's a good idea, it's a part of the instructions actually, your hands should be clean when you put it on." She took Jasmine's arm and they continued their stroll. Jasmine half listened as her mother talked about her love and relationship with Mark. The urge to have the lotion tested increased with each step. Knowing someone gave her mom a gift that had harmed her and the babies renewed her anger.

"Silas," she called. "I need to get away."

"I feel your heat. Breathe, listen to my voice. Follow the cadence, let it ease you."

"Someone got to my mother."

"I know, Jasmine. We'll take care of it, just breathe, allow the anger to flow through your nose. Don't allow your mother to see your fury, it will upset her."

Jasmine watched as Jacques approached them. His smile didn't reach his eyes as he offered his arm to her mother. "There are some beautiful flowers I'd love to show you, Madam."

Her mother glanced at her before hesitantly placing her arm in his.

"*Silas, you're making things worse. She loves Mark, this is going to get messy.*" She turned to take a shortcut that would take her to another corridor, which would lead downstairs. Jasmine reveled in the freedom she now had without Jarcee's constant shadowing. If she had known Silas would have relaxed his restrictions, she would have told him months ago about her energy surges.

"Jacques is her mate; in the end he will have her."

Jasmine refused to debate what she suspected was true. If nothing else, Jacques would outlive Mark and could claim her mom then. *"I'm headed to the lab."*

"Matt is eagerly waiting." He paused. "So am I." His voice deepened and sent a shockwave of lust through her. She stumbled at the throbbing between her legs.

"*Stop that*," she hissed.

"It's been three days."

Lord knows her body knew exactly how long it had been since she had ridden him. "I know and I'm hungry for you. But let's save the kingdom and all that jazz first." She smirked as she placed her hand on a secure door. It opened and welcomed her to the lower level.

Warmth flowed over her like honey on its comb. *"I love you, Sweet Bitch"*

His words touched off a firestorm of need in her. Her breath shortened and her muscles loosened, she swore if he kept it up she'd turn into a puddle of goo.

"Love you too, wolfie."

She exited the elevator. Silas and Matt stood near the entry to the labs. Her mate's eyes blazed royal blue. Tassels of heat danced across her skin as she walked toward him. Their gazes met, the temperature in the corridor went up a notch.

"I'll take this so the two of you can… um, do whatever you need to cool off." Matt held out his hand.

Jasmine tore away her gaze. "I can't give you the container, mom might want it back. I'll pour you some."

"Okay, we'll have to go inside then." Matt waited as she gazed at Silas.

He smiled and took her hand. "Let's save the kingdom," she said.

"Huh?" Matt said with a confused look.

"Nothing. Just check this for the chemicals you mentioned earlier. Also, expand the side effects search. Something is off with her memory and she might not have a clear grasp on what's real."

Silas glanced at her but remained silent.

"Yes, Ma'am. I'll get on that." He took the bottle and poured a liberal amount into three test tubes before returning it to her. "I'd like that email address and her account number as well. One of my men will trace the company. La Patron wants to know if they handled her orders differently. He also wants to know who else is getting this special treatment. Who else are they singling out?"

She gazed at Silas. "Good point. That way you can pinpoint the purpose of some of this."

He nodded and squeezed her hand. "Right now I want to know what exactly they hoped to accomplish by giving a breeder, your mother, poison." His tone turned sarcastic. "I wonder if she is the only breeder receiving this gift."

"Gift?" She snorted. Probably not, but she kept that to herself. "How long before you know something?" she asked Matt as he headed to another section of the lab.

"I'll know within ten to thirty minutes if one of the two poisons I identified earlier are in the lotion. The time it takes depends on how well they've masked them. It'll take longer to identify all the ingredients."

Hearing Matt discuss the poisonous lotion hit her hard. Her mom had brought the weapon that hurt her babies into their home. That reality slammed into her. Sweat broke out on her forehead as dizziness hit her hard, she rocked on the balls of her feet before Silas secured her to him.

"If the two poisons are in the cream, which means..." she whispered and turned into Silas' chest. All along she had been hoping that it had been someone else, even though she'd suspected something was off with her mom. Renee simply did not do subterfuge. She came at you where you could see her. But her mom's memory loss and confusion made her a likely target.

"Which means she has been used without her knowledge." Silas stroked her hair easing her distress. "If what Matt says about the poison is true, we learned another thing about breeders."

Jasmine glanced up at him and waited.

"You women are damned hard to kill."

Chapter 26

JASMINE CLOSED THE DOOR to their suite and dropped onto the sofa. Silas sat next to her and placed her feet on his lap. He removed her shoes and massaged her sore feet.

She dropped her head back, allowing it to rest on the arm of the sofa. "Ummm, that feels good." Struggling to understand everything she learned that day, she peeked at him. "So…someone gave my mother lotion that has been poisoning her for the past four months. The poison is so toxic it transferred to my babies when she held them, which is why they are still sick." She released a long sigh as his hands reached her calves. "It's been too long. Work your… 'I am La Patron' magic and make them well. I miss their energy, their fights and their laughter."

"I have given them all that I have, sweetness. But their temperatures had fallen a bit tonight, which is progress. It will take time, but they are on the mend." His kiss to the top of her foot sent tingles of awareness through her.

"Ummmm, do that again," she murmured. He complied with her request. "The thing that bothers me is how mercenary all of this is. I mean, think about the long-term planning involved in this. For what? I don't think the goal was to poison the children. You?"

Silas shrugged as he continued massaging her leg. "They knew she would eventually come in contact with the pups. Babies," he corrected when she frowned. "But I agree with you, I don't think poisoning the children was the original target."

She relaxed further as he started on her other leg. "None of this makes sense. Corrina started this vendetta against you because her childhood friend died in childbirth. She acted as if you were the only large black wolf with green eyes."

"For the most part, I am. I've never met a wolf with eyes the same color as mine."

She stared at him. "Either there was another wolf or she got her stories mixed up, Silas. Don't try to convince me you had sex with a ten-year-old, I'm not buying it."

He snorted. "I can't lie to you, remember? I had nothing to do with that child. My point is I don't know of another black wolf with green eyes, that's all."

"Have you sent notices to the alphas in the states she targeted?"

"Yes. Most were already on stand-by and the raids started before we sat down for dinner. Most importantly, we confiscated the equipment and secured the building where the bombs and serum was manufactured. Tyrone is working on the list of half-breeds who have been taking the drug. Each alpha will send out letters explaining what happened and offer free shots to wean the breeds off the chemicals as well as work on strengthening the wolves of anyone who wants help." He exhaled. "It's a start."

She nodded. "Corrina Griggs was crazy. Is that what happens when you live a long time, you go crazy?"

"I'm older than her."

"I meant breeders, Silas. Be serious."

He pulled her up and lay on the couch behind her. Cocooned in his warmth, she pushed back against his hardness and released a sigh. She hoped the hot connection would always be this way with them. She wiggled against him.

"Behave, you wanted serious."

She chuckled. "Sorry, I'm serious."

His arm tightened around her. "I don't think so... I believe there are many happy breeders living long productive lives with their mates. We don't know about them yet because of the aggression against them. But I think once we get this war behind us, and we have our public joining, more will surface."

She snuggled against him. "So the secret to long, happy living is being mated, is that your answer?"

"Um hmm, yes, of course."

"Corrina didn't know how all of this got started," she said into the silence.

"No, not directly. There are a few things I have Jacques researching for me. There was a disturbance amongst the early settlers that I had forgotten. Missing women and children, that type of thing. I had no idea this situation had started that far back."

Silas pulled her closer to him and nipped her on the ear. Mimicking her mother from earlier, she giggled.

"You like that?"

"Yeah," she said breathily.

His large palm brushed against her breast.

Her breath hitched at the contact. He then rested his hand on her and pulled her nipple.

"Mmmm... that feels so good. I love when you tease me with your hand." She placed her hand over his and pulled it close. "Right there, right –"

Boom, boom, boom. The building shook and then stopped.

"Shit," Jasmine said, jumping up.

"Damn Merriweather." Silas had jumped up and over the couch, his head tilted up. He had told her earlier he expected some sort of retribution for taking Griggs and raiding the house.

She ran toward the door, yelling over her shoulder. "Babies, then mama."

"I'll send Jacques for Victoria. I've placed a cover over the grounds to stop any more explosives from hitting the compound. I've got to assess the damage." He paused. "Just get my pups below."

She nodded, forgetting to check him for calling her babies pups and unable to swallow around the lump of fear choking her. "This is crazy," she muttered as she turned the corner. Jarcee nodded as she reached the door to the nursery.

Rose was already inside the nursery. "I've got David and Renee ready to go," she said. "We're going to have to roll them to keep the IV's intact."

Jasmine nodded and started to work on Jackie and then Adam. She looked at the nurses who were gathering their things to head for a separate underground tunnel. "Thank you ladies, be safe. La Patron has a security screen around the compound so no other hits will impact the buildings. But he wants everyone in the tunnels until he accesses the damages. I suspect he'll give updates within the hour."

"Thank you, Ma'am." They left the nursery through one door while Jasmine wheeled two small incubators and Rose wheeled the other two out a different door. She watched as Jarcee brought up the rear, making sure no one entered the private corridor. Once they accessed the elevator he remained outside, unable to continue further.

Silas walked through the rubble at the back of the compound. The gym and separate condos had been hit. It would take some time to repair. Froggy and Stefan had been taken to the infirmary for injuries. He was thankful there weren't more people in the gym, but it was late. Tyrese and Tyrone took a group of security to search and scan the forest for proof that the mortars had come from the coverage of green foliage. He expected the police chief any moment, as well as a few investigators. Hopefully, the twins would have some information to give them.

Silas sat on the floor of the gym and looked out the hole in the side of the wall. His fortress had never been attacked before. He'd never taken a direct hit...until now.

"Jasmine, are you and my pups secure?"

"Yes, where's mama?"

He had forgotten. *"Jacques?"*

"Sir?"

"Take Victoria and Mark to the staff tunnels."

"Yes, Sir. I... I was on my way to her suite to check on her, thank you for not making me look like a stalker."

"I understand mates, do what you need to do to keep her safe. You have to include Mark, though."

"Damn."

Silas shook his head and looked at the damage. *"Jacques is on his way to her suite."*

"Any of the wings get hit?"

"Just the outermost buildings."

"You think it was Merriweather?"

"Yeah. I did take his mother."

She didn't laugh as he expected. "You warned me this might happen."

"What?"

"When you asked me to postpone the christening, you said this could happen. I didn't listen. I'm sorry, Silas. More than you could know."

"I feel your pain and your sorrow, Jasmine. I do know, Sweet Bitch. We will work through this together. Merriweather will not win."

"Where are the twins?"

He exhaled. "In the forest searching for clues, they should be back in a few minutes." He waited for her explosion.

"Okay, let me know when they're back safe."

Surprised, but pleased, he spoke, *"Okay."*

"Mama's in the other tunnel?"

"Yes, she doesn't have access to ours, you understand?"

"Yeah, I do. It's just hard. I don't know how to tell her she's being poisoned. I don't even know if she'll understand. Hopefully Mark can help me get through to her."

"Yeah, he needs to know as well."

"Sir?" Jacques called out to him.

"Yes?"

"Victoria isn't waking up. Mark had fallen in the shower, has some sort of bruise on his forehead, but Victoria is unconscious."

"Silas, is that Jacques? I can't hear him clearly. Is something wrong with mama?" He told her what Jacques told him.

"Get her to the hospital or to the infirmary," she demanded.

He hesitated taking the woman to the lab area where the larger infirmary was located. The one in the other tunnel area was rarely staffed because of the wolf's abilities to self-heal. *"The ambulance is on its way along with the police. Shouldn't they take a look at her?"*

"That's fine with me, but they're going to draw blood, might have some questions…I just want her taken care of…please."

"I can't allow Mark in the lab area."

"That's okay. Just have Matt or Dr. Passen look at her. It could be the poison from the drugs."

"Separating Mark and Victoria is going to be tricky, especially with Jacques in the picture."

"Just do it, please."

This was one part of dealing with family Silas could do without.

"Jacques?"

"Sir?"

"Is your mate awake?"

"Not yet, Sir."

"Where is Mark?"

"In the bathroom getting dressed. I helped bandage his head." Silas heard the disgust in Jacques voice and snorted.

"Take Victoria down to the tunnels, right now. Mark is not permitted and I'm only making this allowance for my mate. Matt will look at her. Leave now while he is in the bathroom."

"Yes, Sir."

Silas stood and finished his inspection of the damage. He had just completed the condos when Tyrese called out to him.

"We are returning, Sir."

Silas opened an area so the scouts could enter the compound. He waited until they were inside the damaged gym before cutting off access. Tyrone and Tyrese shifted. Leonidas padded around a bit and then sat nearby. Two other wolves sat next to Leonidas.

"What'd you find?"

"Scents connected to Griggs and Merriweather. They used remotes, cowards," Tyrese spat.

Silas updated them on family matters.

"Mark's going to try and find her," Tyrone said, grinning.

"Security is going to corral him to the EMTs," Silas said. "Where is Griggs?"

"Gone," Tyrone said.

Silas nodded. "Let's find Alfred."

Hank contacted him. "Police called. There's been another explosion on the edge of town at the mill, one dead, two hurt, plus there was quite a bit of property damage. Hold on, another call's coming in." He paused. "Merriweather is melting down in the town square, screaming you killed his family. He's swearing to blow up everything unless you turn yourself in to the Feds. The police are clearing the area but have no idea if he's loaded."

"Damn," Silas murmured. "That man is a pain in my ass." He gazed at the twins, unsure if he should allow them to travel with him.

"What's up?" Tyrese asked, watching him closely.

Leon had shifted and stood further back, but he was alert as well as Tyrone. The other two security men had stepped back to guard the entry, but they would be able to hear him as well.

Silas briefly repeated what Hank said and wasn't surprised by the glimmer of lights in the twins' eyes. They had been sparring in the gym and relished a fight with real adversaries. But this wouldn't be one on one, or one on ten. Merriweather would have someone nearby locked and loaded. Silas doubted the man was on a suicide mission and didn't expect Merriweather to carry explosives.

"Son of a bitch," Tyrone said and then whistled.

"I have an idea," Tyrese said, and then explained.

Silas nodded. Tyrese' plan could work. "Grab what you need and we'll leave in five. I've got to get a couple of things myself." He glanced at Leon. "Be ready in five, you're going with us." He didn't miss the man's feral grin. Silas shook his head at the eagerness they all showed at the prospect of bringing down prey. Youth, he scoffed silently.

Chapter 27

AFTER GIVING JACKIE HER medication, Jasmine discovered the container was empty, fortunately she'd had enough to give each child their prescribed doses. There were more meds in the nursery. Once the children were asleep and Rose lay on the sofa watching a video, Jasmine decided to leave.

"I'm going to grab another bottle of meds for the next round. Silas and the guys will be in town for a while checking the damage. It won't take me long, you need anything from upstairs?" she asked, thinking she would check on her mom while she was out.

"No, I'm good. They're going to be asleep for a few hours, I'll probably doze off myself before the movie finishes."

"Okay, be back in a bit." She left the suite and after signing herself out of the maximum security area, headed for the nursery. The corridors were eerily quiet. Most personnel were in the separate tunnel and hadn't been released yet. She had broken protocol by leaving her space but she'd need the medication in a few hours, better to get it now rather than risk falling asleep and forgetting until it was too late.

The private elevator arrived near the nursery and she noticed Jarcee standing in the shadows. He came to attention when she stepped off.

Waving him down, she offered a brief explanation. "I forgot the children's meds."

He nodded and lagged behind her. Inside the nursery, she grabbed two bottles of the medicine, a few additional blankets and clothes, which she stuffed into a diaper bag. The high security area was fully stocked with food and diapers, but Renee preferred the blanket Jasmine pulled from the shelf, along with a few other particulars.

"Got it." She hefted the bag over her shoulder and returned the way she had come. Once she entered the elevator, Jarcee nodded and returned to his post. Instead of stopping the elevator on the maximum security floor, she headed down to the labs with the infirmary to check on her mom. This elevator stopped in the rear of the laboratory, closer to Asia than the front where her mom had been taken. Thinking this would only take a few moments, Jasmine headed toward the front of the area. She had just turned a corner when she saw Mark. Smiling, she shook her head. She had told Silas the man would try to find her mom.

She raised her hand to call out to him, thinking they could walk the rest of the way together, when he stopped in front of Asia's cubicle.

Puzzled, Jasmine stopped and watched as he placed something metallic on the door. Seconds later he punched keys on the security pad that would allow access into the room. Jasmine's breath caught as the door opened and Asia flew out of the room like a tornado. She hit Mark so hard in the chest, the sound echoed in the hall. He swung and she ducked and hit him again.

"Jasmine?" Silas called.

"Watching something here. Take care of what you're doing."

"Are you in trouble?"

She scoffed as the fight intensified. *"No, Mark and Asia are fighting."*

"What?" he yelled.

"Yeah, I'll get back with you. Focus on the bombs, Silas. Trust me, I got this." she said with more confidence than she felt.

"I'm sending security."

"Don't insult me. I said I had this. Leave it to me."

"Okay, just don't burn down the building, and we will discuss why you are not where I asked you to be when I return."

"Because I'm a grown woman, Silas, and your mate. It's my job to put out fires, not start them. Go away, the fight's getting interesting."

Mark stumbled, but didn't fall. Instead, he bulked up like the incredible Hulk and returned the hit. Jasmine's hand flew to her mouth as Asia went from a slender size eight to five times her size, with a huge snout, pointy ears, razor looking claws, and long sharp teeth. She made snapping and barking sounds that sent a chill of excitement down Jasmine's spine. Mark had his hands full fighting Asia's two-legged wolf.

The two combatants fought in earnest. Gone was the man who'd fawned over her mother the past few days. Mark's confident movements landed powerful blows. Even blind, Asia fought with speed and cunning, drawing blood from her opponent. But it became obvious her blindness was a major handicap. When Mark picked Asia up and slammed her onto the ground, the snapping sound, coupled with the loud scream of pain, catapulted Jasmine into action.

One moment she watched in horrified silence, the next she was airborne, heading for Mark. Her fist slammed into his jaw, knocking him off his feet as he flew backward and skidded across the floor. Running, she grabbed the much larger man by his tattered shirt and punched him in the face again and again. He pushed her back, causing her to stumble.

Standing shakily, he shook his head, snarled and ran at her. Fire raced up her back as she braced her feet apart and then jumped out of the way when he reached her. Spinning, she watched as he tried to stop and fell short. Before he could regroup, she ran forward, jumped and kicked him in the back. He hit the ground.

"Ooof," he groaned.

Jasmine touched his foot and sent the fire trapped inside her into his body. She watched as he shook on the floor like a fish out of water. This man had entered her home under false pretenses. She removed her hand.

"Did you give my mom the poison?"

"Fuck you."

No he didn't. Growling, she touched his foot with hers again and took the fire up a notch. Bastard. He screamed worse than a girl. She removed her foot.

"Why did you try to kill my mama?"

"Didn't try...to kill her. I love...love her. Had no choice."

Jasmine heard a sound behind her and saw Asia standing slowly. Her heart went out for the young woman. Moving toward her, she took Asia's hand and led her back to Mark.

"You love my mama? But you tried to kill my babies? How does that work?"

He made a sound that was a mixture of sobbing and laughing. "You don't get a choice. They...never mind. You already know about the poison in the lotion. There are some pills too. She's going through withdrawal. I... I couldn't keep doing it."

Jasmine eyed the man on the floor with a raised brow as his body shrank into the Mark she was accustomed to seeing. "You were sent here to spy on my mate?"

"No."

Asia stepped forward a bit, bent down and touched his neck before standing. "He was sent to kill me."

Shock raced through Jasmine. Her foot slammed down on his.

His body jumped and jerked as she shot more heat into him. When she stopped, his sobs filled the air. "You came to kill Asia?" Jasmine asked through gritted teeth. Her fury leapt at the idea that he'd try to destroy Asia after the woman had been through so much.

"I...I can't say."

Jasmine's foot rose to hit his again, Asia stopped her.

"He truly cannot speak those words, his mind and mouth will not allow him to betray his mission. Ask whatever you can now because they are recharging him and his *other* will soon be in control again."

Jasmine thought quickly. "Who started this war?"

"I do not know."

"Do you have metal inside you?" She couldn't think of anything, her thoughts were scattered. She squeezed Asia's hand for help.

"No."

"Are they sending others for me?" Asia asked. Jasmine released a breath. That was a good question.

"Yes. Until you are destroyed, don't know why."

"How many are nearby? In the town, in the state?" Asia asked, her voice calm.

"None in town. Twenty in the state." He paused. "Arrgh…" he groaned.

"Is there an attack planned on the compound?" Asia asked as Mark's upper body rose and fell with ragged breathing.

"Not yet."

"He is being recharged and soon will not be able to think on his own, the only thing he will be concerned with is the completion of the mission. If you will permit me, I will kill him, but you need to be safe inside my room," Asia said.

Jasmine stared at the young woman. "Go in your room and lock the damn door." She eyed Mark. His body was changing. Asia hadn't moved.

Leaning closer to Asia's face, Jasmine growled. "Go to your room. Do it now."

Asia dropped her hand, scampered backward, felt the wall until the metal of her door was beneath her palm. She pulled it closed. Satisfied her charge was out of the way; Jasmine backed up and prepared to bring down her mom's fiancé.

She watched as Mark bulked, and leapt up, hazy-eyed. She wondered if he could see. The next moment he bypassed her and ran toward Asia's room and pulled on the door. It didn't give. From her peripheral vision she saw Jarcee and another guard standing in the shadows. She and Silas would have a long talk on trust later on.

Mark slapped the door as if he could make a dent in the thick metal. It was as if he didn't see anyone else. Inhaling, she calmed and pulled all of her energy to the center. If she could save Mark she would, but seeing him like this, drooling with erratic movements, she doubted he would ever be in his right mind again.

The warm breeze of her energy enveloped and filled her until she vibrated from the sheer beauty of it. Instead of fearing who she was, mate of La Patron – aka First Bitch, she embraced his fire, his purpose, his destiny. A roar of energy whipped through her as she fought to retain control. Silas' soft words of encouragement rolled down her spine and lifted her higher. Through the shine of energy she sighted Mark, raised her hand and pointed. His back bowed as she dragged him from the door and pushed him to his knees.

Anger at what her babies and mother suffered raced through her. Not so much at Mark, according to Asia, he may have been a pawn as she had been, but at those pulling his strings.

"Silas?"

"Yes, Sweet Bitch."

"Stop flirting. I want to send a message to whoever sent Mark. What do you suggest?"

"Hmmm… great idea, and another reason women are much scarier than men in war."

"*Silas*," she snapped.

"Go inside his mind, find the mechanism they are using to control him and fry it. They will feel the hit…it may also kill him or turn him into a vegetable." He paused. "I scanned him often and nothing ever came up, hmm."

"Talk to Asia, she felt the necklace he has on and knew his mission. I see Jarcee, by the way."

"He won't interfere. I thought it would be good for others to see why we are a perfect match. Kick ass, Sweet Bitch."

She disconnected and thought of the mental connection inside Mark, within seconds she saw the small metal patch. "I'm sorry, Mark," she whispered just before she sent a blast of energy directly to the miniscule plate.

His mouth flew open as his body jerked a few times, and then he slumped over onto the ground with a loud thud.

Chapter 28

"SIR?" TYRESE CALLED TO Silas, pulling him from the conversation with Jarcee. The man had been in awe of Jasmine's abilities and swore she was a mini-version of the Goddess. Asia had been equally wowed by Jasmine ordering her inside for protection. No one had ever offered protection to the young bitch before. Although, according to Asia, there was no offering involved. The young bitch had asked him if he was sure Jasmine wasn't part wolf. His mate had racked up a large fan club in a short space of time. He was pleased she now embraced her mantle as his mate and protected those under their care.

Turning, he watched Tyrese jog toward him. "Ready?"

Tyrese grinned. "Oh yeah."

Silas nodded as adrenaline pumped through his body at the prospect of the hunt. "Let's go." He shifted into his wolf along with the Tyrese, Tyrone, and Leon. They took off toward town. Silas stopped two miles out where Tyrese had stashed equipment and shifted again. He sent out energy and located two bodies with explosives. Silas encircled the two bodies with energy, preventing them from moving or contacting anyone.

Tyrone and Leon shifted to their human forms, grabbed the equipment and went in search of their targets. Scanning the minds of the men carrying the explosives, it was as Silas suspected, young half-breeds who had been forced into servitude. Griggs used and abused those she claimed to protect. Tyrone and Leon deactivated the explosives and left the breeds in a drug-induced sleep so they couldn't be utilized.

Silas repeated the process, and within an hour, ten half-breeds had been spared. There was one more body with explosives, but it was human. Had

Merriweather armed himself? Silas didn't think so, but he couldn't be sure. Instead of leaving it to chance, he surrounded the human in an energy bubble and tightened it so that if he exploded it would only kill him.

The four of them shifted and ran into town to meet Merriweather. At the edge of town they shifted and strode toward the rotunda in the middle of the county seat.

"Shit," Tyrone murmured from behind Silas.

Silas echoed his sentiments. Attached to the swing set at the park was the police captain. Merriweather had attached two small bombs to the man's chest and placed gray tape across his mouth. This was the human Silas had wrapped in energy. A forlorn look of acceptance graced the captain's face. Silas' energy lashed out in search of Merriweather and found no signs of the man. The ground shook. He spun and stepped forward to get a better view. The twins and Leonidas stepped behind him at first and then moved to his side. Leonidas released a low whistle. Silas brow rose as ten amped up hybrids walked toward them. He sought their wolves and met with static interference. Strange. He sought to take control of the wolves again and met static resistance. It was as if their signals were blocked and they could not receive a transmission.

"If you participate in this fight in any way, Sir Knight, I will blow up the captain," Merriweather's voice blasted into the silence from some point beyond Silas' vision. "I have an audience and they want a show."

Silas glanced at the eagerness in the twins' eyes as they shifted into their wolves. He fought his wolf's demands to shift all the way.

Within seconds the onslaught of hybrid wolves attacked, and from the outside it appeared they had the upper hand.

Silas sent Hank a message. "Pinpoint Merriweather, I want him."

"Yes, Sir."

Leon jumped back snarling as he landed on his four paws outside the huddle. The first hybrid flew through the air and landed with a thud. Leon jumped on the wolf before it could rise and with a snap of his strong jaw broke his neck, tossing the beast aside. Seconds later another hybrid was tossed aside and Leon repeated his actions. It wasn't until four of the hybrids had been destroyed that Silas got a glimpse of the real fighting. Tyrone and Tyrese moved in blurred precision, attacking so fast it was hard for the hybrids to touch them. Leon had been in their way and it made sense for him to be on the outside.

"Sir, he's off-site in a home outside of town. I didn't pick up any signs of explosives and there is one other body with him."

Silas grinned, Merriweather had made the same mistake so many others made, he had underestimated his opponent. "Send in a covert crew to pick him up. I want to know who's watching this fight, and any other data you can pick up. I want him and the person with him alive and brought here for justice."

"Yes, Sir."

The numbers were even now, three for three. Tyrese and Leon shifted to their two legged hybrid form. This was the first time Silas had seen Leon's hybrid in action although he had given Dr. Passen permission to give Leon the shot. He was shorter than Tyrese and not as fast but still a good fighter.

But Tyrone was the real surprise. He shifted into something Silas had never seen before. He stood on two legs in a crouched position, larger than Leon but not as big as Tyrese. He was faster than everyone left on the battlefield and fought with daunting ferocity. Tyrone jumped over his opponent and hit the hybrid with a series of punches that were so fast the only thing Silas saw was the resulting jerking of the hybrid as the blows landed. The hybrid jumped up and flipped behind Tyrone only to discover Tyrone had flipped and was now behind him.

The sound of flesh hitting flesh filled the air.

Leon knocked his opponent to the ground but the beast jumped right back up with remarkable reflexes and landed a punch in Leon's gut, which sent him stumbling back a bit. When the hybrid charged, Leon was prepared and slammed his fist into his opponent's throat, which would have killed a human. The half-beast grabbed his throat as he staggered backward, leaving himself open for Leon to pummel his chest and gut. When the hybrid doubled over, Leon quickly got behind him and wrapped his arm around its neck. A hybrid grabbed Tyrese and tried to place him in a choke hold. Tyrese flipped the hybrid, who was almost double his size, over his head and punched him in the face. The sound of crunching bones hit the air. The hybrid pushed Tyrese back, jumped up and charged him. Tyrese ducked out of the way of the outstretched arms, and landed a punch in the beast's gut. Silas looked on in approval as the loud sound of air leaving the hybrid reached him. The hybrid fell to the ground and rolled over, trying to breathe. Tyrese grabbed him by his hair, pulled him up and powered down with his elbow into the skull.

Silas stood with his arms crossed, evaluating the fighting techniques of each man, and found little he would correct or change. A moment later, Tyrone crushed the skull of the hybrid he'd been fighting. He reared back and released a loud howl as he tossed the beast aside. A few moments later, Leon joined in, and then Tyrese. Impressed with the level of skill he'd witnessed, Silas' howl merged with theirs.

Tyrone shifted into human, his need to run buffeted Silas. He gazed at the three men and waved them off. "Go run, get it out of your systems. The police will clean up this mess."

The three turned and ran toward the outskirts of town where they would shift. Silas turned to Captain Samson. "Be patient."

The captain gave a half nod.

"We got him, Sir. Security is bringing him and his guest to you. You can release the captain, the bomb's deactivated. The man he's with is a doctor, like Passen. I pulled as much data from his laptop as I could before it was remotely destroyed. He's one of the men from the other team, Sir. Seems Merriweather was playing both sides."

Silas had suspected that when he saw the hybrids. There were too many of them, plus Griggs hadn't been interested in improving or changing half-breeds. "*Thanks.*" He released the captain.

"My men are bringing Merriweather to me now. I plan to kill him, so if that's a problem for you, you need to leave now."

The captain wiped his mouth with the back of his hand. There were still sticky patches of white glue on his face. "If you'd allow it, I'd shoot him my damn self. Son of a bitch sent those assholes into the station and jumped me. I didn't even hear them coming." He ran his hand over his short cropped hair. "I'll go inside, wait it out." He pointed to the pile of broken bodies. "What do you want me to do with those?"

"Get rid of them." Silas glanced at the heap and noticed the gleam of metal on the necks of each one. "Hold on." He stepped to the one Tyrone had killed and yanked off the necklace. Mark had worn a gold circle similar to this. Silas had assumed it was jewelry. Could it be more? Was this what Asia had mentioned to Jasmine?

"Take off as many of these as you can," he told the captain. "I want to have these examined."

"Yes, Sir." They worked quickly and in silence until they had collected the gold bands. "Keep these with you." Silas handed the ones he'd collected to the captain. "I'll pick them up after."

The captain accepted the additional bands and headed inside the building. Silas leaned against a tree in the shadows as he waited for Merriweather to arrive.

"Jasmine?"

"Hmmm?"

"You asleep?"

"Kinda, the TV's watching me."

"How's your mom?"

"Not good. Mark wasn't lying; she's going through withdrawal and is in a lot of pain. She cursed Jacques out, snapped at me, and cried asking for Mark. We decided to wait until she's through all this before I tell her he's dead. Pity, I think he really loved her, well as much as he could love someone with that thing in his head."

"Yeah."

"They set her up from the beginning, chose her because she was my mom, and then tried to destroy her."

"Or they wanted to use her as a guinea pig for a new product. Maybe they wanted to see how the poison affected breeders, you never know with those assholes. I'm sure quite a few humans already died testing that stuff."

"Hmm...more stuff I don't want to think about right now."

He chuckled imagining her lying on the sofa in the family room waiting for him. *"I've got one more thing to do before picking up where we left off."*

The smile she sent him slid across his chest and spread out. *"You left me hanging...again."* A picture of her pouting lips filled his vision. He chuckled.

"An emergency arose, but I promise to make it up to you." He deepened his voice, enjoying the shiver she allowed him to feel through their connection.

"You better. My skin is all prickly and stuff, is that normal?"

"Yeah. You need to release a different kind of energy. I'll be in a similar state when I get there, so be prepared."

She growled.

He purred and she laughed. *"Hurry home, I need you."*

He straightened as a large dark Suburban pulled into the parking lot. *"You can bet on it."* He disconnected as one of his security members stepped out of the van and moved to the side. Silas ran a scan, and sent the man verification. The other door opened and the process was repeated.

One of the security men opened the back door and pulled a blindfolded and bound Merriweather from the truck. Silas waited for the other occupant to be removed from the truck.

"This one is dead, Sir."

Silas shook his head at the waste. "Pull him out and toss him on the pile with the others." He waited until his instructions had been carried out. "Go inside and ask the captain if he needs your help moving the bodies. If he does, assist him and then leave. If not, return to the compound. Silas ignored Merriweather, who had been pushed to the ground and lay struggling. A glint of metal caught Silas' eye. Merriweather wore one of the gold collars. Did the man have to be free of the metal bands that were wrapped around his body to activate his hybrid beast?

Excitement rose inside his chest. Instead of killing the bastard outright, Silas would allow his hybrid to fight. The prospect of beating Merriweather's ass before destroying him was a pleasurable bonus. He stooped next to the man and ripped off the duct tape that served as a blindfold. Beads of bloods formed where the tape pulled off skin. Not wanting to hear the man's voice, Silas left the tape covering his mouth in place.

"Hello, Alfred. I understand you've been trying to arrange a meeting with me." The man's eyes narrowed as he stiffened. Silas fingered the gold band around the man's neck, enjoying the pungent smell of fear that wafted to his nostrils. "So you want to be a super soldier, huh? Sold your poor mama out, didn't you? She thought she had all of those hybrids on drugs, ready to step into the public and tell the world about wolves." Silas chuckled at the surprised glint in his nemesis' eyes. "You played her like an old violin. Strange thing happened when my alphas hit all those safe houses, few of the breeders had any idea what was going on, many never gave their pups the shots. You exaggerated the numbers for Corrina, didn't you? You played double agent and gave away her secrets to the highest bidder."

Disgusted with the stench of greed rising from the man, Silas stood. "You're garbage, Merriweather. You mean nothing to no one. If the men you worked for valued you, they would have executed you like they did the good doctor." He ignored the surprised expression in Alfred's eyes. "They used you and your mother to stall for time. They never intended for the world to know about us or what we can do. Not when they are trying to mimic me and my abilities. Her plan was doomed from the outset, they gave her enough rope until she hung herself."

Merriweather jerked against the metal rings holding him.

The captain stepped out the building, followed by the two security workers. In silence they headed to the back of the Suburban, opened the doors, and tossed the bodies inside. When they finished, the captain held up a bag.

"*Take that to the lab, give it to Dr. Passen,*" Silas said to security. The man accepted the bag from the captain. The three men entered the truck and drove off. He looked down at Merriweather and smiled. "Time for justice to be served, wolf-style." The man struggled against the metal bands in earnest.

Silas strode to the middle of the street and called his people to him. Within minutes, the street was crowded with full-bloods and half-breeds, with more on the way. Silas noticed that the twins and Leon pushed their way to the front, becoming a barrier between him and the people.

He held up his hand and the noise died. "Tonight another assault was thrown against our people." He went on to tell them what had happened with the explosions and the incident with Mark. He appreciated the concerned comments regarding the health of his pups and his mate. Most were in awe over Jasmine's abilities, and some wore masks of doubt. No matter, they would all soon learn his mate was not one to be trifled with.

The burning need for retribution rose from the masses as a tantalizing fragrance wafting toward him. He glanced over his shoulder at Merriweather. The man met his gaze with a defiant stare. Silas exhaled as the realization that his personal desire to beat the man within an inch of his life was not going to happen.

"One thing these…our enemies forgot. We are pack. I am pack." He slapped his chest. The crowd roared in approval. "You are pack." He pointed to the crowd. They screamed in agreement. "We are pack." His voice rose as the crowd yelled and howled.

"Coming after me…meaningless. We are connected, we are one. We live and fight as one. So here is the message we send to our enemies, come for one… come for all."

"Come for one, come for all," the crowd chanted repeatedly.

Tyrese looked over his shoulder at Silas with a grin.

Silas held up his arms, the crowd quieted. "Alfred Merriweather and his mother Corrina Griggs have been judged guilty of crimes against our nation. The bombs…that killed so many of our people…they are the ones who created and placed them in people, often without the person's permission. You remember Detective Jennings..." He pointed to the police station. "They did that."

Growls and snapping of teeth filled the air. Some shifted and moved closer to Merriweather. Silas ignored the scent of fear wafting from the man. The crimes the man committed were against the many and Silas wanted to show those who attacked him that there would be a price paid for their actions.

"Release his bands." Tyrone and Tyrese walked to Merriweather, stood him up amongst the jeers and calls for vengeance. More had shifted and moved closer. The moment Merriweather was free, he looked at the growing crowd and then Silas.

"Killing me won't help. I can help you. I know how to find them, I can take you to them...I'm telling you, I can help you win this thing." The man's head whipped from Silas to the crowd who had moved closer.

"No you can't. They didn't trust you with anything of value, by now everything you think you know has been changed. You couldn't contact them if your life depended on it. Lucky for you, it doesn't. We will find our enemies and eliminate them just as we will eliminate you."

Merriweather's eyes widened and then he shifted into a hulk-sized creature. His eyes slid to Silas and then at the pack of wolves closing in on him.

"Kill you." He pointed at Silas and took off running.

Silas shifted and led the pack of wolves after him. Merriweather may have been big, but he was fast. He ran through the town knocking down everything in his path. Silas and the wolves jumped over or ran around the obstacles. Merriweather made it to the edge of the woods. Silas grew tired of the chase, shifted into his hybrid and jumped. He landed on the man's back, the force of the impact sent Merriweather sprawling forward a foot or so before his face hit the ground. Before Silas could reach his neck, the man jumped up, shaking off a couple of wolves who had attacked his arms and legs. Swinging wildly, he missed the wolves who darted back and forth, in and out. Silas jumped again, this time his large canines punctured Merriweather's neck. The man grabbed Silas and tried to pull him off, but Silas had been leading pack wars for too long. He ignored the blows to his body and dug in while the rest of the pack attacked other areas of Merriweather's body. Weakening, his opponent fell to his knees, and Silas released his grip and moved out of the way, silently granting his pack permission to finish the kill. It didn't take long for the man to be ripped to pieces.

Blood glistening on his snout, Silas released a victory howl. A chorus of howls followed his as his pack rejoiced in defeating another of their enemies. Afterward, Silas took off running into the woods beneath the moonlit sky. The pack followed, and for the first time in months, his wolf led his pack. A glorious sense of purpose filled him as yips and howls filled the air. He had allowed his enemy to stop him from being himself. Harder he ran, muscles stretching as his mate's words returned to him. "We have wolves and all that goes with that..." He had missed the simplicity of her statement, just be who you are. Pack. He scented prey and headed in that direction. Soon the large buck came into view. Adrenaline surged through him as the buck raced away. The chase was on.

Chapter 29

JASMINE WATCHED SILAS AS he strode into the room. There was something different about him. She couldn't quite put her finger on what it was. He stopped, checked on the four small cribs, and placed kisses on the cheeks of each child. His vibrant eyes glowed blue-green when he turned in her direction.

Everything within her tightened and throbbed at his deliberate approach. She waited for him to speak.

He didn't.

Instead, he crawled up to her from the foot of the bed, reminding her that her man was indeed a predator. Her thighs quivered when he reached them. The heat in his gaze stole her breath. While staring into her eyes, he pulled the cover from her and placed his warm hand on her breast. When he rubbed her nipple, his palm had a rougher texture than normal, the friction sent waves of pleasure to her core.

"Mmm," she moaned, opening herself to him.

He pulled her nipple. She shuddered as he pinched it and then ran his lip across the tight bud. Reaching up, she pulled his head down, wanting to keep his mouth on her breast. "Yeah, right there," she whispered as moisture trickled from between her thighs. He lavished each breast with loving affection, sending a heat wave of need through her. With bent legs, she widened them in invitation. "Now Silas. Now."

Instead of moving to do her bidding, he roughly claimed her mouth with his lips to hers. His tongue sought and secured entranced. A moan escaped from her throat at the pleasure. He placed his questing fingers at her entrance. Hungry to be filled, she rolled her hips against his hand. He got the message and touched her in earnest until his fingers filled her. In and out, he thrust his tongue and fingers, mimicking a dance that never grew old. Her body responded, releasing more fluid in preparation.

She grabbed his hair and pulled. "Now," she growled, needing him with a desperation she couldn't describe. His scent, his touch, his taste inundated her senses. She had no idea where he stopped and she began, nor did it matter. Not now. The blinding need to join with him rode her hard.

He topped her and slid forward, filling and stretching her in one thrust with his hard thickness. Once fully seated, he stopped. In symphonic harmony, they both sighed.

"Good," he grunted in a garbled voice.

She held his hips in place with her hand. "Damn good." He moved and it got better. Thrust for thrust, she met him as they journeyed together toward fulfillment. He had left himself wide open, allowing her to see and feel what she meant to him. Her breath hitched at the depth of his commitment. Pouring all the love in her heart through their link, he shuddered and then quickened his pace. His body stroked faster, deeper, harder inside her, hitting against her velvety walls. Fire spread throughout her body destroying her defenses, leaving her open to him on every level.

Caught in the maelstrom of their emotions, she rose higher, tightening, until she flew over the edge in a blinding flash as her orgasm tore through her. He thickened inside her. She held him tighter, eager to receive all of him. His body pulsed as he came with a loud cry, releasing his seed deep within her body. He tensed, shuddered, and then relaxed on top of her. She wrapped her legs around him to keep him close a bit longer.

"Good?" he muttered into her neck, as she found the strength to stroke his hair.

"Always, baby," she said softly, and then placed a kiss on his head. He was so precious to her, she could not imagine life without her wolf. She exhaled into the comfort of their joining.

"Must have been good tonight…in town," she said, softly stroking him.

"It was, but it paled in comparison to what we just shared. I love you, Jasmine." He leaned up and met her gaze. "Thank you for mating with me. I want the ceremony, forget our enemies. I want the world to know you are my mate, my Sweet Bitch. Say yes."

Unable to speak, she nodded as tears of joy streamed from her eyes.

Chapter 30

SILAS AND JASMINE SAT in the room with Victoria. After three days under the watchful care of Matt and Jacques, she had broken her addiction. Her eyes were clearer than Jasmine had seen since her arrival at the compound, and her mental capabilities were back on track. She sat up in bed, gazing at Jasmine and Silas.

"You're a wolf…I mean you can change into a wolf." She pointed at Silas. He nodded. She turned her attention to Jasmine. "You gave birth to half-breed babies?" She shook her head. "One day they will shift into wolves, is that right?"

"Yes, Mom."

"The twins are half-breed wolves and so is Rose?"

"Yes," Jasmine said, searching for her depleted well of patience. Her mom had not been the best patient the last couple of days.

"And Silas is your mate, the one person created for you?" The skepticism in her voice rubbed Jasmine the wrong way. Just as she was about to answer, Silas stepped in.

"Yes, just as you have a mate. That one person who will complete you so that you will stop searching. Aren't you tired of looking for someone to love you unconditionally? Someone you can be yourself with?"

Her mom stared at Silas and then laughed. "You sound like one of those dating commercials. Okay…I'll bite." She paused and then said in a shy voice. "Yes…yes, I want a man who completes me, who totally gets me in every way. I've been searching my whole life for the right man," she ended dryly, rolling her eyes.

Jasmine bit back a laugh at her mom's antics. This was the Victoria she had grown up with. That woman had always been a force to be reckoned with.

"Listen, I believe the wolf thing because I've seen them before. No need to discuss that further." Her mother waved down any questions. "We need to keep that quiet, believe me I understand that my grandchildren are special. I'm damn proud and will do my part to keep them safe." She closed her eyes. "I loved Mark. It's hard to believe he was used like that, but I saw the footage and have to accept he was not the person I thought he was. In time, I might be ready to take on another lover, but not right now."

Understanding, Jasmine met her mother's gaze and nodded. "No problem. I just want you to get better, you've been through a lot. The poison is still in your system, it'll take a couple of weeks to fully flush it out. And then you'll need to take supplements to rebuild your strength."

"I know. Thank you for ... well, for everything. Especially that well-edited explanation you gave Renee. I couldn't take another of her give women a try speeches that she gives me after every break-up. I'd rather have her believe I was sick and that Mark had died from exposure, than to see her pity over another bad choice I made."

Jasmine rubbed her mom's arm in commiseration. Renee had forgiven Jasmine's bad treatment during her visit when she discovered her mom had contracted an almost fatal disease. Jasmine wound up as a heroine battling germs to save her children in Renee and Mandy's eyes. Mark's demise had been glossed over in deference to their mother's health.

Silas stood. "We ask that you stay as long as you wish, you never really had a chance to get to know our babies."

Noticing her mom's drowsiness, Jasmine rose as well. "Of course she's sticking around a bit, I need some help and she's offered to give it to me."

Her mom frowned. "I did? When?"

"When you didn't make it to Germany to help with the twins. You promised to help with my next batch. I'm calling you on it, now."

Her mom laughed.

Silas smiled.

Jasmine grinned as she and Silas left the room hand in hand. She nodded to Jacques, who walked in and sat in one of the chairs. He pulled out a book and read while her mom drifted to sleep. Tomorrow, her man and her sons would track down the lab and shut it down. She wanted her life to return to normal. Leaning into her mate, she sighed at his low growl.

Forget normal she thought gazing at his wolf hiding behind his eyes, it was overrated anyway.

The End

A Note from Sydney:

Hello and thanks for taking the time to read my fourth book in the La Patron series. I love paranormal books and characters in general and shifter stories in particular. Throw in the romantic element, strong Alpha characters who bend beneath the power of love and I'm over the moon. Sighs...

Jasmine pushes for the christening of her babies and that's okay, totally human but the consequences have devastating effects. Silas didn't understand Jasmine's refusal in kicking all of her family members out of the compound, in his mind there are no gray areas. Not where his pups are concerned anyway. I handled Jasmine's defense of her mother and subsequent discovery of her mom being victimized, in the same manner I would have done things if I were her. No one messes with my mom. Author privilege I suppose. (smiles) Consequently, Jasmine redeemed herself in the end by handling the source of her mom's problem directly.

You're invited to journey with me through the six and counting books in this series. If you like fast paced action, suspense and great love connections like me, you won't be disappointed. Feel free to drop me a line, SydneyAddae@msn.com or join La Patrons' Den, my Facebook group where discussions regarding Silas and the Wolf Nation abound.

For more information about Silas Knight and the Wolf Nation, I'd like to give you a *Free Companion PDF Booklet* with personal messages from Silas and Jasmine, as well as their family tree. To receive your Free Booklet and Free Book, go to my website www.SydneyAddae.com and join Knights Chronicles, my reading group, for fresh news on my Works in Progress.

La Patron, the Alpha's Alpha is my first paranormal series and I'd like to ask a favor. When you finish reading, please leave a review, whatever your opinion, I assure you I appreciate it.

Thanks again
Sydney

You've finished this story, get ready for the next! The following books are in the La Patron Series, enjoy!
Birth Series

BirthRight
BirthControl
BirthMark
BirthStone
BirthDate
BirthSign

Sword Series

Sword of Inquest
Sword of Mercy
Sword of Justice

Holiday Series

La Patron's Christmas
La Patron's Christmas 2
La Patron's New Year
Christmas in the Nation

KnightForce Series

KnightForce 1
KnightForce Deuces
KnightForce Tres'
KnightForce Damian
KnightForce Ethan
Angus

LaPatron's Den Series

Jackie's Journey (La Patron's Den Book 1)

Alpha Awakening – Adam (La Patron's Den Book 2)

Renee's Renegade (La Patron's Den Book 3)

David's Dilemma (La Patron's Den Book 4)

Rise of the Wolf Nation Series

Knight Rescue - Rise of Wolf Nation 1

Knight Defense (Rise of Wolf Nation 2)

BlackWolf Series

BlackWolf Legacy

BlackWolf Preserved

BlackWolf Redemption

The Leviticus Club (The Olympus Project Book 1)
Altered Destiny
Family Ties
Booksets:
La Patron Series Books 1-3
La Patron Series Books 4-6
Sword Series
KnightForce Series Books 1-3
KnightForce Series Books 4-6
A Walk in the Nation (Three Stories to Tease Your Imagination

Other Books by Sydney Addae:
Last in Line (Vampires)
Bear with Me (Bear Shifter)
Jewel's Bear (Bear Shifter)
Do Over: Shelly's Surrender
Do Over: Rashan's Recovery
Secret of the Red Stone

www.SydneyAddae.com

Made in the USA
Monee, IL
01 December 2021